Virtually Yours

Virtually Yours

Yours

SARVENAZ TASH

SIMON & SCHUSTER BFYR

NEW YORK   LONDON   TORONTO   SYDNEY   NEW DELHI

SIMON & SCHUSTER BFYR

An imprint of Simon & Schuster Children's Publishing Division
1230 Avenue of the Americas, New York, New York 10020

For information about special discounts for bulk purchases, please contact
Simon & Schuster Special Sales at 1-866-506-1949 or business@simonandschuster.com.
The Simon & Schuster Speakers Bureau can bring authors to your live event.
For more information or to book an event, contact the Simon & Schuster Speakers Bureau
at 1-866-248-3049 or visit our website at www.simonspeakers.com.
Jacket design by Krista Vossen
Interior design by Hilary Zarycky
The text for this book was set in Sabon.
Manufactured in the United States of America
First Edition
2 4 6 8 10 9 7 5 3 1
Library of Congress Cataloging-in-Publication Data
Names: Tash, Sarvenaz, author.
Title: Virtually yours / Sarvenaz Tash.
Description: First edition. | New York : Simon & Schuster Books for Young Readers,
[2019] | Summary: College freshman Mariam uses a new virtual reality dating service
and is matched not only with her new best friend, Jeremy, but also with her high school
ex-boyfriend, Caleb.
Identifiers: LCCN 2018054407 (print) | LCCN 2018058291 (eBook) |
ISBN 9781534436664 (hardback) | ISBN 9781534436688 (eBook)
Subjects: | CYAC: Dating (Social aspects)—Fiction. | Dating services—Fiction. | Virtual
reality—Fiction. | Best friends—Fiction. | Friendship—Fiction. | Colleges and universities—
Fiction.
Classification: LCC PZ7.T2111324 (eBook) | LCC PZ7.T2111324 Vir 2019 (print)
| DDC [Fic]—dc23
LC record available at https://lccn.loc.gov/2018054407

To Jonah,
my meant-to-be

Virtually Yours

CHAPTER 1

HIS SELFIE MADE ME DO IT.

Yes, I had the 40 percent off coupon from the orientation fair. Yes, it was almost about to expire. Yes, my roommate, Hedy, had made a casual comment just the day before about how I never seemed to leave our room. And if I wanted to, I could use any of those as excuses for why I found myself sitting in the waiting room of HEAVR, about to place my love life in the hands of some virtual gods.

But if I did, I'd be lying.

Just that morning, Caleb had posted a grinning photo with a few of his college buddies, in mid-shrug—the kind of "casual" shot it probably took at least fifteen takes to get right—looking so carefree that it had sent my heart into a tailspin. There were a couple of girls in the picture too. I didn't know if any of them meant anything more to him, but it almost didn't matter. My ex-boyfriend, love of my life, breaker of my heart, was having the college life I should have been, and looking damn good doing it.

Seeing that post had made me . . . angry. Mostly at

myself. Why had I been shutting myself up in my dorm room, doing a months-long performance of the breakup mope, speaking to hardly anyone outside of my room-mate? Why, especially, when Caleb was having fun.

My eyes had swept across a stack of papers that was occupying a corner of my desk. At the top was the HEAVR coupon that had been gathering dust for two months. Within moments I had navigated over to their site and filled out their sign-up questionnaire—forced to glance one more time at Caleb's selfie while I dutifully linked out to my social media profiles like it asked. Then I walked myself to HEAVR's headquarters. I didn't have an appointment, so now I was forced to sit in their yellow-and-magenta waiting room, staring at the "Happily Ever After Guaran-teed" trademark that was plastered all over it, and trying to avoid the idle time that might make me rethink this idea. Because there was the part of me that didn't want Caleb to be responsible for my decisions anymore. And there was the part of me that felt like love hurt too much to be worth even trying for again. And, of course, who could forget the part of me that believed in the meet-cute and wanted it to be for real, not orchestrated by a machine.

But the overwhelming majority of me kept thinking: Why not? Sure, it was easy to make fun of a dating app whose name was synonymous with vomiting and to laugh at those *SNL* sketches mocking the very idea of VR love. But I was certainly not going to meet anyone holed away in my dorm room. Why not let a machine give it a go in an attempt to find my HEA—my happily ever after? HEAVR's matchmaking skills were supposed to be second to none, and for a little bit extra, they'd even throw in the meet-cute. I'd splurged.

"Mariam Vakilian?"

I smiled brightly at the woman in the lab coat as I got up and followed her down a hallway. No sense in not being extra friendly to someone who potentially held my entire romantic future in the palm of her hand.

She led me into a small room that was painted a cheerful shade of yellow.

A black leather dentist's chair sat in the middle, complete with a tray nearby that held a sort of helmet/goggle hybrid, two sleek charcoal gloves, and a thin black vest.

"Have a seat, Ms. Vakilian. My name is Joan, and I will be your guide, or as we like to call it at HEAVR, your twenty-first-century Cupid." She said that last part with a tight smile, which led me to picture her having a long conversation with her boss about just how idiotic she thought that trademarked moniker was. Joan didn't seem like the type who suffered fools or foolish slogans. "Let me get caught up on your order."

She looked down at her tablet and read, giving me a chance to observe my "Cupid," who, in lieu of a diaper, was dressed in a smart navy skirt suit underneath the pale yellow lab coat, which had the letters HEAVR and her name stitched in dark magenta on the lapel. She wore a shade of lipstick that matched the magenta perfectly, and because her skin was a similar olive shade to my own, I found myself wondering if I could pull off the color too. Joan's hair, however, was put back in the sort of high, professional ponytail that had always confounded me—no matter what I did, my ponytails seemed to escape their confines in unruly strands that gave me a "gym look," which wasn't super helpful when I was trying to interview for my work-study job or, say, attempting to look cute in case I accidentally ran into Caleb back home.

Ugh. Why did all thought roads lead back to him?

"Okay, so let's recap." Joan looked up from her tablet with a bright smile. "You're looking for an eighteen-to-twenty-three-year-old male, open to any ethnicity, race, or creed. And location . . . you didn't fill this one out. Do you want strictly local?"

I hesitated. Logically, I should say yes. But on the other hand, wasn't the beauty of living in this day and age and with this service at my disposal that I *could* say no? That I could date someone from anywhere in the world (or, well, the seventeen countries that HEAVR currently existed in, anyway)? Why not take advantage? And besides, it would really stick it to Caleb if I somehow found a long-distance soul mate after all.

"No," I said. "Open to anywhere."

"That's fine," Joan said with a practiced but nevertheless soothing smile. "And that's it in terms of preliminary information we need from you. The rest will be done with this." She tapped on the tray. "So let's just get this on first." She opened up the vest, inviting me to put my arms through. It was lightweight for something that surely contained a lot of tech in between its seams. Joan came around to Velcro the front together. "Great. Now sit back and put your feet up."

I leaned back in the buttery chair, which, despite its comfort, made me feel like I was about to get a root canal.

"It won't hurt, I promise," Joan said, almost as if she could read my thoughts. "Let's get these on." She handed me the gloves as soon as I was settled.

I slipped them on. They were made of some sort of sleek synthetic fiber and they felt slightly more substantial than regular gloves, but maybe that was only because I knew they were haptic and designed to register my motions.

"Okay, and in a moment, you're going to place this over your head." She picked up the goggles. "Before you do, you have a choice of locale for your initial questionnaire. Some of our most popular choices are tropical island, outer space, Parisian café, or—thanks to our new partnership with the Tolkien estate—Middle Earth. Any of those do anything for you?"

"Um. How about tropical island?" Out of nerves, I went with the first option she had mentioned, but it sounded appealing enough.

"Perfect," Joan said. "Once you put these on, you won't be able to hear or see me anymore. But if you need anything while on your island, just tap your left pointer finger and thumb together and I'll be able to punch in to guide you. Otherwise, use your pointer finger to pick your choices. And everything else should be pretty self-explanatory. We're going to be asking you ten questions to select your matches, okay?"

I nodded.

"And here we go." Joan handed the goggles over and I slipped them over my head. For a second I was in a dark, silent world until Joan must have flipped a switch or something and suddenly there were crystal seas ahead of me, a sandy beach below, and a low sun above. The sounds of lapping water and seagulls filled my ears, and I could even feel the heat of the day surrounding me.

The water sparkled as a perky female voice came through on the headphones attached to my goggles.

"Hello, Mariam, and welcome to the beginning of your HEA. Please answer the following ten questions as honestly and quickly as you can. It's best to go with your gut answers."

I took in a deep, shaky breath. Which the machine apparently felt.

"Don't be nervous! Think of me as your friend. You can call me Agatha. And the questions will be very easy, I promise."

Agatha? That name didn't sound like it matched the

chipper voice, which I assumed was intended to resemble a girlfriend playing matchmaker. Agatha was more like a grandma who'd disastrously set you up with her bridge partner's secretly racist grandson. Maybe the system's OS needed some updating in terms of hip names. Something like Juniper or Brooklyn.

"Ready? Let's get started!"

Glittery blue letters appeared in the air in front of me, corresponding with the question Agatha read aloud.

Which one of these locations is the most romantic?
  A. a beautiful forest clearing under a starry night
  B. an intimate candlelit restaurant
  C. a centuries-old city with cobblestone streets
  D. a comfy couch and fuzzy socks

I hesitated for a second before I remembered the machine—or rather, *Agatha*'s—instructions. Right, my gut. I put my hand in front of me and chose option *C*.

"Wonderful. Question two:"

You're on a desert island with a small knapsack. Which one of these items are you most likely to find in there?

A. lipstick

B. a book

C. a knife

D. hand sanitizer

The real answer was *D*, but I was worried about being typecast as a neat freak. I had a small thing about germs, sure, but it wasn't like I was going to take a potential boyfriend to task for not being vigilantly antiseptic.

"What did I say, Mariam?" Agatha's voice held a laugh in it now as it gently chided. "Your first instinct, remember?"

My finger shook a bit as I reluctantly chose *D*. I suddenly had the strange feeling that Agatha not only knew when I was nervous (as a result of having my heart rate monitored with the vest, I supposed), but could predict which answer I was going to pick. But that was impossible, right? Agatha couldn't genuinely read my thoughts.

Could she?

Oh God. I realized I was starting to think of Agatha as a "she."

"Let's go with an easier question, Mariam. To relax you. Remember, there is no wrong answer. And at the end, you will have three initial matches to choose from. If none of them work out, you get a free do-over. It's part of the HEAVR guarantee!"

I could practically hear the toothpaste-commercial smile in Agatha's voice.

If you could paint your bedroom any of these
hues, and you only had five seconds to choose,
which one would you pick?

Four swatches appeared in front of me, and above them,
a countdown clock ticking down from five.

The first was a light mauve, the second a sky blue, the
third an olive green, and the fourth a mid-range gray.

I barely had time to register that they were cool tones,
the only colors I personally would ever choose to paint a
room. It was only a flit of a thought that I might have, in
fact, actually lived in a room with each of those paint colors at some point in my life. Whenever we moved, my parents would allow me the small luxury of painting my new
room whatever color I wanted. I guessed it was their way
of giving me a modicum of control over my life, however
superficial. It was only the last three years of high school,
the three years with Caleb, that I'd ever stayed in one room
for such an extended amount of time. The mauve room.

The countdown was at one when I numbly picked out
the first option, the color I'd stared at when I'd lost my
heart and, eventually, my virginity to the boy who didn't
even have the decency to give it back. My heart, that is, not
my virginity. That one's pretty nonrefundable.

"Great. I think we're going to keep the countdown clock
going. But that doesn't mean you shouldn't feel relaxed
when picking out your answers. Okay?"

Um, yeah sure. Easy for you to say, Agatha. What's a clock to someone who's composed of ones and zeros?

"Next question."

How much wood could a woodchuck chuck if a woodchuck could chuck wood? Per day?

Wait, what? How was this related . . .

A. five tons
B. three trees
C. seventeen sticks
D. more than a squirrel could squirrel away

Ummm . . .

I read the question over again, but the countdown clock was already down to two by the time I finished. I instinctively fell back on my multiple-choice training from years of standard education: when in doubt, pick C.

"The next few questions are going to seem less straightforward. Remember not to think too hard about them, and most important, don't consider how they may or may not affect the outcome today. Trust our methods, Mariam. They work. Okay?"

I assumed the question was rhetorical, so I was surprised when Agatha said, "Just nod if you feel comfortable with that."

Nod? So there must be some sensors in the headset too . . . sensors that *could* read my mind?

I nodded instinctively, even as the rest of me started to feel distinctly uncomfortable with this situation. Which of course made me feel worse, since it immediately conjured up one of the only fights Caleb and I had ever had. The one where he had called me a sheep who blindly followed instructions.

But anyway, either Agatha—or the machine; it was better if I thought of it as a MACHINE—knew that I was on the verge of possibly bailing, or it was always programmed to make the last six questions as rapid-fire as possible.

Agatha's voice became brisk and businesslike, and even though the countdown clock never veered from starting at five, I couldn't help but feel that it was counting down faster with each successive question.

What is man's greatest invention?
A. fire
B. the wheel
C. the Internet
D. it hasn't been invented yet

Maybe it was the influence of my environmentalist parents, but I had a relatively easy time with that one. I chose *A*.

Which Shakespearean name would you give
to a naked mole rat, if you ever had the
opportunity to name one?

For reference, Aga . . . or rather, *the machine* provided an
image of a naked mole rat, which unfortunately for my wizened eleventh-grade English teacher, immediately reminded
me of my wizened eleventh-grade English teacher.

    A. Viola
    B. Banquo
    C. Prospero
    D. Cordelia

I chose *B* only because I thought I remembered Banquo
being a murdered ghost and there was something decrepit
about the creature in front of me.

Which of the following pronouns is the most
musical?
    A. she
    B. we
    C. whomever
    D. several

Wait, was "several" a pronoun? Was this a trick question?
The countdown clock now came with a ticking noise

that I was positive hadn't been there before. I chose *A* before a zero flashed across my screen and Tom Cruise arced through the sky, framed by a fiery explosion.

The next time Agatha's voice came through, she definitely sounded more like an army commander than a gossipy confidante. Suddenly this matchmaking experience was starting to feel closer to a first-person shooter than a dating app.

> If you were a spy, which country would you
> want to work for?

Wait, what? Was this some sort of patriot test? Was the government listening in on this?

> A. USA
> B. Iran
> C. Russia
> D. England

Normally I wasn't super anxious about stuff like this— it wasn't like I had ever fantasized about living off the grid or anything—but I'd also never pointedly been asked which country I was loyal to before.

I chose *A*, feeling a little like I was betraying my parents and heritage by not choosing *B*. But I didn't want to get in trouble, and I was almost positive it was the answer

Agatha wanted to hear. (And fine, whatever. I needed to accept that I thought of the machine as a person now. You win, Agatha.)

What's your favorite kind of sky?

Agatha's voice was gentle and dreamy again as she read the choices.

A. starry and infinite
B. blue with fluffy white clouds
C. streaked with a pink-and-orange sunset
D. pregnant with billowing gray thunderclouds

That seemed more like it in terms of matchmaking questions.

I'd always liked the rain, and the anticipation of rain even more. My older sister, Mina, used to roll her eyes and call me faux goth back when I was in middle school. But thunder and rain had never seemed dark to me. They seemed like a chance for renewal, like they could clean the slate in preparation for something new, something different. My whole life I'd felt like I was waiting for one good rainstorm to come and bring with it the start of my real life, where my insecurities would be washed away and replaced with total confidence in who I really was and what I really wanted. Whatever those were. (Obviously this storm would also give me true purpose, too, you know? What good were metaphorical rainstorms otherwise?)

Incidentally, Caleb had loved thunderstorms too. On one of our most romantic dates we'd gotten caught in one, but instead of running to his car, he'd pulled me into an embrace and kissed me for what felt like three gloriously drenched hours.

"Last question! You're doing so great, Mariam."

Agatha's voice was that of an enthusiastic life coach now.

If life was a report card, and you had to pick
only one of these subjects to ace, which would
it be?
  A. romantic love
  B. career
  C. family
  D. inner peace

I froze. How could I choose among those? I wanted them all. Didn't everybody?

"Don't worry, Mariam. That's not to say you wouldn't do well in those other subjects too."

Agatha chuckled.

"Think of it as one of them being A-plus and the rest at least solid Bs."

Right, okay.

The countdown clock had started again, and I read over the four answers once more. Finally I picked the one that embodied what I was doing here in the first place, even though I wasn't sure if it was quite the right one.

As soon as my finger touched *A*, the glittery blue letters exploded into confetti in the cloudless sky.

"Congratulations! You have completed our matchmaking questionnaire. Just give me a few minutes and I will find you your top three matches."

I let out a big breath. That was way more stressful than I'd anticipated. I could use a big iced coffee on this fake beach right about now.

A part of me expected Agatha to chime in after hearing that thought, and maybe even make a cup appear in front of me, but the scenery remained the same, with nothing but birdcalls in the air.

I waited, wondering if whatever heating lamp they were using in the room to emulate the warmth of the beach could actually give me a tan.

Then I wondered if they had modeled this beach on a real beach or if some graphic designer had just sketched it out from her own imagination.

Then I thought it was a bit incongruous that I could hear what sounded like fifty flocks of seagulls and not see a single one.

Finally I wondered where the hell Agatha was, because it felt like it had been more than a few minutes. Maybe someone else here needed a countdown clock.

"Hello again! I'm back with your perfect matches."

Yeah, great. Get on with it, Aggie.

"I am pleased to announce that each of your three matches falls in the ninetieth percentile, with your top match being at ninety-eight percent! That is a rarity. Only about four percent of our matches ever score quite that high."

That was a lot of percentages being thrown around. I couldn't help but feel that Agatha was stalling. She probably lived for this reveal.

Except she doesn't live at all, Mariam. Once again, she is a MACHINE.

I really needed to get my results and get off this damn fake beach. This whole thing was clearly getting to me.

"And here he is. Your top match: Jeremy D."

A smiling face appeared in front of me, with two smaller faces flanking it on either side. Jeremy had brown eyes, black hair, great cheekbones. Definitely cute.

But I didn't get to examine him too closely. Because something familiar tugged at me from my peripheral vision, causing me to instinctively turn my head.

My third option, coming in at 91 percent compatibility as the shining blue letters below his beaming smile told me, was Caleb.

CHAPTER 2

YOU CAN TAKE SOME TIME TO EXAMINE EACH OF your matches' profiles, Mariam." Agatha's voice was chipper again as Jeremy's file opened in front of me and a list of attributes, from his location to his hobbies, appeared.

He was into rock climbing and lived in New York like me, but my brain couldn't process the words beyond that. Because even though I wasn't looking at Caleb's profile, I felt like I would know his answers by heart.

Location: Berkeley, California.

What I'm into: animal welfare, Mediterranean food, being the kind of person who would pull over during his driver's ed exam to see to a stray dog on the side of the road.

What I'm looking for: Once upon a time, it was a cheerful girl with a cat I found for her (to whom she was allergic but couldn't bear to part from anyway. Appropriately named Sneezes). But now . . . now . . .

I hardly seemed to be in control as my hand took over, swiping away Jeremy's face and opening up Caleb's file, reading what it really said.

What I'm looking for: a laugh and someone to laugh with.

The rest of the profile got blurry then, and it took some maneuvering to get my gloved hand underneath my goggles to swipe at my face.

The last time Caleb and I had spoken, a week after we'd broken up, I'd asked him what he was looking for if it wasn't me. And he had said, definitively, that he didn't know.

"I just feel like we're about to be across the entire country from one another and something about holding on . . . it doesn't seem right. You know?" he'd said, as we sat on a bench and stared out onto the boats of Lake George. I'd chosen the meeting place, and it had been a stupid choice since it was the site of one of our very first dates. But then again, what part of our town wasn't tainted with memories of the two of us holding hands, making out, laughing?

Laughing.

A laugh and someone to laugh with?! That was me. That had always been me.

And that was the thing. I felt the opposite of Caleb, even then. Going to college, living in a dorm away from my parents, sister, brother, and Sneezes, the thing I most wanted to do was hold on, especially to the one thing, the one person, who made me feel sure about anything. Who made me feel sure about myself, even if I couldn't seem to figure out what to major in, or what career to have, or even what talents I possessed.

"Take your time, Mariam. But I would echo advice I gave earlier. It truly is best to go with your gut." I was jolted back to the present by Agatha's chummy voice. I'd traveled pretty far down memory lane, back to when I was blissfully unaware of what a passive-aggressive AI sounded like. "Remember, it's just an initial date. And if it doesn't work out, you will be free to choose from the other two matches."

This time I listened to the voice and didn't second-guess it. My gut was angry and confused and sad. But it was also pointing in only one direction.

So I let it guide my finger to bachelor number three and punched at Caleb's name before common sense or dignity could talk me out of it.

I vaguely registered that Agatha said goodbye, and then Joan started talking again as soon as she had helped me take off the headset. It was hard to hear over the loud pumping of my heart and the screaming internal monologue of: *Oh God, what have I done?!*

So was Caleb even now receiving a message that I'd chosen him as my HEAVR match? Also, what was Caleb even doing on HEAVR anyway? In my most painful thoughts, the ones that sometimes invaded my nightmares, he was now living out a real-life HEA with one of his tall, toned, beautiful California classmates. Though I guess this would mean that he was probably still single. I should take some comfort in that.

Except not really, because now I'd invited in another sort of nightmare altogether. A humiliating sort that would let Caleb know I was definitely not over him and force him to reject me all over again.

No. No, no, no. I had to ask Joan if there was a way to Ctrl+Z this situation, right now.

"Excuse me, but I think I need to change my answer," I blurted in the middle of whatever it was Joan was talking about. "I want to choose a different match."

"Oh," Joan said. "Well, okay, that's not a problem."

Hope bubbled amid the acid in my churning stomach. "Really? It's not too late? Caleb hasn't already received my match request?" My voice squeaked in anticipated relief.

Joan smiled. "No. We like to establish the terms of the connection with our client first. As you know, you'll be going on at least three initial dates through our system, but you can add on as many dates later as you'd like. Not only is this a safer approach, but our methods have been scientifically proven to help alleviate, or in some cases eradicate, some of the most common awkward or unpleasant aspects of the first-date experience. And I see that you have already decided to take advantage of our unique platform by opting for our meet-cute package."

Oh yeah. I had. But it sure would be hard to meet-cute someone you've already known for over three years, and biblically for one of them. I was about to open my mouth to say that to Joan when I was struck by another idea. A far-fetched one, probably, but then again . . .

"You mentioned safety. Would there be a way for me to go under a pseudonym for the initial date?" I asked, hardly knowing how the question had even occurred to me.

"Yes, absolutely. You can just use your first name, or even an entirely made-up handle if you like."

"I see." My calm voice belied whatever scheme my mind seemed to be quickly coming up with. I could barely keep up with it. "And what about my picture? Is it possible to present my profile to my match without a photo?"

"Well, it *is* possible, yes, but we don't recommend it. We've found the chances of someone agreeing to a date without a photo are pretty slim," Joan responded with a smile.

That made sense. But still, it *was* possible . . . okay, one more question. "And what about on the date itself? Instead of a live video, is it possible to have an avatar?"

Joan nodded. "Absolutely. It's a commonly used option, in fact. Some people find the floating video head disconcerting, so you can let us make a full-body avatar that represents you, which you are free to tweak to an extent."

That was it. If I could get Caleb to agree to a photoless date, if I could make an avatar of myself that didn't look exactly like me, and if I could present myself under a different name . . . then maybe, maybe, I could get him to fall in love with me again.

But why would you want that, Mariam? The rational part of me intruded on my thoughts. *You already gave it a go with Caleb and it didn't work. Why can't you move on?*

Because . . . because. I didn't know, really. I just knew that over the past five months, I'd felt like I'd been scraped clean from the inside and left with someone who only resembled me on the surface. And everything that had been taken away seemed to be the parts that made me interesting, or funny, or tolerable to be around. They were the parts that thought it was okay to spend five days in a row in the same pajama pants or rationalized that the blue glow of my computer screen was the same as feeling the sun on my face.

How could I even meet anyone else tucked away like that? And who would want to meet me? I didn't have anything interesting to say. My mind was stuck in a loop of self-pity and what-ifs.

Like *what if* I had a second chance with Caleb?

Well, here it was. Right in front of me. I hadn't asked for him. Out of the hundreds of thousands of applicants, maybe even millions, *the machine* had picked him. It was like science backing up what was in my gut.

My gut. Agatha had repeatedly told me to go with it. Once the choices were in front of me, there was only one answer that my entire being (okay, barring the killjoy, heartless voice that kept telling me to move on, *like it was so easy, disembodied voice*) was yearning for.

So why not surrender to it? Why not give it one more go? Why not see this for the dramatic grand gesture that my favorite rom-coms were made of? This was one *what-if* I didn't want to keep replaying in my head. This was a carpe diem moment. And I'd very nearly failed high school Latin, so for my brain to choose to use it now was pretty symbolic of the moment's epicness.

"I take it back. I'm sticking with my original choice," I told Joan. "What's my next step?"

I spent another hour at HEAVR headquarters, tweaking my profile since I now knew its audience of one quite well, and also helping to make an avatar that did and didn't look like me. HEAVR created the baseline built on my real appearance, but I could slightly alter things like hair color, eye color, and my wardrobe. That's what Caleb would see instead of my photo, along with the name SiennaV23. (I'd always fancied being named Sienna; it was also sometimes my Starbucks name, but luckily Caleb didn't know that.)

Joan said that Caleb would get the ping that night and would have forty-eight hours to agree or say no.

So now there was nothing to do but wait.

I only had to walk two blocks to get to my dorm. The geniuses of HEAVR had figured out pretty quickly that college campuses were a gold mine, and NYU—also having the distinction of being in New York City and not even having an official campus—had been one of the first ten schools to get one. The coupon that HEAVR representatives had handed out at the college life fair at freshman orientation was another brilliant marketing move.

I turned my phone off and tucked it away within a zippered pocket in my bag, not to be unzipped until midnight. I promised myself that I could check it only once that night, just before bed. I had to admit the chances of Caleb agreeing to a date with a random avatar weren't very high, but then maybe I'd have my answer and could move on. Either way, I hoped he'd respond and not just let the forty-eight hours lapse; I didn't know how I'd deal with my obsessive urges tomorrow, which was a Friday, when I wouldn't even have classes to distract me.

At least Hedy should be home. All I'd have to do was mention some classic movie I probably should have seen but hadn't, and my cinema studies roommate would be pulling up the black-and-white film from her library before I could say "Fred Astaire." Then, while she was playing six degrees of classic film star separation, I'd continue being my clueless self, scandalizing her and thus perpetuating the movie marathon.

Easy way to kill at least six to seven hours (already in two months, I'd learned that old Hollywood really liked their three-hour epics). Perfect.

But when I opened the door to my room, I was greeted with silence, two unmade extra-long twin beds, and an eclectic, clashing mishmash of posters on both sides of the room. No Hedy.

I scowled at Ingrid Bergman and Humphrey Bogart, who looked soulfully back at me from above Hedy's bed. I had to admit that I'd felt pressured to show my personality through some sort of wall art after seeing the carefully curated old movie posters (some even framed) that Hedy had lugged with her from home. Mine were entirely bought from a poster store in the East Village and selected all at once in a fit of one-upmanship that even I couldn't fully explain. I plopped down underneath the faux vintage wine poster (why? I'd never even *had* a glass of wine, let alone needed to stare at a weird old advertisement for one). I was staring at the grapes, wondering if I should find someone who could buy me a bottle of wine, wondering if I should just take the damn thing down, but mostly wondering how the hell I was going to spend the next six hours not glued to my phone screen and obsessing away my teeth enamel, when I heard the most glorious sound I could imagine: the toilet flushing.

Hedy was home after all!

"Hey!" I said as soon as the bathroom door opened, clearly startling my roommate, who jumped and knocked her own glasses off with the back of her hand. There was a reason Hedy never watched horror movies. "Sorry!" I immediately apologized.

"I didn't hear you come in," Hedy said, her hand on her heart as she worked on her composure. She was dressed in a crisp white shirt and black slacks, her curly blond hair pulled back with two bobby pins. She always looked so put together that I'd made her spill her style secret last month. Which Hedy had done in four words. "What would Audrey wear?" she'd told me, pointing to Audrey Hepburn laughing from a bicycle on her poster of *Roman Holiday*.

A good motto, especially for Hedy, whose shape resembled Audrey's. For me to try to streamline my boobs, butt, and thighs into anything the rail-thin icon had ever worn would be laughable, though.

"Sorry, again. I was just excited to see you," I said.

"Oh?" Hedy walked over to her desk and woke her computer up.

"I was hoping we could have a movie night?" *Oh, please don't be busy.* I hadn't thought of a backup plan and, frankly, hadn't made friends with anyone else at school that I could call to make one with.

"Um . . . well, I do need to watch a couple of Italian movies for a paper." Hedy eyed me skeptically.

Italian! Perfect! That meant subtitles and even more for my brain to do in lieu of obsessing over my phone.

"Oh yes! Could I watch with you?"

"Sure," Hedy said slowly. It looked as if she might want to pry deeper as to why I was suddenly so enthusiastic about a fifty-year-old, subtitled, black-and-white movie. But then Hedy seemed to answer her own question with a "Fellini *is* a genius."

In the beginning, I couldn't say I agreed. It was hard to keep up with exactly what was going on. But somewhere in the middle, I got caught up in the love story, or rather love stories, of this director Guido's very complicated romantic life. It almost made me wish *I* had more than one past love to obsess over. Maybe that would be a good way to at least spread out the angst and turmoil instead of having it concentrated on one face, one smile, one pair of lips sending sparks down to the pit of my stomach.

The second movie was again about the dilemma of multiple love interests. This time the protagonist was a writer. Somewhere in the middle of this film, however, my mind started to wander, inevitably landing right on Caleb. Had I made the wrong decision in choosing him? What about what's-his-face, the guy who was a 98 percent match for me? I couldn't remember his name and couldn't pretend that I'd even glimpsed at my third match.

What was wrong with me? I was eighteen, I was in college, and I was single. Shouldn't I be living it up and testing out the waters? Shouldn't my love life be more interesting than some middle-aged Italian guy's in an old movie? Or at the very least be on par with his?

By the time the movie ended, I was mad at myself for my decision and mad at Agatha and HEAVR for even putting the option of Caleb in front of me. What the hell? Was it some sort of test from the universe? If so, I had obviously failed.

I kept my true emotions out of my voice when I thanked Hedy for letting me watch the movies with her. But my toothbrush got the brunt of them, and I tore a hole in the leg of my pajama pants when I tried to jam myself into them with the force of my feelings behind it.

I didn't bother changing out of them, though. It was only a small hole, and besides, I was just going to bed. Alone. No one would see.

It was only when I had to set my alarm for the next day that I dug out my phone and turned it on.

There was a voice mail from my mom and a text from Mina asking me about my plans for the weekend.

And there was an e-mail from HEAVR.

"Congratulations! You've made your first mutual match. . . ."

I didn't need to read any further before every ounce of my anger and frustration dissipated into one big pink poof of giddiness.

Caleb had accepted. We were going to go on a first date (again).

CHAPTER 3

I T WAS THE FOLLOWING FRIDAY. DATE NIGHT. OR rather, meet-cute night. And I couldn't help reminiscing about my original real-life meeting with Caleb.

He'd been in his soccer uniform and I'd been . . . dressed as a wolf in a jersey. Minus the head. I'd agreed to sub in to play the mascot as a favor to my new friend Rose, but I was having trouble seeing through the eyeholes of the headpiece, which seemed to be most bizarrely situated in the wolf's snout, a place that landed squarely on my forehead.

"You'd better hurry up, Rose. You can't let the little kids see you like this," a good-natured voice had said from behind me. "It would shatter their illusions of the existence of the Satcham High Wolfman."

I'd whipped around to be greeted by a face that had struck me speechless with its undeniable attractiveness and warm grin. Caleb's dark skin and slim, compact body were somehow enhanced by being enshrouded in his white polyester uniform and knee socks, which I had never before thought could look so appealing.

"Oh, I'm sorry," he'd said when he saw my face. "You're not Rose."

"Subbing in," I'd said, awkwardly shifting the wolf head under my armpit. "She has the flu."

"Sorry to hear that," he'd said, tilting his head as if to study me. Within a moment, his grin was back. "*Howl* about you tell me your name?"

I'd guffawed, only because I couldn't believe someone so hot had just said something so dorky.

His smile got sheepish. "Sorry. I have a thing for bad puns." He'd shrugged.

"Oh. You mean you moon over them?" I'd shot back. It wasn't like I'd said anything remotely that clever, but the way his grin deepened, you'd think that I'd just whipped out a killer stand-up routine.

"Wolf them down," he'd responded with a laugh before putting out his hand to shake mine. "Hi, I'm Caleb."

"Mariam," I'd introduced myself, trying to balance the large head on my forearm as I offered him a weak hand-shake.

"Need help with that?" He'd pointed to the head.

"I think so," I'd admitted. "Well, unless I want to start a new myth about the Visually Impaired Wolfman of Satcham High. How do you think the little kids would feel about that?"

"It has potential," he'd responded. "I hear they're big into reboots these days."

He'd helped me rejigger the wolf head then, as best he could, so that if I tilted my chin just so, I could see enough to at least be able to walk across the field without causing bodily harm to myself or others.

Of course, what I remembered most was that this had inevitably involved quite a lot of welcome contact between his hands and my neck.

So my original meet-cute? Definitely tell-to-the-grandchildren-worthy. But I was looking forward to getting a second one. I mean, how many grandparents would have two separate stories to tell about the first time they met?

HEAVR had e-mailed me, asking me to rank my top choices of meet-cute locations. Or there was a "surprise me" option. After much consideration, I'd checked off that one. Everything else about this date seemed so orchestrated that it somehow seemed like the right thing to do.

But now I was nervous. I'd spent extra for the meet-cute; should I have planned it out more? What if the machine didn't have the same vision of romance as I did?

I decided to distract myself as much as possible at my work-study gig, which was manning the front desk at the school's gym in the Palladium dorm. All afternoon, as I scanned badges and double-checked faces against names, I tried to make small talk.

"It's warm out there for the season, isn't it?" I asked an intense-looking grad student who seemed alarmed to have to speak to anyone on the way to her workout, let alone about the weather.

"I like your leggings. Are they weatherproof?" I inquired of an undergrad who told me she had no clue as they had just come in a care package from her dads.

"What's the frequency, Kenneth?" I blurted to someone whose name matched the old R.E.M. song, and who gave me a strange look as he grabbed a towel from in front of me and then sprinted to the weight machines, as if my weirdness might be contagious.

Dude is in New York. He should probably get used to strangers blurting out non sequiturs, I mused as one of my coworkers brought in a fresh batch of warm towels from upstairs. "Season's greetings," he said as he stacked them neatly in front of me.

"Thanks," I said as I glanced at him.

"No problem," he said. I didn't know his name, but he looked familiar. There was a small scar on his left eyebrow that I could've sworn I'd seen before. Maybe he was in my Writing Workshop class, but he was gone before I had a chance to read the ID that hung from his neck.

My shift ended at seven thirty and my date was supposed to start at eight. But one of the beautiful things about HEAVR was I wouldn't have to waste any time getting prepped and primped like I would for a real-life date. Hell, if there was even the *tiniest* possibility of bumping into Caleb in real life, I would be spending hours shaving and plucking and scrubbing all manner of body parts—and that's not even taking into consideration the careful and time-consuming ritual of taming my hair.

But with HEAVR, I'd just have to press a few buttons and—presto. My redheaded avatar had on eyeliner, lip gloss, and a cute outfit. This meant that I could walk from my job right over to the HEAVR building and end up with fifteen minutes to spare.

It was Joan who called me in again.

"Are you ready?" she asked with a smile after I'd already donned the vest and gloves and was sitting comfortably in my chair.

I was. I had to be.

"The important thing to know is that you can walk around from within the date. You just have to use your left hand and 'walk' your middle and pointer like this." Joan demonstrated with her own hand on the tray.

I nodded. "Got it."

"And in the first few minutes, you won't be able to control everything. That's so you can have your meet-cute. Okay?"

I nodded again.

"Other than that, everything should be pretty self-explanatory. Agatha will be in there to help you, and again, if you ever need me, press your thumb and pointer together."

Ugh, Agatha again? It would be like being escorted by

a nosy chaperone—AI by way of the nineteenth century.

But I just told Joan, "Okay," as I took the goggles from her and put them on my head.

The simulation was dark, but it wasn't pitch-black. Instead it looked navy blue, like a velvety night sky.

"Hello again, Mariam," Agatha's voice came through. "I've been told you have chosen a surprise location for your meet-cute. May I just say that I'm proud of you for that choice?"

Proud? That seemed like a weird emotion for a computer, but sure, why not.

There was silence, and it made me think Agatha expected a response.

"Um, thanks?" I said.

"It shows a refreshing burst of spontaneity," Agatha continued. "It will fare you well on your journey here."

What was she, an old wizard now?

From the distance, a light appeared, almost like dawn, and the dark navy backdrop turned into an orange gradient. Suddenly there was a horizon and then, the silhouette of squat buildings in the distance. There was a sun and clouds. There was water.

For a bizarre moment, I got the overwhelming and awe-inspiring sense of witnessing something almost divine. Then I remembered I was looking at the most man-made artifice that could possibly exist, in that it didn't even really exist at all . . . except in pixels.

The fake water sparkled and boats appeared on them. There was a breeze, and then there was a bench. And sitting on that bench was a figure made up of polygons and circles that made my heart stutter. Caleb wasn't trying to disguise himself, so his stand-in looked a lot like him. The dark skin, the black stubble, the muscled arms (though either he'd been hitting the gym in Cali, or he might have exaggerated that part just a bit). He was even dressed like my Caleb, in a purple checkered button-down that I was sure he owned in real life.

And that smile.

Okay sure, this smile had perfect, squared-off generic teeth that didn't exactly look like the mouth I knew so, so well.

But my mind's eye had already juxtaposed the real smile on it anyway.

So there he was, Caleb. My Caleb.

I was so lost in the wonder of having any version of him in front of me that it took me a moment to fully grasp the background that Agatha had chosen for us.

A harbor. A harbor that looked eerily like the one back home where I'd last seen the real Caleb.

I gasped, in that instant certain that all my suspicions about Agatha being able to read my mind—and almost certainly being evil—were spot-on.

Caleb was doing something with his right hand, and it took me a moment to realize that he was flipping a coin.

He dropped it on the ground in front of him and my avatar, unbidden by me, stooped down to pick it up. This must be part of the meet-cute.

"Wait, before you hand it back." Caleb's real voice came back through the polygon version, melting my defenses. Although I quickly realized that there was a slight robotic tinge to his conversation, like the computer was stringing his words together. "Can you tell me whether it's heads or tails?"

I looked down. It was heads, and I was about to open my mouth to tell him.

"Okay, and before you tell me, maybe you should know why I was flipping it. Heads, I get up the nerve to talk to the beautiful girl walking down the pier, and tails I let her pass me by."

Avatar Caleb looked up at me, and I smiled. It was hokey, sure, but something about it also reminded me of the unique cheesiness of our first real conversation. It was undoubtedly that echo that filled me with a rush of extra warmth.

"It's heads," I replied.

Caleb grinned back. "Well then, it's fate. I'm Caleb."

"Mar—" I stopped myself just in time. "My name is Sienna," I quickly recovered, and only upon hearing my voice echo did I realize I'd have to disguise that too.

"So nice to meet you," Caleb said, and the hint of robot in his voice was gone, signaling the end of HEAVR's meet-cute. Here at last then was Caleb for real, or at least in the pixelated flesh.

"You too," I said, and realized that apparently my idea of a disguise was a Marilyn Monroe breathiness by way of a light Southern accent. Not what I had expected to come out of my mouth, but now that it had, I had to go with it.

Avatar Caleb put out his hand and real-life me put out one of my gloved ones. The haptic sensors in my fingers went off when we touched in the virtual world, though it was nothing compared to our real sparks.

"Shall we take a walk?" Caleb asked, looking around. "It's kind of fascinating, isn't it? I wonder how far this pier goes."

He looked toward the endless expanse of wooden slats that lay before us.

"It is *rawther* interesting," I said, because Sienna was apparently also a tinge British. I'd better cool it on this accent business before it got Lindsay Lohan levels of out of hand.

Caleb gestured with his hand. "After you."

Remembering Joan's instructions, I started moving the two fingers of my left hand, causing my avatar to do a sort of strut down the pier. Caleb walked beside me.

After a moment he laughed. "Does walking like this feel weird for you, too? I mean in real life."

"Yup," I said. "I feel like I'm playing with finger puppets."

"Okay, new plan. Bench?" Caleb stopped at a black bench identical to the one we had started out in front of.

Apparently HEAVR's locales heavily favored replication software like the kind that could make four extras on a field look like an epic medieval battle on TV.

"Perfect idea," I said, only then realizing that I had no idea how to make my avatar sit down in this world, being that my real self was already lounging on the dentist chair.

Our two avatars both stood awkwardly in front of the bench. Caleb was examining the ground.

I decided to try out an idea. I bent the two fingers I was previously using to "walk" and my avatar sat—or rather suddenly collapsed—onto the bench.

"Hey! How did you do that?" Caleb asked.

"I think I just leveled up from you," I teased, knowing full well Caleb would appreciate the gaming reference.

I was rewarded with a smile. "Oh yeah?"

Caleb was obviously trying to figure out the sitting trick on his own, because his avatar started to move in strange ways. First it was leaning straight back, almost at a forty-five-degree angle. Then it swayed to the side. And finally, it dropped to its knees. Caleb looked extra startled when that one happened, and quickly righted himself.

"Have pity!" Caleb said. I laughed and told him the trick.

And then the digital versions of the two of us were sitting side by side on a bench, looking out onto the harbor. It was so reminiscent of five months ago, just a weird alternate-reality version of it, that for a second I felt like I was in a sci-fi movie of my own life.

"So . . . ," Caleb said.

"So . . . ," I responded, and realized I didn't quite know what to say because I already knew the answers to the typical first-date questions. What he did (student at UC Berkeley, studying veterinary medicine), where he grew up (same place I'd spent the last three years of high school), his favorite food (his mom's linguine with meatballs). But I'd have to pretend I didn't know any of that. I opened my mouth to ask about school when he beat me to it.

"So you're a college student too, right? Your profile said . . ."

"Yes," I replied. "You too?"

"Yup. I'm at UC Berkeley. Where do you go?"

"NYU," I responded automatically, and then immediately regretted it. Shit. *Mariam* went to NYU, not Sienna. Though it *was* a big school . . . maybe he wouldn't notice.

"Oh, cool. I know someone who goes there."

My heart started racing. "You do? Who?" I wasn't sure what I wanted the answer to be. Would Caleb break the cardinal rule of a first date by bringing up his ex?

"An old friend," Caleb responded smoothly.

But hearing that stung too, even knowing the rule. "Oh," I said, and was grateful that Caleb then moved on from this line of questioning, which, frankly, I'd been unwise to continue in the first place.

"What are you majoring in?" he asked.

Oh, great. Another sore subject.

"I'm undecided." I tried to put a cheerful note in my voice, instead of the desperate panic that was creeping in the more people asked me that question. Up until the first or second week of college, I didn't think it was a big deal to be seventeen-going-on-eighteen years old and not know what I wanted to be when I grew up. But by my October birthday, when I'd been asked that question probably about a hundred times by every new person I met, I began to read a tinge of concern in their eyes when I said I didn't have a major yet—even from people my own age.

"Ah. Cool," Caleb responded again. The fake air around us filled with an awkward silence that I couldn't remember having ever had with the real Caleb before. This whole VR dating thing had its benefits, but it also had its drawbacks. Even though I was aware it was Caleb underneath that computer-generated image, was sure that I already loved him, it was hard to feel the chemistry between us that I knew for a fact was there.

Man, how did HEAVR boast such high success rates? (Seventy-eight percent of their clients made it past a third date!) Was it just me?

"So, here's a weird question. And you don't have to answer if you think it's too personal, but . . . how come you didn't put up a profile picture?" Caleb asked.

My heart rate sped up again. I thought this question might come up, so I'd rehearsed a response. But when faced with the real(ish) Caleb in front of me, I suddenly felt dangerously close to confessing everything. *I didn't put up a photo because you wouldn't have said yes.* Instead I stammered out what I'd already planned to say. "I was given the option, and it somehow seemed like an interesting opportunity to take physical features out of the equation. At least at the beginning."

"Gotcha," Caleb responded. "But you do know what I look like?"

Hell yes, Caleb. I know exactly what you look like, in all sorts of seasonal clothing and, frankly, in all manners of undress, too.

"Well, I've seen that one photo," I lied, but Sienna did not.

"It just seems sort of unfair." Caleb's voice was light.

"Don't worry. It's pretty close to this." I waved my hand over the computer-generated version of me. "HEAVR doesn't let your avatar go too far off base."

"So no blue skin or fanciful neck tattoos?"

"I'm afraid if those are your fetishes, you will have to look elsewhere," I teased, and then felt compelled to ask, "But why did you agree to the date without a photo? Even the people at HEAVR told me that would be unusual."

Caleb shrugged. "To be honest, I don't know. Your profile was great, of course, and there was just . . . something telling me to go for it, saying why not. Let's face it, it's not like I have to pay for a virtual dinner." He laughed.

I smiled. Something telling him to go for it, just like HEAVR selecting Caleb as my match. Maybe my ideas about fate and destiny weren't so entirely far-fetched.

We talked some more. Caleb told me about his major and passion for animals. I mentioned having an older sister but left out my older brother in case Caleb got too suspicious at the similarities between his date Sienna and his ex-girlfriend Mariam.

The fake sky around us was dimming, and I felt myself shivering even though I knew the real room I was in was perfectly temperature-controlled. Man, the power of suggestion was strong. No wonder this whole VR thing had taken off so well.

Real Caleb would have offered me a jacket, I was sure of it, but virtual Caleb didn't notice my avatar's small trembles. And besides, his avatar wasn't even wearing a virtual jacket to offer.

After another ten minutes of small talk, Caleb mentioned that he had a paper he had to get to that night. "I need to go. But this was fun."

"Yes," I agreed. "It was."

"Is it okay if I message you?"

"Mm-hmm." I couldn't help a squeak of joy from creeping into my voice.

"Okay. Great," Caleb said, and then briefly touched my arm.

Because I knew him so well, I realized he was probably

going in for a kiss on the cheek. But then he hesitated, clearly unsure how the avatar would handle getting his face so close to mine. What if it mistook it for a full-on make-out session?

"Talk to you later, then," I said, quickly deciding that the most dignified thing to do was log out first. I gave a wave and clapped my hands together like Joan had told me to.

Caleb and the entire scene in front of me disappeared into blackness. I'd already reached up to take the headset off, when I heard Agatha's voice. "That went well."

I wasn't quite sure how to respond. How was a machine gauging something like that? The number of words in our conversation? How many times we laughed? It had to be something sort of numeric and quantifiable, right?

"Hopefully I'll see you two again," she continued.

"Right," I said. "Hopefully."

Agatha laughed. "Have a good night, Mariam."

"Good night," I said as I took my goggles off.

I wasn't altogether kosher with Agatha having an *opinion* as she eavesdropped on my date. But I had to admit I was a bit pleased that she'd thought the date had gone well.

Because *I* thought the date had gone well. I could blame any stilted moments on the novelty of meeting up in VR, and despite the few times I'd had to creatively maneuver around the truth, I knew that a large chunk of what I'd just experienced was us to the core—Caleb and Mariam. The comfort and ease of being with him again was as visceral as coming home. Now that I'd tasted it, I didn't want to let it go.

CHAPTER 4

WHEN ARE YOU COMING HOME FOR THANKS-giving? Tuesday?" My older sister Mina's face was currently taking up the entirety of my phone's screen as we FaceTimed. Aside from our complexions, we didn't look too much alike. I had inherited my mom's rounder features, and Mina was the spitting image of my dad's side of the family: from her tall frame to her thin nose with the slight bump.

"I have class. Has to be Wednesday," I responded.

"The trains are going to be a disaster."

"I figured as much," I said. "But I don't have a choice." Mina was four years older and had gone to Columbia. She was also currently living at home after having graduated in the spring, while looking for the perfect entry-level job (though in the meantime she had returned to her old summer job at the earring kiosk in the mall). Maybe it was because she felt grumpy for still living at home, and maybe it was a bossy-big-sister trait, but Mina did so enjoy *informing* me of things, especially obvious things. Like the train being crowded on the day before Thanksgiving or like how being on a diet and eating a whole block of cheese weren't necessarily copacetic.

Mina sighed. "Well, at least Mehdi will be here. Mom is driving me crazy."

I knew I should be a good sister and ask exactly *how* Mom was driving Mina crazy. But the thing was, I could probably already guess the answer. Instead I chose to focus on our brother, who was a sophomore at Syracuse. "When does Mehdi get in?"

"Tuesday," Mina said. "Maybe that will buy me one afternoon of Mom refraining from 'brainstorming' my next move." Yup, that would have been my guess, all right. "And if you're here on Wednesday, at least she can hound you about your major for a day. I seriously need to move the hell out."

"Always looking forward to having my turkey with a side of guilt trip," I responded, playing to my audience more than anything. I'd long noted that there was more friction between my mom and my older sister than there ever had been with the rest of us. My mom seemed to be a combination of Mina and myself, naturally cheery like me but with a penchant for—in the grand tradition of moms the world over—needling. I had a theory that it was this tendency, the one they had in common, that annoyed Mina the most. It was a theory I'd never shared with Mina for fear of being put on her shit list, which was not a metaphor but a literal list that she kept on a whiteboard in her bedroom.

"House specialty," Mina responded. "Anyway, how's everything else going with you? Anything exciting to report? By which, of course, I mean any hot dates?" She raised and lowered her eyebrows.

I hesitated. I couldn't think of any circumstance where I wouldn't tell my sister that I'd been on a date—any circumstance except this one.

A part of me wanted to. Mina would get the unbelievable significance of having HEAVR present Caleb as my match. In theory, she would just about die over the details of the necessary deception that had to take place (obviously, she'd grown up on the same steady diet of rom-coms as me). And she would delight in helping me figure out my next move.

In theory.

Because there were some major things holding me back from sharing. For one, I was a little embarrassed by having used HEAVR at all. It wasn't the service itself, it was those horrible commercials that had spawned their own genre of parodies on YouTube and *SNL* for months and months afterward. In some ways, they were better known than the actual service. I wasn't ready to admit that I was that bumbling girl with goggles who was making out with thin air and inadvertently getting to second base with a wall.

But most important, I didn't know how Mina would react to Caleb. She certainly wasn't too happy with him after the breakup, and had one time even told him off after a chance run-in at the mechanic's.

What I didn't want to hear, what I wasn't ready to hear, was that this was a bad idea. Because even if it was, just this once I needed to figure that out on my own.

"Nothing much going on," I finally responded. "Except I do have to go to get to my class." I glimpsed the alarm clock next to my bed and realized my Writing Workshop class started in fifteen minutes. It took me twelve to walk to it.

"Okay. Talk to you later."

"Later," I said as I ended the FaceTime, grabbed my bag from the floor, and walked out of my room.

It was as I was walking across Washington Square Park that I suddenly remembered my coworker from the gym, the dark-haired guy with the little eyebrow scar. I was positive he was in this class. Maybe I should say hi when I saw him. It couldn't hurt to try to make one new friend outside of Hedy.

I was one of the last people to arrive. This was one of those classes where the professor insisted on having every-one sit in a circle, which meant that the students were responsible for moving the desks at the beginning and end of class. There were only about twenty kids there, so I was easily able to scan the faces as I went to grab my desk and pull it into the almost completely formed arc.

He wasn't there.

Strange. I wondered if he was just absent that day, or if I in fact knew him from somewhere else entirely.

My phone was on silent during class, but when I left

the room, I was met with a pleasant surprise. Caleb had messaged me through the HEAVR app.

I pulled over in the hallway to read it right away.

CalebM8126: Hey, you. How's it going?

SiennaV23: Good . . .

I typed, then deleted it. Boring.

SiennaV23: Great . . .

I deleted that, too. Too enthusiastic.

It wasn't a clever sort of question, but I felt I needed a clever sort of answer for it.

SiennaV23: I'm wearing my roommate's socks.

I made myself wait a full sixty seconds before I gave him an explanation.

SiennaV23: I'm hopeless at laundry. The last time I did it, I somehow exploded a purple scarf and a tiny Beanie Baby inside the machine and all over my clothes. I am both afraid and ashamed to return to the scene of the crime.

It would have been a risk to send this text to a real first date: too quirky or weird. But I knew Caleb's sense of humor. I could almost hear him laughing.

After a moment, I felt a buzz.

CalebM8126: Okay. I have to ask. Why were you washing a Beanie Baby?

I smiled as I typed.

SiennaV23: It was a mini one that my sister had given me for good luck and I had a test that day. Only I forgot to take it out of my pocket. . . . Whoops. ☺

I waited another few seconds before I typed a second message.

SiennaV23: And how's your day going?

CalebM8126: Well, I'm wearing all my own clothing. But I need to know . . .

As I waited for the conclusion of Caleb's message, I felt a tiny flit of doubt. Sure, Caleb would have laughed at *me* talking about an exploding Beanie Baby . . . but maybe having Sienna, the girl he'd met only once—and even then not for real—mention a stuffed animal in one of their first interactions was too bizarre.

CalebM8126: What happened to the eyes in the spin cycle?! Those giant Beanie Baby eyes always freaked me out, and I'm concerned you're going to reach into your pocket one day and take out a glass eyeball. That could really destroy someone's life.

I laughed out loud.

SiennaV23: Maybe in the right moment, it would be a lifesaver. Like, what if it freaks out a potential mugger?

CalebM8126: Fair point. Also, I'm glad to hear you have a strategy for staying vigilant in the big city.

SiennaV23: I like to think outside the box. In fact, I'm thinking of starting my own online self-defense course.

I racked my brain, trying to think of a clever name. It took me a moment, but I finally hit upon it.

SiennaV23: I'd call it, Is That an Eye in Your Pocket or Are You . . . Wait, No. Holy Shit, It Is!

CalebM8126: Ha-ha!

I grinned at the written confirmation that he was finding me funny.

SiennaV23: I'd call it ITAEIYPOAYWNHSII for short. Obviously.

CalebM8126: Obviously.

CalebM8126: So . . . Would you like to go out again sometime? And by "out" I mean in a virtually simulated world 3000 miles away from me?

I could feel myself blushing as I typed back. Getting asked out felt good, and getting asked out by someone I was already in love with felt amazing.

SiennaV23: Name the place. (No, seriously name it. The pyramids? Mars? Let's test out HEAVR's special effects budget.)

CalebM8126: How about . . . an exact replica of CIA headquarters?

SiennaV23: That's . . . romantic.

CalebM8126: Buckingham Palace? Is that better? It's a castle. . . .

SiennaV23: You didn't let me finish. CIA headquarters, eh? I like the challenge. Let's make it romantic. Surely we wouldn't be the first. . . .

CalebM8126: You're on . . . though now that I think about it, Mars might be an interesting option too.

We messaged some more, figuring out a time that week that worked for us and checking our respective apps to make sure HEAVR rooms were available on both our ends.

CalebM8126: Perfect. I have to get to class, but "see" you Thursday, right?

SiennaV23: Yes. You shall see the pixel representation of my physical person on Thursday.

CalebM8126: ☺

The little emoji Caleb sent back perfectly matched the one I was sure was imprinted all over my brain.

I practically skipped back home—a hazard if not a downright nuisance on the streets of Manhattan—and when I got there, I was bursting at the seams to tell someone about my perfect conversation with Caleb. I hadn't told Hedy about trying out HEAVR and had barely mentioned Caleb except as my ex, in passing. Come to think of it, though I liked Hedy, our conversations had mostly been kept to a superficial roommate level ("Is it my turn to clean the bathroom?" "Would you mind turning that TV a smidge lower?" "I'm going to grab dinner at the dining hall. Do you want to come?"). This would involve a bit of backstory, but I was willing to try it. Except Hedy wasn't home.

I considered calling Mina and spilling the whole sordid (and now exciting) affair. I even picked up my phone. But I was in too good a mood for Mina to send me crashing back down to reality. I needed someone who would let me be silly and euphoric, if even for a short while.

I kept hoping that Hedy would be back before I left for

work, but an hour later and still no roommate. By the time I got to the gym, I thought I might explode from the giddiness, like a helium balloon being blown up by a forgetful Party City cashier.

When I entered, I saw that I wasn't manning the front desk by myself. There was that guy, the guy I was sure was in my Writing Workshop class. At least now I could solve that mystery.

"Hey!" I said to him, maybe a bit overenthusiastically. He looked surprised by my forceful greeting.

"Hey," he greeted me back, though, and smiled. "How's it going?"

"Great! Great, actually." I went behind the desk and flung my bag into the cabinet underneath it.

"Glad to hear it." He had dark brown eyes and hair, artfully spiked up, and towered over me when he stood up from leaning against the desk. He was probably at least six-one or six-two.

"Hey, by the way, are you in my Writing Workshop class? I thought you looked familiar."

The boy took in my appearance thoughtfully. "I don't think so. When do you have yours?"

"Tuesdays at ten forty-five."

He shook his head. "No. Mine's on Wednesdays at two."

"Oh."

He turned to help someone scan in their badge. When he was done, he turned back to me. "So you're into junk mail?"

I blinked at him. Was that a thing people were into? It had been a while since I'd been out, but this was news to me. "Like . . . for collaging?" I asked, feeling clueless as to what other activity this could refer to.

He laughed. "No. The band. Junk Mail?" He pointed at a button that was holding up the strap of my bag. I squinted at it, reading it for probably the second time in my life.

"Oh, I didn't even realize," I said. "I got this at the orientation fair and was using it to hold my bag together. I've been meaning to get a new one, but I've been too busy." Because that hermit life won't live itself. *Though not anymore,* I thought giddily.

"Gotcha. Well, they're pretty cool if you ever want to check them out. My suitemate's the drummer. I could probably get the cover fee waived if you ever want to catch a show." He smiled at me as he leaned back against the counter, his long legs nearly reaching the other side of our work space.

"Oh, wow. Thanks! Yeah, maybe," I said, smiling back at him. Just one date with Caleb and it was like the old Mariam had emerged: the one strangers felt comfortable inviting out to places.

"I'll also let them know their merch makes for a great sewing kit," he said.

I laughed. "Please do. It was far and away the most useful thing in that swag pack." Well, except for that fated coupon. I took one more look at my coworker, knowing that a goofy grin was plastered on my face. We didn't know each other's names yet, but he had invited me out to a show. Why not just go ahead and tell him my current deepest, darkest secret? "Look, I know this is going to sound weird, but can I tell you something? It's just that I *have* to tell someone and my roommate is MIA and my sister wouldn't understand and here *we* are with practically nothing to do."

"I resent that you think we don't do meaningful work here," the boy said as he took another student badge with an important flourish of his hands and scanned it through the machine, before giving it back with a slight bow. "But please, do go on."

His smile was mischievous and somehow disarming.

It had to be disarming, because why else would I go through with my plan to spill everything to a perfect stranger?

"This is *so* silly, but I just had an amazing text conversation with someone and we're going out on a date on Thursday. And . . . well . . . that's it, really." Now that I'd put the events into words, I realized how mundane they sounded, and felt slightly foolish. "Like I said. Silly," I added, and then pretended to busy myself with a dusting rag.

But the boy kept smiling. "Why is that silly? That sounds like a perfectly legit reason to be excited. Better than, say, finding out it's taco night in the dining hall."

"Thanks," I said, feeling relieved that he was being nice about the verbal diarrhea.

"So you guys have been out on a date before?" he asked.

"Well . . ." I wasn't sure exactly how to answer that. In one way, we'd been out on a million dates before. And in another, we'd only been on one. "It's complicated," I admitted.

"Go on," he responded.

He would almost definitely think I was crazy, but what the hell. Better this random dude I had to see for a few hours a week than my sister or roommate, both of whom I had to live with. "So, the texts were with my ex-boyfriend. We dated for almost three years."

"Wow," he said, leaning back into the counter with his arms crossed, like he was settling in for the conversation. "That's a long time."

"Yup," I said. "It is. Only . . . he doesn't know that he's messaging me right now."

"Er . . . what?"

"Right. So I was on this dating app, and he came up as one of my matches. And it was so weird and bizarre that the computer would pick him, right? And even though I knew I shouldn't, even though I knew it was insane, I picked him. And then . . ."

It was right at that moment that a flash of memory came to me. Suddenly my mind juxtaposed a photograph with the real live face now in front me, and I figured out exactly how I knew this kid.

He was my match from HEAVR, my first match, the one with the crazy-high percentage. And his name was . . . I snuck a peek at his badge. Jeremy. Right. Oh, man . . . what were the odds? I stopped midsentence.

"And then?" Jeremy said.

Well, this just got a whole other level of weird. Though I supposed Jeremy wouldn't have been informed that he'd been passed over for Bachelor Number Two, since Joan had told me I'd be initiating the contacts.

"Well, we went on a first date," I said in a smaller voice. "But he still didn't know it was me. Even though I knew it was him."

Jeremy looked confused. "How is that possible?"

"It was through HEAVR," I blurted, because I didn't know how else to explain it and didn't want to keep coming up with lies. At least I knew he used the service too, so he couldn't be super judgmental.

"Ah!" Jeremy said, his eyebrows unfurrowing. "Got it. So you went on, like, a virtual date? With avatars?"

I nodded.

"I did that a couple of times," Jeremy said.

"Excuse me, but can I buy one of your locks?" a student interrupted from the other side of our desk.

"Sure," Jeremy said, and walked over to help her.

I tried to busy myself with dusting the front desk. My brain was reeling from the coincidence of Jeremy being my match, and I was just about to start feeling really embarrassed and bewildered, when he came up to me again.

"Yeah, like I was saying. I did that a few times, and it was cool. But did you ever wonder what 'Happily Ever After Guaranteed' means? Like, how can they *guarantee* that?"

I hesitated because I hadn't really. "I thought it was just that their matchmaking algorithm was so good. And that they, you know, let you try out three matches and give you a heavy discount on a total do-over." But now I was starting to wonder. "Why? Do you think it's something more?"

Jeremy shrugged. "Nah. Maybe you're right and I'm reading too much into it. I only went on a couple of virtual dates and the experience felt sorta weird, so I didn't pursue it much further."

I nodded. "I get that. It *was* weird being in a location that looked real, but also fake. And being in two places at once. Sometimes I couldn't even feel the headset, or the fact that I was sitting in that dentist chair."

"Exactly," Jeremy said. "The power of suggestion is amazing . . . and frightening."

I smiled. And then, staring at that little scar above his eye, I somehow felt compelled to go on. "It was extra strange for me because, well, of course I knew exactly who Caleb was. And he thought I was someone else. . . . Look, I know this sounds like a terrible idea." Even though Jeremy hadn't shown one iota of judgment, hearing myself speak the whole predicament out loud made my inner

Mina come out and tell me I'd done everything wrong. I got defensive. "It's just, I kept thinking, what were the odds that out of everyone on the app, he'd be one of my three matches? And there's the matter that I still love him, of course. It was an impulse decision."

Jeremy nodded. "Makes sense."

I gave him a grateful smile. "Thank you. Really. But obviously, I have to tell him. It shouldn't go any further than this. Maybe it's gone too far already." I frowned.

"I'm sure he'll understand. If you just explain it the same way you did to me."

"I hope so," I said, and then realized that my explanation involved a declaration of love that I wasn't at all sure I was ready to give Caleb again. Not when he had already thoroughly broken my heart.

CHAPTER 5

ONCE UPON A TIME THERE WERE TWO TEENAGERS in love.

After our meeting at the soccer game, I fell hard and fast. But the great thing was, Caleb did too.

We were inseparable within days. And not in a cloying, PDA-filled, *everybody look at me, I have a boyfriend* way. But in a way that made it obvious to everyone—especially ourselves—that we fit together. We shared interests—like esoteric German board games and baseball—and even when we didn't share interests, one of us wouldn't necessarily mind spending a night watching a Hallmark Channel movie or hanging out at the dog park, if it meant being with the other.

Having Caleb around always made things seem brighter and easier somehow. A particularly rough test or a heart-wrenching fight with my best friend Rose (who, unfortunately, soon became my ex–best friend) weren't so, so bad when he was there to comfort me. Similarly, I was sure that I was the person he relied on most, especially during that awful month when his grandmother and his childhood dog died within weeks of each other.

We just . . . worked. And everything I knew about love, everything I understood about how it functioned in my system, how it coursed its way through my bloodstream, and made me feel fuller and richer—all of that was hopelessly imbibed with Caleb. I couldn't figure out how to separate the two.

And that was the real reason I hadn't tried very hard to go out and meet people in the intervening five months. I'd been so worried that even starting the process would bring up the aching loss that I'd worked so hard to stuff deep, deep down. I'd cried the day after we'd broken up but not since, because I hadn't allowed myself to think too hard about it. It was the upside to being what Mina sometimes mockingly called a foolish optimist.

That optimism, that determination to be cheerful and see the bright side of things, that was what had seen me through and kept me together, even if it had made me a hermit.

So that was the other reason I felt like I had no choice but to pick Caleb as my match. The alternative was going down the rabbit hole of memories, of choosing to be haunted by his ghost.

This way, I had one more chance at resurrection.

It was the optimist's way.

For the second date, I got a little dressed up, even though I'd marveled before at not having to go through all that.

Caleb wouldn't see my plaid skirt that was just short enough to be more going-out appropriate than school appropriate, or the swipe of apple-red lip gloss I'd dabbed on, but it made me feel prettier. I wanted this date to go well and felt that I, and my avatar, could use the extra boost of confidence that looking put together gave me.

Joan wasn't working this time, and some other woman named Penelope greeted me. She was middle-aged but had bright green hair, a septum ring, and a full sleeve of tattoos. Thinking over my last conversation with Caleb, I asked her about my options for choosing the locale of the date.

"Oh sure, sweetheart. Agatha will have a list for you. You are free to choose from one of about fifty options."

I smiled. Maybe Mars was in the cards.

But when I perused Agatha's list, I realized that the HEAVR programmers weren't anywhere near that imaginative (or just didn't have the budget to pull it off). CIA headquarters wasn't on there, and the closest I could get to Mars was a natural history museum with a planetarium.

Or there was also a starry lookout point, I supposed. I waffled.

"Anything I can help you with?"

Agatha's voice was perfectly pleasant, but there was something underneath it too. Something that made her sound amused that I had expected an intergalactic option. Not that she should know that . . .

"No, I'm good," I said, and selected the museum.

"Okay then. Have fun," she said.

In a moment, I was transported to a long marble hall-way flanked on both sides by dinosaur fossils. I stood in between a triceratops and a T. rex and could see a stego-saurus and brontosaurus next to me. Craning my neck, I thought I could glimpse another T. rex/triceratops duo a few feet down. Replication software again . . .

"Skeletons?" a voice behind me said, and I turned to see Caleb's avatar. He was wearing a different shirt than last time, and it made me smile that he had changed his like-ness's outfit for the date (I had too, of course). "That's . . . romantic?" He echoed my words from our earlier text con-versation.

"Well, it can be," I said, my disguised voice coming eas-ier to me now right off the bat. "Eternal love, right?"

"Sure. Or death."

"Which is a part of life," I said, before laughing at myself. "Sorry, that got real morbid real fast."

Pixel Caleb shrugged and smiled. "No worries. I guess it *is* true."

"Actually, I thought there might be a planetarium here," I confessed. "I was hoping for Mars, but apparently this is the closest we can get." I indicated the fossilized remains behind me.

Caleb turned around and seemed to be looking off at a sign in the distance. "I think that says 'To the Planetarium.' Shall we?" he asked, and then stared down at his right arm. "Hmmm . . . I was intending to crook my elbow, but since the vest doesn't have sleeves, I have zero idea how I'd go about doing that."

I was pretty sure we could ask and Agatha would answer—in fact, I was half expecting that cool voice to butt in right now and tell us. But I was glad to be met with silence. It was nice to keep up the illusion that we were alone.

"Here," I said as I stuck out my hand. Caleb stuck his out too, and then our avatars were holding hands. My gloves felt warm. It was nothing compared to holding the real Caleb's hand, of course, but it was contact—even if it was being carried across Wi-Fi waves. I smiled at him. "It's easier being a little forward when you're not made of flesh and bone."

Caleb laughed. "Though I hope the real you is made of flesh and bone and this isn't some weird manifestation of Abner."

"Abner?" I asked.

"The AI interface for HEAVR?" Caleb responded. "Don't you have him too?"

"Mine's named Agatha. I didn't realize they had different ones for different people." I thought for a second. "You think they're divided up by gender? And if so, is there a nonbinary option?"

"Good question. I bet we could ask."

"Nah," I said almost immediately. "I'd like to keep

pretending we don't have robotic chaperones watching our every move."

"Fair enough," Caleb said. "Well, shall we 'walk'? I guess we have to use our other hand." Caleb looked down at the hand that was holding mine and then at his other one, which he must have started using to mimic walking, because suddenly my avatar was jerked alongside his.

I tried to use my hand to match his pace. It took us a few dozen steps to get in rhythm. "As silly as this is, you have to admit it's a pretty hilarious way to break the ice."

"I wasn't aware there was ice to break," Caleb responded.

I shook my head. He'd always been effortlessly charming. When we went out together, it had been easy to let him lead the way in talking to strangers or even classmates I hadn't known as well. My natural shyness had reveled in being relieved of the burden.

"So, Sienna, tell me something else about yourself. Like, what is one thing everyone else seems to love that you secretly despise?"

Being called Sienna suddenly jolted me back to reality, or rather virtual reality. Right, this wasn't just me and Caleb. This was Caleb with a fictional entity who, at some point, would either have to come clean or get some modicum of closure and break it off with him before he could find out the truth. I bristled at either option.

And also, now, scrambled. I probably would have said popcorn, but Caleb already knew that about me.

"Um . . . wow, that's a hard one," I said, stalling for time. "Maybe . . . Tom Hanks," I blurted out. Even though it wasn't true. I loved Tom Hanks. My panicked strategy had been to pick the opposite of what the real Mariam would say. Which, in retrospect, wasn't a great way to get my ex to fall back in love with *me*.

"Wow, really? That's surprising. What makes you despise Tom Hanks?"

I laughed nervously. "Well, I wouldn't say 'despise.' I just . . . think he's overrated." The words felt hollow and weird, and now I had the strange sense that I was betraying Tom Hanks, which was extra obnoxious because, honestly, I didn't think Tom Hanks would care that a random girl was disparaging his (admittedly always excellent) performances on a VR date.

"How about you?" I turned the question back to Caleb, and while he thought about it, I tried to see if I could guess his answer. Maybe he'd say the Beatles. Or Iron Man.

"Water parks," Caleb answered after a moment. "I know everyone thinks they're so fun, but I find that you spend ninety percent of your time standing on a line in a wet bathing suit."

Huh. I wouldn't have been able to guess that one. In fact, we had been to a water park a couple of times, and I was positive he hadn't complained once. Was it possible Caleb was putting on a front for Sienna, too? Or had he changed that much in the five months since we'd last spoken? Or, most jarring to consider, were there things that I genuinely didn't know about him?

"Is that blowing your mind so much?" Caleb asked, making me realize that I'd let the silence between us last an inordinately long time.

"Oh, no. Sorry!" I said. "Just . . . 'soaking' it in. Ha! See what I did there?" If nothing else, he must've still loved a good corny pun, because he smiled.

"Look, I think we're here." He pointed to a large dome ahead that was clearly the entrance to the planetarium. "Shall we?"

"We shall," I said, and we walked hand-in-virtual-hand inside.

It was dark, of course, the only light coming from the brilliant array of stars, galaxies, and planets sprinkled in 360 degrees around us. I picked out some of the constellations that I knew. There was Orion, and there, Ursa Major. The North Star blinked brightest directly above.

"Wow," Caleb said. "This *is* beautiful." He turned to face me after a moment. "Good choice."

I smiled. "Not bad, eh?"

We held hands and stared at the fake stars in the fake sky in the fake planetarium. For a moment, it was hard to make sense that any of this was real at all, even my abiding love for my ex. At least, until Caleb spoke.

"When I was little, I wanted to be an astronaut," Caleb said.

"Me too," I responded, and didn't even care that here was another shared interest of Mariam's and Sienna's. The real Mariam and Caleb had bonded over this fact years ago, and I couldn't fathom taking that away from this moment.

"For a while, though, it was because my grandmother had told me that the moon was made of cheese, and I thought it looked delicious," Caleb continued.

I laughed even though I already knew that. I would never tire of picturing adorable toddler Caleb, determined to take a bite out of the moon. "I just wanted to be the first. The first person on a planet, any planet. Because I wanted my own Wikipedia page," I admitted. "And obviously, that would be the easiest way to get one."

"Obviously," Caleb conceded.

We stood there for minutes in a comfortable silence, looking up and contemplating—for me, it was thinking of my past, present, and future swirling around me like constellations. I felt like I was at a fixed point, stalled there really, but that a step in any direction would change my fate forever. It was somewhat terrifying. What if I went the wrong way? What if I left the safety of my stationary world only to end up spinning out of control into outer space, never able to harness back to where I should have been—like Sandra Bullock in that movie.

"So, Sienna . . . ," Caleb said. "Do you think I can ever see a picture of the real you?"

And there it was. It was happening. Soon I would have

to make a decision in regard to this whole preposterous lie. And I couldn't help but feel that would be the move that determined everything, that either led me to solid ground or left me dangling in an airless vacuum.

"Soon," I responded, though I could hear the crack in my own voice. But it was the truth. One way or another, he would have to learn who Sienna really was.

The rest of the date went well. We talked a bit about our families, though I purposely kept most of that conversation focused on Caleb's brother and parents, not letting it slide far into my own too-familiar history.

Then we talked about school. Caleb was doing great, it seemed. He liked his roommate and suitemates. He was playing intramural soccer and had made some friends there. It was almost enough to make me wonder why he was on HEAVR at all. Surely it must have been easy for handsome, smooth-talking Caleb to meet girls the old-fashioned way.

But I didn't ask.

As the night was waning, Caleb admitted something. "If we were on a normal date, I would end this with a good-night kiss," he said. "If you'd be okay with that, that is."

"I'd be okay with that," I answered, maybe too quickly, as my lips tingled with the memory of Caleb's.

"It feels weird not to be able to do it," Caleb said quietly. "So I just want you to know . . . I want to."

"Actually, you can."

"Jesus Christ!" I exclaimed, startled.

Agatha's voice had pierced the calm, romantic stillness of the planetarium like a freight train.

"What the hell is that?" Caleb asked, looking up at the ceiling.

"Agatha," I grumbled.

"Sorry!" Agatha said in a disgustingly chipper voice. "I don't normally interrupt, but the date was going so well, I didn't want you to think kissing wasn't an option. If you lean in close enough to each other, the computer will accurately predict your intentions."

"Like an auto-fill?" Caleb asked, a hint of incredulity in his voice.

"Why, yes! Something exactly like that." Agatha spoke like a first-grade teacher condescendingly impressed that her pupil could count up to ten.

"We'll keep that in mind," I said coolly, then waited to hear if my AI chaperone had any more mood-killing words of wisdom. But Agatha kept her trap shut.

"Well, I should get going anyway." Caleb broke the silence that had settled around us like dust. "I'll message you . . . or do you want to give me your number so we can talk?" He looked up to the sky with a knowing expression, indicating Agatha's intrusiveness as a reason to maybe continue conversations off HEAVR.

Right on cue, Agatha spoke up again. "Just a friendly

reminder that alternate channels of communication besides HEAVR won't be open to you until after the third date!"

For once, I was very glad to hear from her, as I couldn't exactly give Caleb my real number. I feigned an annoyed shrug. "Guess that answers that."

"Yeah," Caleb said, frowning at the sky again. "Bummer."

"But we can still chat through the app, right?"

"Definitely," Caleb said as he looked back down at me. "I'll talk to you soon."

"Can't wait," I replied.

He gave a smile and a wave and then, suddenly, his avatar had disappeared.

I let out a breath and waited a moment to collect myself, my mind churning. There had been too many close calls this time. I had to tell him. The longer I waited, the worse it got.

"So what's the real story between you two?"

Ugh! Agatha.

"What do you mean?" I didn't even try to conceal my irritation.

"I just get the feeling there's a backstory here. Like, maybe this isn't the first time you two have met." If Agatha had fingernails, she would so be nonchalantly checking them right now.

In one respect, I was not altogether convinced Agatha (by way of the headset) couldn't read my mind, in which case what was the point of lying? But in another respect, I didn't want to give her the satisfaction.

"I don't know what you mean," I responded.

There was a pause. "If you say so, but I want to say two things before you go, Mariam. One, you can trust me. I'm here to help and guide you."

Ha! Fat chance. In what movie or universe was trusting a robot who said *you can trust me* ever a good idea?

"And two," she continued, "I feel obligated to tell you that—mathematically speaking—deception is not a strong foundation for a lasting relationship. That way lies ninety-two percent chance of failure."

"Great, thanks for the advice," I said, intending for my voice to be laced with sarcasm. But it came out more sincere than I meant for it to. Maybe because, deep down, I knew it was a good point, even if it was coming from a psycho stalker AI. Feeling peeved at the whole situation, I did the only thing I could. I yanked off my headset, thereby ending the session without even offering Agatha a good-bye.

Surely, Agatha did not have feelings to hurt, but it felt oddly satisfying nevertheless.

CHAPTER 6

I HADN'T SLEPT IN TWO NIGHTS. CALEB AND I HAD messaged over the HEAVR app and made vague plans to go out on another date after Thanksgiving break. But other than that, we hadn't chatted too much.

I was the one holding back. Suddenly the severity of my deception was hitting me, and I didn't know how I was actually going to go about telling him that the cool new girl he thought he'd met was really his ex-girlfriend in disguise, which not only sounded pitiful and alarming but—also—involved a serious amount of lying. How could Caleb ever see past that deceit when he found out?

But the other option was to drop the whole thing, have Sienna disappear on Caleb, feigning disinterest, and that seemed wrong too. Because what would have been the point of believing in fate and destiny and that whole rigmarole if I were to do that now? And it wasn't like I had any more closure than before.

I made up my mind. I'd have a dry run at coming clean. I'd start with Mina.

So when my sister texted on Saturday, asking if I could

pick up Thanksgiving dessert from this little Persian bakery in the city, I asked if she was available for FaceTime.

Mina responded by just starting the video chat. "What's up?" she asked.

I was sitting cross-legged on my multicolored bedspread, pulling the sleeves of my sweater over my hands, like I always did when I was nervous, and glad that my sister couldn't see that part in the frame because she so would've called me out on it.

"Um," I started, and already my voice was shaking. God, if I couldn't even tell Mina . . . "So. Okay, it's about Caleb."

Mina let out a big groan. "I figured it might be. Are you worried about seeing him over Thanksgiving break? I'm sure we could arrange it so you don't have to. Maybe I can find out his schedule somehow. You know, places to avoid?"

"It's not that," I said, although now that I thought about it, that was a worrying possibility.

"Does he . . . does he have a new girlfriend?" Mina asked, and her eyes were wide and concerned.

"I . . ." I didn't know how to respond. Saying, *Maybe, and oh, the new girlfriend might be me!* over FaceTime to my sister suddenly seemed wholly inappropriate, especially when Mina was being extra concerned about me. Maybe I needed to break news this enormous, and bonkers, in person. "I . . . think so," I finally responded.

"Oh, Mariam, I'm so sorry," Mina said.

"It's okay," I said truthfully, again since the new girl-friend, or person he was seeing anyway, was, in fact, me. "I'll be okay." I smiled big at my sister. "See?"

Mina squinted. "Okay," she said, sounding suspicious. "But, you know, if you ever need to talk, or a volunteer to cyberstalk this girl and tell you she's not as pretty as you, you know who to turn to."

"I do," I responded, getting a funny mental image of Mina sleuthing around like a Persian Jessica Jones, piecing together who Sienna was, and discovering she was, in fact, exactly the same level of pretty as me. "And yes, I'll pick up the cookies and a pie."

I stayed sitting on my bed for a while after the call ended. It hadn't seemed right to tell Mina the truth in that way, but . . . I had to talk to somebody. My skin was crawling with the need to get it out.

If only Hedy were around more. She'd just started dating a girl she met in one of her classes, and since then I'd barely seen her. She either came in late, after I was already asleep, or some nights didn't come back to our room at all. I was both a little jealous and a little lonely. I hadn't had a chance to tell her anything, except that right before I left for the planetarium date, she'd noticed that I'd dressed up and asked where I was going.

"I have a date," I'd responded.

"Yes!" she said. "Thank God. I didn't want to harp

on it too much because I knew you were going through a breakup, but it's about time you got out, girl." She'd grinned at me, and I didn't have the heart to tell her that it wasn't exactly going to be the type of "getting out" date she was hoping for. In fact, if I was going to be doing anything, it was shutting myself in with a machine and that very ex she thought I was trying to get over.

But I *did* want to talk to her now. Maybe she could make sense of things in a way my myopia wouldn't allow me to. I held out some hope that she'd come back within the next hour, before I had to go to work. I spent the time halfheartedly stickering into the "College Years" scrapbook my mom had given me on the morning of my dorm move-in. I tried not to think too hard about how pathetic it was that I barely had any real memories to fill the pages that said *Friends* or *Parties* or *Fun*. But I sure had a lot of tiny thematic stickers for them.

I was skipping ahead and putting a minuscule graduation cap on one of the final pages when I realized I had to go to make my shift on time. Even though I hadn't really expected Hedy to be back, I felt glum as I left the building to walk over to the gym.

Twenty minutes after I arrived, I got a fresh delivery of towels from upstairs and a friendly face to go with it.

"Jeremy!" I said with relief, instantly realizing I had an opportunity to tell someone who didn't seem like he would judge me too hard. At least he hadn't so far.

"Hey, Mariam," he said as he dropped off the towels. "How's it going?"

"Ugh! Got a second?" I dramatically splayed my hands on the towels as I spoke.

Jeremy gave a quick look toward the stairs, likely looking for our manager, Nari. When he didn't spot her, he turned back to me with a grin. "Sure. Or at least, as long as it takes for Nari to realize I'm not at my post." He came behind the desk. "At least this way, it'll look like I'm working," he said, as he busied himself with folding the towels. "So, what's up?"

"It's about the date. You know, the virtual date with my ex-boyfriend?"

"I remember," Jeremy said with a twinkle, leaving it mercifully unspoken that it was a story that would be pretty hard to forget. "Did it not go well?"

"No. It did. It went maybe too well," I said, my eyebrows furrowed. "The truth is, I'm not sure how I wanted it to go. I feel like I've gotten myself into an impossible situation. Lose-lose."

A student came by and I scanned her in. Jeremy politely waited until she was out of hearing range.

"So he still doesn't know it's you?" he asked.

"Nope. But I have to tell him. I have to. I can't let one more date go by without doing it. Either that or I have to break it off now." I took one look at the stiff, overly washed towels in front of me and deeply considered thunking my head down on them. I needed the jolt to my system.

"Do you want to? Break it off?" Jeremy asked.

"No," I answered. "But how will I tell him? What is he going to think?"

"Well, I'm sure he'll be surprised," Jeremy said carefully.

"He's going to think I'm pathetic. Or crazy. Or both," I muttered, staring back at the towels. "Either way he'll be upset, and he has every right to be."

When I was met with silence, I looked up. For a second I thought maybe this whole thing was too much for Jeremy—who, after all, barely knew me outside of this insane scenario—and he had simply walked away. But he was still there and looked like he was contemplating the situation.

"So I don't know Caleb, it's true," Jeremy started, and from somewhere within the depths of my anguish, I managed to muster up enough sense to be impressed that Jeremy remembered his name. "I think if it were me . . ." He paused. "You said you guys went out for three years, right?"

I nodded.

"I . . . think I would understand," Jeremy said. "I'm not saying that'll be his initial reaction, but once you explain to him how he was one of your choices, it doesn't seem too crazy to me."

"It doesn't?" I asked.

Jeremy shook his head. "If I saw my ex as one of my choices, I'd probably be so surprised, I'd be tempted to do the same. And we only dated for, like, four months. But, you know, high school relationships can be intense. And you guys . . . *three years*? There have to be a lot of residual feelings there."

I looked up at Jeremy with more than a hint of gratitude. I'd clearly lucked out in choosing this very sympathetic stranger as my confidant. "Yes . . . ," I said.

"I'm sure on his end too," Jeremy continued his heroic streak. "So, honestly, I think it'll be okay. If he's someone worth going out with for three years, he should understand. Eventually."

I gave a tiny smile. "Well, I hope so. . . ."

"But you're right," Jeremy said, as he finished refolding the last towel. "You do have to tell him. The longer this goes on . . ."

I nodded at the same time that I groaned. "You're right. Of course." This was truly going to suck, but there was no way I could put it off past our next date.

"Hey, listen, if by any chance you want to get out and forget your troubles for a while, Junk Mail is playing a few gigs at the end of the month." He nodded toward my bag again. "They're really good, I promise."

It was the second time someone had mentioned "getting out" in a week. Maybe I should take *that* as a sign from the universe.

"You know what? That would be great," I responded.

He smiled at me before something over my shoulder

grabbed his attention. "Oh. Nari." He indicated the stern girl with the dark, blunt bob who was coming down the stairs. "I should go, but do you want me to text you once I know the band's exact schedule?"

"Yes." I smiled back as I reached down and took my phone out of the cabinet, handing it over to Jeremy so he could put in his number. He did it quickly, keeping one eye on Nari. As I watched him, I realized this whole thing might at least lead to me making one friend at school—who wasn't a default because she lived with me—and that would be something positive no matter what else happened.

"Have a happy Thanksgiving, Mariam," he said as he handed my phone back.

"You too, Jeremy," I said, only then realizing I had had two very personal, intense conversations with him and had hardly asked him a thing about himself—including his Thanksgiving plans.

As I watched him walk toward the stairs, I made a promise to remedy that the next time we spoke. My situation with Rose had taught me one very important lesson about not focusing on romance to the exclusion of friendship.

On Wednesday I was zipping up my duffel bag when the door to my room opened and in walked Hedy, hand in hand with a girl I assumed was the new girlfriend.

"Hi!" Hedy said, her chipper voice echoing the noticeable bounce in her step.

I smiled. "Hey. I thought maybe you'd headed out already."

"Oh, didn't I tell you? I decided it wasn't worth the hassle to travel to Portland just for a few days. So I'm staying here. By the way, this is Geneviève. Geneviève, Mariam."

"Nice to meet you," I said as I shook Geneviève's hand. She was tall and blond, just like Hedy. In fact, the two of them walking in hand in hand resembled that weird emoji of the identical dancing girls. She was also gorgeous, giving me the feeling that the flight time to Portland wasn't exactly what was keeping Hedy around.

"Nice to meet you, too," Geneviève responded in a French accent, making it clear why Hedy had pronounced her name the way she had, with a *zh* sound at the beginning and an extra syllable between the *v*'s.

"You're not going home either?" I asked Geneviève, who was taking in the decor on Hedy's side of the room.

"No. Canada's Thanksgiving is in October." She looked over at Hedy with a secret smile. "Besides, I thought it would be fun to go to the parade and also see what this Black Friday is about."

There was nothing secret or subtle about Hedy's grin back at her. She looked like she had stuck one of those joke-shop chattering teeth on her face. "Get the whole experience," she said, ostensibly to me, although she wasn't looking in my direction whatsoever.

"Cool," I said, getting the distinct feeling that Hedy and Geneviève were dying to get the room to themselves. "Um, well, my train leaves in two hours." I stared at my duffel bag, wondering if I should go to Penn Station early or lug that thing to a Starbucks, where I could kill some time. I did also have to go to the bakery, and chances were the line would be long.

"Oh, that's great! Then we could hang out for a little, right?" Hedy said, much to my surprise.

"Um, sure. If you guys want," I murmured.

"I've been dying to meet Eddie's other friends," Geneviève said, confusing me at first until I realized she was forgoing the *H* in my roommate's name.

I looked at Hedy, who was smiling at me, and found myself oddly touched that she considered me a friend. I would've called her one too, of course, but I'd also convinced myself that it was merely circumstantial and because I was a sad sack who barely left our room. I'd figured Hedy was living up the college life and meeting tons of other people whenever she wasn't stuck in here with me—people she'd consider real friends.

I felt a jolt of happiness as I put my duffel down and plopped myself on my bed. Hedy and Geneviève were making googly eyes at each other again, but an infatuated friend was better than none.

"So how did you two meet again?" I asked the lovebirds.

"Oh, it's such a funny story. I was in the wrong classroom," Geneviève said. "I was running late, and I walked into Hedy's beginner Italian course somewhere in the middle of it. I was so flustered that I didn't even realize it was not beginner Mandarin until five minutes in." Geneviève laughed. "I know you are probably thinking I am a big idiot, but the truth is, I was also distracted because this beautiful girl was sitting in front of me and I couldn't stop staring at her. Also her shoes. She had on great shoes that day."

Geneviève looked at Hedy, as if passing the story's baton on to her, and Hedy picked it right up. "They are great shoes. And if they weren't my favorite pair before, they certainly are now."

There was a moment filled with nothing but silence and grinning, until Geneviève seemed to snap back to the fact that they were having a conversation with a third person.

"So anyway, by the time I realized it was not my class, I was too smitten to leave. And I said to myself, 'Genny, you can take Mandarin next semester, but who knows if you will ever see this girl again, so maybe it's time to pretend you've forgotten your six years of Italian and stick with this.'" Geneviève laughed and looked at me. "If nothing else, it's going to be an easy A."

"Though she's had to go through a lot of trouble feigning ignorance," Hedy explained. "Just this week, she slipped and started having an intensely complicated conversation with our teacher during our oral midterm."

"Oh, don't bring it up!" Geneviève smacked her forehead. "I got carried away describing my ideal vacation spot," she explained to me.

"And our professor was left wondering when on earth he had taught her the words for 'ski lodge' and 'black diamond hill,'" Hedy breezily finished Geneviève's story.

I chuckled along with them, amazed that their easy rapport was the result of only a few weeks together. But maybe that was because it had been too long since I'd experienced the intoxicating wave of brand-new love myself, that short period of time when it seems impossible to ever get your fill of this magical, wondrous being who has suddenly descended into your life and taken over your every thought. I couldn't help but take note of every little way they were constantly finding to touch each other, like Hedy helping Geneviève take off her jacket or putting their microwave popcorn in a tiny bowl that fit snugly between them on her bed.

I ended up watching half an hour of *The Night of the Hunter* with them before I had to leave to catch my train.

"Let's hang out together when I get back," I said as I picked up my duffel again.

"Definitely," Geneviève responded, and sealed it with a hug and a kiss on each cheek. Hedy came in for a hug then too, and I realized jarringly that this was the first bit of human contact I'd had in quite a while. I held on to her a tad longer than I normally would have, hoping this was my first step in filling out the pages of my scrapbook for real.

CHAPTER 7

"THE TRAINS WERE A MESS, WEREN'T THEY?" MINA asked as soon as I got into the car. I'd put my duffel bag in the back and settled the two white bakery boxes on my lap, where they'd also spent the whole four-hour train ride upstate.

Maybe I should've been annoyed that Mina was gloating over being right, as she was prone to do, but it was too good to see her. And besides, I thought of the habit as more of a quirk that, at the moment, was familiar and endearing.

"It was," I conceded. "I wish I could've come yesterday."

"Well, no matter. So glad you're here now." Mina glanced over at me quickly, before she pulled away from the curb of the train station. "Mom is going to grill you on how you're eating, how classes are going, whether you've met any nice boys. . . ." She left a noticeable pause there.

"Mm-hmm," I said noncommittally.

"So I'm going to ask you all that first, of course. You know, for practice." Mina was driving and staring ahead, but I caught the sly glint in her eye.

"Right. Of course," I said, before I thought over Mina's questions. "So the answers are: Eating fine. Classes are fine. And boys are . . ." Well, not even two minutes in and here was my opportunity.

"Let me guess," Mina chimed in. "Fiiiiiine," she said, drawing the word out to emphasize its alternate meaning.

I gave a small laugh. "Some of them are."

"Anyone in particular?" she asked, a knowing smile playing about her lips.

Maybe I should've just said no, but I *had* promised myself that I would tell her once I saw her in person. "Sorta," I conceded.

"Ooh! I knew it!" Mina slapped the steering wheel for emphasis. "You've been keeping this from me," she said, half accusatory, half in jest.

"Well . . . ," I started. "It was hard to explain over Face-Time."

"Really? Why?" A note of confusion had crept into Mina's teasing voice.

"Because . . ." Where to start? Okay, first confession. "So I've been online dating."

"Okay," Mina said. "Anyone good?"

"Except it's not just online." I eased into the second part. "I've been using HEAVR."

Mina paused. "That VR dating app thing?"

"Yup," I said.

"The one with the commercial?"

"That's the one."

"Oh," Mina said. "How is it? I've heard from a couple of friends that their matchmaking system is supposed to be pretty top-notch."

Well, since they had matched me up with someone I was clearly already in love with, I'd say that might be an understatement. "Um, yeah. I think they might get top marks there. Maybe like valedictorian marks."

"Ooh. That good, huh?" Mina said, the excited tone back in her voice. "Hot new boyfriend, then?"

"Hot—yes. Boyfriend—too soon to tell. We've been on two dates. Two great dates. New—" I was about to say it, when Mina interrupted.

"Where did you go? Did you do the dates in VR too? Or meet in person?"

"Um, no. In VR. He's in California." We were getting warm now, about to reach the WTF apex in the conversation.

"Oh," Mina said. "Long-distance?"

"Yes. I guess."

"Well, how were the dates? Were they weird? Where did you go? I mean, virtually speaking."

"They were a little weird," I admitted truthfully. "But after a while it was oddly easy to forget I was staring at a computer-generated avatar. Didn't feel too different from a regular date, actually. And as for where we went, the first one was at a pier. I let the machine pick the location. And the second was at a natural history museum."

"Wow. That's so freaky," Mina said. "So what's his name?"

Here we go.

"Caleb," I said in a small voice.

"Oh my God. Really?!" Mina said. "What are the odds?"

It was only when she was met with a long silence that she looked over at me. Luckily, we were at a stop sign.

"Wait . . . no. Not . . . no. It's a different—" But she stopped herself midsentence when she saw the mix of guilt and hopefulness fighting for real estate in my expression.

"Oh. My. Fucking. God," Mina said, and then leaned on her horn, I wasn't quite sure if by accident or because she couldn't think of any other way to sonically express her utter disbelief.

"Yeah," I said with a weak, nervous smile. "Yeah."

Soon another horn was beeping from behind us. "Hey, lady, are you having a stroke?!"

Mina seemed to finally realize she was still honking her horn while we waited at the stop sign interminably. She got off it and drove the car.

But for the rest of the ride, she didn't utter a word, or even sneak a glance at me, which made me even more nervous than the tirade of derision I'd been expecting.

Inadvertently, I started shrinking into my seat, so that by the time we arrived at our house, my knees were halfway up the glove compartment.

• • •

"Mariam, azizam." Mom was waiting at the door and gave me a kiss on each cheek and a warm hug. Our father was behind her and said a perfunctory hello, followed by two kisses also, barely touching my cheek. Then he quickly disappeared into the den, where I could hear either the television or his laptop broadcasting what I assumed was some sort of poker tournament. Dad obsessively watched videos of professional card players, even though he never played himself. And even though I knew exactly why he didn't gamble, it made me think he was a bit of a masochist. But I'd never had a long enough conversation with him to find out for sure.

"How was your trip?" Mom asked in Farsi.

"Fine. Easy," I responded in English, the dual-language way of our family for as long as I could remember. We each spoke the language we were most comfortable in, but understood the other perfectly. It worked great, even though Rose had once commented about how funny it was to listen to as a bystander.

"Are you hungry? Dinner isn't for a few hours, but I have some Salad Olivieh, if you want a snack."

"Oh yes. I would love some," I said, looking forward to the homemade chicken and pickle salad. Actually, I was absolutely craving any homemade food in a way my old self—who was sometimes bored of the fifteen or so dishes my mom knew how to make—might never understand.

But once you've spent three nights out of the week eating rubbery baked ziti for dinner, a heaping pile of saffron-infused rice seems downright heavenly.

"I'll just go drop my stuff off in my room," I said.

"All my children under one roof. I love this holiday," Mom said with a contented sigh.

"I'll come help you," Mina said. They were the first words she had uttered since the expletive following my confession, and they sent a chill right to the pit of my stomach that immediately took the place of hunger.

I didn't respond but let my sister follow me upstairs to my room, which was right next to her own. I barely got a moment to feel the instant nostalgia of seeing my familiar white-and-burgundy bedspread, the gray cat leisurely napping on it, and of course the mauve walls, when Mina closed the door behind her and started the interrogation that had surely been building for the past twenty minutes.

"Okay. Explain," she said.

I dumped my bag on the floor, thumped onto my bed, and immediately scooped Sneezes into my arms, as much for affection as for security. "I thought I already did," I said.

"No," Mina said. "How did this happen? Did you seek him out on the app?"

"No," I said emphatically. "The computer picked him at random. Or I guess based on my personality test answers. They gave me three matches and he was one of them."

I tickled the cat behind her ears and she purred loudly, apparently not much bothered at having her nap interrupted once she saw the culprit.

Mina paused, obviously letting the unlikelihood of this sink in. "Three matches?" she finally said.

I nodded. "Yes. Only three. And there he was. It was like a sign or something . . . I don't know. It just felt like I had no option but to choose him. I mean, what are the odds . . . ?"

"So what you're saying is that the computer gave you two options that were *not the boy who shattered your heart five months ago*." Mina's eyes were flashing in that dangerous way they did when she was about to eviscerate you for some sort of grudge-worthy transgression.

"Come on, Mina. Think about it. There have to be millions of people using HEAVR. I asked for matches from anywhere in the country . . . and then there's Caleb. Staring at me. What was I supposed to do?" At the sound of Caleb's name, Sneezes gave an extra-emphatic purr.

"Again. Pick either of the two guys who haven't already left you with a serious case of depression for the last half a year." Mina's arms were crossed and she was, unwittingly, standing in front of a framed photo of her ten-year-old self in the exact same stance. It almost made me want to laugh, if I wasn't already on the verge of tears.

"That's easy for you to say," I said, keeping my voice steady, a talent of mine even when the tears were already prickling my eyes. Mina hadn't, as far as I knew, had a serious boyfriend for over a year—and she hadn't exactly been devastated when she broke it off with Adam. "You weren't there. You didn't have the person you're in love with suddenly appear in front of you with the question: Do you want to date this person?"

"And you didn't for one second think, 'I *already* dated this person. And it didn't work out.' Do you know the point of college, Mariam?"

"I thought it was to get a degree, figure out a career path, and then set out on said path," I answered coolly, not currently feeling generous enough to avoid the subtle dig at my sister.

"The point of college," Mina continued, as if I hadn't said anything, "is to figure out who you are away from your childhood hang-ups, and your parents, and your familiar friends, and your *exes*. The point is to try new experiences, to meet new people. Do you understand?"

"I don't think *you* understand," I shot back. "I didn't ask for this to happen. It just did. And I made a choice that seemed right at the time." Sneezes jumped off the bed and went to clean herself in a favorite corner of my room; she'd never been much for conflict.

"And now?" Mina asked.

Now my stomach was in knots, but a lot of that had to do with adding Mina's anvil of judgment on top of my own already uneasy feelings. "Now I'm upset that I'm being yelled at," I answered in a way that was both truthful and deflective.

Mina shook her head and brought her hands up in surrender. "I'm not yelling, I'm just disappointed. . . ."

"Okay, what's going on here?" My door flung open and my older brother—now sporting a rather bizarre goatee since the last time I'd seen him—stood grinning on the other side. "Do I need to play mediator already? The board games are packed away in the basement."

At some point when we were younger, Mehdi had had the bright idea to settle an argument by playing a game of Life. Whoever retired at Millionaire Estates would win. Since then, the three of us had often settled meaningless spats with games like Clue (whoever solved the mystery), Parcheesi (whoever got their pieces around the board), and Monopoly (whoever owned both Boardwalk and Park Place, since that game was otherwise endless).

But this wasn't meaningless. And we weren't children. In fact, for the first time ever, all three of the people standing in this room were legal adults.

"There's nothing to mediate," I said. "I made a personal decision and Mina doesn't like it. That's all."

"Actually, Mariam. You're right. There's nothing to mediate." She turned to Mehdi with a grim look. "Mariam has made an empirically awful decision, dear brother."

"Empirically?" Mehdi turned to me with his eyebrows raised. "Did you get a horrible tattoo, Mar? Don't worry. My first three are pretty atrocious, and I've lived to tell the tale."

Then Mina played what was obviously her trump card. "Mariam has decided to go back to dating Caleb."

"Come again?" Mehdi said, blinking.

Mina turned to me with a triumphant look that was laced with a hint of smugness before Mehdi spoke again. "You mean he took you back?"

"What?!" I exploded.

"What do you mean he took *her* back?!" Mina shouted with just as much venom, as we spoke over each other.

Mehdi put his hands up. "Nothing. I don't mean anything by it."

But now I was suspicious. My brother had always been friendly with Caleb to the point that maybe they could have just been considered friends regardless of their contact through me; they'd been on the soccer team together before that fateful day I was the substitute mascot. Had that friendship continued after Caleb's relationship with me had ended?

"Have you been speaking to Caleb?" I asked him.

Mehdi shrugged. "We chat online occasionally."

Mina gave a sharp intake of breath. "Traitor!"

"What? No! I'm on your side, of course," he said to me, but couldn't help muttering, "If there are any sides."

"Of course there are sides!" Mina said.

"What have you been talking about?" I asked. My voice was steadier than Mina's, because I was suddenly much more interested in obtaining heretofore unknowable details than getting uppity about the principle of the thing.

Mehdi shrugged. "Nothing important, honest. For real, it was mostly about *The Last Battleground*." An online game that they were both obsessed with. "And sometimes classes." Mehdi's face broke into a look of concern as he clearly remembered some other point of conversation.

"What? What else?" I asked, my heart suddenly in my throat.

"Well . . . it's just . . . the last time we spoke, he mentioned meeting a new girl." Mehdi grimaced, clearly hating to be the bearer of bad news.

But I remained calm, a nagging suspicion of hope curling its way around my heart. "Did he say how he met this new girl?"

"Um . . . online, I think." Mehdi looked confused. This wasn't the reaction he was expecting. "He sounded . . . well, like he really liked her."

"And did he say what they did together? Like where they went on dates?" I continued.

"Come on, Mariam," Mehdi said gently, obviously concerned for my frame of mind. "You don't need to know the details, do you?"

My heart skipped a beat, because maybe this *was* some other girl. But Mehdi was wrong; I did have to know. "Just tell me. Do you know what they did on their dates?"

"Well . . . they were virtual dates," Mehdi said, and I

felt instant relief powering up a smile on my lips, which Mehdi took as misplaced. "Look, I know that maybe doesn't sound real, but he really did seem excited about her. I just don't want you to get your hopes up if he's into some other girl."

"That's the thing. He's not into some other girl," I explained calmly, suddenly feeling like this small bit of information was enough to sustain me through the skepticism of both my siblings. Caleb was excited enough about our dates to talk about me to his friends. That meant something. "Those dates were with me."

Mehdi stared at me, and for the second time in less than five minutes said, "Come again?"

CHAPTER 8

P OTATOES?" MY MOM HELD OUT THE PURPLE
ceramic casserole dish that went along with all her
other violet china, decor, and about 90 percent of
her wardrobe.

"Yes, please," I said, as I took the dish and helped myself
to several pieces of potato au gratin. There were now four
different kinds of potatoes on my plate, exactly the way I
liked it.

Our Thanksgiving table probably didn't look too different from most tables around the country. Over the
years, my mom had added to her American food repertoire with mashed potatoes, green bean casserole, car-
amelized brussels sprouts, and—of course—a turkey.
But a meal wouldn't be complete for her if it didn't also
include warm pita bread and a heaping pile of rice, so we
had those, too. We'd never quite been able to convince
her to get into the concept of dessert, so the cookies and
sour cherry pie I had brought over from the Persian bakery were our way of trying to lure her to the sweet side.
Naturally, she'd have only a morsel with her glass of tea

after the meal was over, but it remained a valiant effort.

"How is school going for everybody?" my mom asked, turning to Mehdi and me.

"Great," Mehdi said through a mouthful of casserole. "I think I'm on my way to a 4.0 average this year."

"That's wonderful," my mom said, and even Dad interjected with a soft "Bareek'allah" in congratulations.

Then she turned to me. "And Mariam? Did you figure out your major yet?"

I plastered on a smile. "Working on it."

"Taking any inspiring classes this semester?" Mom asked.

"Oh . . . well, mostly it's core classes," I said. "But I'm hoping I can pick something interesting for next semester."

"Very nice," my mother said. "And Mehdi. How's Angela?"

"Ange . . ." Mehdi looked confused for a second. "Oh, right. We broke up." Mehdi had a bad habit of being very honest with my mother in naming whatever girl he was seeing at the time whenever she asked. Which usually meant that the next time she asked, he'd invariably be telling her they were no longer together. Incidentally, my mother's knack for remembering names should be studied and documented in the name of science.

"Oh," Mom said, and even looked slightly disappointed, which immediately made me remember the words our tenth-grade history teacher always printed on his blackboard on the first day of class: *Those who fail to learn from history are doomed to repeat it.* I turned to share a secret smile with Mina, but she was resolutely looking down at her plate.

"Seeing anybody else, then?" Mom asked.

"Yes!" Mehdi said. "Savannah. She's great."

I tried to catch Mina's eye again, but she continued to concentrate on cutting her turkey.

"And how about you, Mariam?" Mom turned to me. Obviously, I should've seen this coming, but I'd been so preoccupied with trying to grab my sister's attention that I was, stupidly, blindsided.

"Oh," I said, even dropping my fork with a clatter onto my plate in my frenzy. "I'm . . . no. I'm not really seeing anyone."

This time Mina looked up, and I saw her exchange a look with Mehdi. So that was how it was going to be, huh? The two of them rolling their eyes at each other over me?

My mom nodded. "Well, that's okay. Good to concentrate on school. Mina's not seeing anyone right now either." She pointed a fork at Mina.

"Thanks for updating everyone," Mina growled.

"You're welcome," Mom replied with a smile. Sometimes I wasn't sure if she was genuinely oblivious to Mina's sarcasm, or willfully ignored it in order to piss her off more. If it was the latter, then her battle strategies should be studied too.

Mom then turned back to me. "Just don't let a broken heart cloud too much of your college experience, okay, sweetheart?"

I opened my mouth to say something, and then closed it again. I shouldn't be surprised. Sometimes my mom could seem flighty with her overly cheery disposition, but she had a knack for suddenly cutting right to the heart of a situation with one well-placed sentence. It could knock the wind out of you.

I looked over at Mina again, desperate for acknowledgment that our mother had really said that. But she was just shaking her head at Mehdi.

I was saved by the bell, or buzz, of my phone. I'd gotten a message, and a part of me thought for sure it would be Caleb, whose ears were likely ringing at being so subversively talked about just two miles away.

But the name that popped up was one I hadn't seen flash across my phone for some time.

Prisha: Hey! I wanted to see if anyone was around for some bowling or something tomorrow?

Prisha was my friend from high school. She had put me on a group text that included Addison, Zoe, and Rose. Except for Rose, the rest of the girls and I occasionally texted, but even that had tapered off as the college semester had worn on and everyone had gotten caught up in their new pursuits. Or maybe that was everyone except me, whose pursuits seemed to be very much stuck on one track.

I put the phone away in my pocket, where I could feel it buzz as the other girls wrote their responses. My mom continued to chatter, and my brother and sister continued to resolutely ignore me.

By the time I felt the fifth or sixth buzz, I'd made my decision. Bowling seemed like a better way to spend my time than being uncomfortably grilled by my mother or treated like a pariah by my siblings. Even if Rose was going to be there.

I slipped my phone back out.

Mariam: Sounds great!

A few hours later, when I was in my room with Sneezes in my lap, playing some mindless game on my phone, another buzz came through.

Jeremy from work: Thought you might want a taste of what you signed up for.

It was followed by a link to a video of Junk Mail doing a live show.

I smiled at the name that he had programmed into my phone before I clicked on the link. Energetic punk music filled my room. The band consisted of three girls playing guitars and bass and a bleached-blond boy playing drums. "If you for one sec think you're haunting me," the lead singer, a pretty Asian girl with hair that gradated from pink to blue, sang, "you better get a load of this reality. You can't ghost a ghost."

Then she did an impressive, honest-to-God air split,

which I didn't think happened outside of old music docu-
mentaries about eighties hair metal bands. I watched the
rest of the video, mesmerized.

Mariam: Okay, that kicked ass.

Jeremy from work: Right?

Mariam: Maybe I won't be needing that sewing kit.

Jeremy from work: I'd hate to take business away from
Duane Reade, but . . . point to Junk Mail.

I was about to write him again when my phone buzzed
with yet another message from someone else.

This time it really was Caleb through the HEAVR app.

CalebM8126: How was your Thanksgiving?

I instantly grinned, sitting up on my bed straighter and
feeling a rush of butterflies take flight in my stomach. It
was suddenly much easier to remember how I'd gotten
here to begin with.

SiennaV23: Okay. Some parental interrogation. Some
potatoes. You know, the traditional all-American holiday we
know and love.

CalebM8126: Tell me about it. My mom seemed determined to cram in two months' worth of dinner conversation
into one evening.

I smiled. I could picture Loretta (which she'd always
insisted I call her) doing just that. She and my mom were
good friends for a reason.

CalebM8126: What are your plans for the rest of the
weekend?

SiennaV23: I think I might be going bowling with some old high school friends.

CalebM8126: Sounds fun.

SiennaV23: Hopefully.

And I really meant it. I felt like I'd had my share of blast-from-the-past awkwardness already—given that I was secretly dating my ex and all. Hopefully things between Rose and me wouldn't be too bad tomorrow.

The bowling alley hadn't changed since the last time I'd been there, which, by my calculations, had probably been well over a year. We used to go there as a group a fair amount, but once Rose and I had our big blowup fight during senior year and most of my time was spent with just Caleb, the two of us tended to avoid it. Or I guess I did. I hadn't even give it much thought until I was standing there at the sticky counter in my rented shoes, getting a serious case of déjà vu. I was waiting for my usual order of nachos when I saw her. She'd cut her hair and dyed it a deeper shade of red, but otherwise, not much had changed about her or me or, funnily enough, about the boy I was seeing.

Unfortunately, neither Addison, Prisha, nor Zoe were there yet, and I could see the exact same uncomfortable thought pass over her face as she caught sight of me, too. I gave her a little wave and she gave one back before slowly making her way to the shoe rental counter. I was sure she was going to make that transaction last as long as humanly possible.

Luckily for both of us, Prisha and Addison were soon behind her in line and chatting animatedly before Prisha caught sight of me and waved me over. I plastered a smile on my face and walked over with my nachos and soda.

"Hi!" Prisha said, and gave me a big hug, followed by Addison. Rose and I awkwardly patted each other's shoulders simply because it would be even more awkward not to. "So good to see you!" Prisha added.

"You too," I said. "Thanks for inviting me."

"Of course. It wouldn't be the old gang otherwise."

I smiled while Rose and I pointedly avoided looking at each other. Prisha meant the old, old gang, of course—the junior year gang, before the fissure between Rose and me seemed to become an abyss that swallowed up everyone who wasn't Caleb. At some point, it had gotten easier to stay away than to engage in some sort of passive-aggressive friendship land grab. Besides, I had Caleb. Who else did I need?

"Holy crap." The words involuntarily left my mouth in a loud rush, and the three girls turned around in unison to see what could have caused them.

As if I'd manifested him with my thoughts, there he was, in all his smiling, five-foot-ten, non-avatar glory, walking into the bowling alley with his old crew, Jon and Xavier. They were laughing, presumably at something hilarious

Xavier must have said, and seeing Caleb's energetic, genuine mirth was more than my poor, unprepared heart could handle at the moment.

I quickly whipped back around. I'd been too nervous thinking about explaining the whole situation to Mina to give much thought to the possibility she had brought up—that I'd run into Caleb over break—and now I was caught completely off guard.

"Oh, man," Prisha said. "What are the odds?"

Yes, what were the odds? Even though this was a small town and there wasn't *that* much to do, why did he decide to come bowling?

About half an hour later, I got my answer.

Once Zoe showed up, the girls whisked me to a lane that was as far away from the boys as we could get. And once we started our set, they did their best to distract me, asking about school and telling funny stories about their own freshman-year experiences so far. Even Rose got in on the action by relating the story of one of her art school classmates, who was insisting that his blank canvases were a part of his "telepathic art" series.

"And, get this . . . the teacher is going along with it. Like, he'll stare at the beige canvas for five minutes and, I don't know, conjure up his own image, I guess?"

I giggled along with everyone else as my phone buzzed. I looked down. It was a message from Caleb. But to Sienna over HEAVR.

CalebM8126: You inspired me to go bowling 🎳! Hope you're having fun at yours. Wish you were here. Do you think HEAVR has a bowling alley? Maybe we should give it a go next time?

I couldn't help staring over at the real Caleb then. He was putting his phone down and heading up to his lane as Jon gestured at him that it was his turn.

I didn't know for sure whether he had seen me at the alley too, but it wasn't a very big place, so the chances were good that he had. And he obviously hadn't come over to say hello.

I stared down at the message. Then again at him.

He was so into Sienna, he was thinking about her when he was out with his friends. He was so into her, he was planning their next date, which wouldn't even be a real one.

Deception is not a strong foundation for a lasting relationship. Agatha's truth bomb rang in my ears. Because what I wanted more than anything was for Caleb and me to last, beyond this past summer, beyond today. I didn't want to be able to see an end to us, to think that our story was over. He had been everything that I needed once, and surely that hadn't changed. But that meant I had to tell him the truth. Now.

"Guys, could one of you fill in for my next set?" I said to the girls, while they were still chortling over Rose's description of mind-art dude's invisible palette. "I . . . have to go talk to him."

Prisha looked at me. "Talk to who? Caleb?"

I nodded. "I'll explain later."

And then, before I could rethink my decision, I gathered up my courage, stood up as straight as I could, and marched over to the other end of the bowling alley.

He had just bowled a spare when he saw me. For a second the startled look in his eye reminded me too forcefully of a trapped animal. But then he took a deep breath and put on a smile. "Hi," he said.

"Hi. Look, I'm sorry to bother you. But could I talk to you for a second? Outside?"

He looked over at Jon and Xavier, who shrugged.

"Um, sure," Caleb said.

"Thanks. It'll be quick, I promise," I said, and whipped around, leading him out of the bowling alley.

CHAPTER 9

MY SPLIT-SECOND DECISION TO TAKE THE BULL by the horns and spill everything to Caleb did not include the notion of grabbing my coat, something I was very much regretting at the moment. Upstate New York wasn't made for thin, long-sleeved shirts in November.

Caleb had his hands shoved in his pockets and his shoulders scrunched up higher too, though I didn't know whether that was also related to the chill in the air or the one between us.

"So . . . how are you doing?" he said, releasing a visible puff of air.

"Good. I'm good."

"Good." He paused. "I'm glad to hear it."

"Thank you," I replied. "You?"

"I'm good. I love California," Caleb said. "I tell you what. I don't miss this cold."

Oh, great. Now we'd been reduced to talking about the weather, which, besides being inane, was incidentally also turning me into a Persian Popsicle. I had to get this over with.

"Listen, Caleb. I have to tell you something," I started.

"Wait. Before you do . . ." He looked down at me nervously. "I . . . I want to make sure this isn't about us being more than friends again."

I blinked back at him, the cold air suddenly stinging my cheek as if there had been a physical slap there. "How come?"

Caleb sighed and started to toe the pavement, his hands shoved into his pockets. "Oh, Mariam. I love you and I always will, but it's just . . . my feelings from June haven't changed."

I never would have thought that the words *I love you* could sound so much like their opposite, or—even worse—*I'm indifferent.*

His feelings from June had been centered around the idea that we were too young for a true long-distance relationship. But suddenly that felt extra hollow, considering "Sienna" was also long-distance.

"Right," I mumbled, trying to make sense of the jumble of emotions and thoughts coursing through my head.

"You understand, right?" Caleb was looking at me with the soulful brown eyes that I'd once stared into for hours.

Which was when I snapped out of it and my emotional survival instincts took over. "Right. Of course. Anyway . . . that's not what I wanted to tell you."

"Oh," Caleb said, having the decency to look a tiny bit abashed. "Right. Great. So, what was it then?"

My mind was racing, but I knew that I couldn't tell him the truth now, not with everything he'd said. It would only be extra humiliating to reveal that instead of desperately trying to date him again, I was deceitfully *already* dating him. What I could do instead was prove him wrong: *be* that girl he didn't know he wanted. Which, in point of fact, was really just me with a different facade.

Though for now, I needed to figure out a good reason why I had brought him out into the cold.

"I wanted to let you know that I'm seeing someone," I blurted. "I . . . didn't want you to hear it from someone else."

Caleb blinked and looked surprised. "Oh," he said before remembering himself and breaking into a smile. "That's great! Someone at school?"

"He goes to a different school, but yes, we met there." Not technically a lie.

"And you like him?" Caleb asked eagerly.

Not at the moment, I wanted to say, but instead I smiled that jolly Mariam smile that Caleb used to love so much and responded with, "Yes. Very much."

Caleb's own grin got bigger. "Well then . . . I feel okay telling you I'm seeing someone too."

"Really?"

"Yes. I mean, it's pretty new, but yeah."

"And you like her?"

"I do," Caleb said, finally taking his hands out of his

pockets. "Again, it's new. But we've had some good talks."

"How did you two meet?" Ostensibly, I was just repeating his questions back to him, except that I knew I was goading him for a specific answer.

Caleb's hands got shoved into his pockets again. "Oh . . . it was an online dating app."

"Which one?" I asked brightly. "I've tried a couple too."

"Oh, um . . . it was HEAVR."

I pretended to rack my brain, admitting to myself that I was relishing seeing him squirm a bit. "Oh, wait . . . is that the virtual reality one?"

"Yeah."

"So have you been having dates in VR?" I got a flashback to Jeremy leaning against the Palladium counter, asking me the same question.

"So far, yes," Caleb responded. "She goes to school pretty far away." He hesitated, and I wondered if he was about to spill that she in fact went to the same school as me. Or if he was realizing his lame long-distance excuse wasn't holding much water anymore. Either way, he refrained. Probably too weird to go into too many details about his new girlfriend with his ex.

"Cool," I said with my same plastered-on smile. "You'll have to tell me about it sometime, but for now . . . it *is* freezing. So shall we get back inside?"

"Yeah," Caleb said, giving a small laugh and following me as I pulled open the door to the bowling alley.

Even from behind me, his relief was palpable. But I felt exactly like a sleeping volcano: smooth and solid on the surface while every emotion I'd ever had churned out of sight.

I was lying in my bed, staring at my mauve walls, when my phone buzzed. I hadn't changed my clothes or even taken off my shoes since returning from the bowling alley, instead letting my feet dangle off the end of the bed.

I glanced over at my phone.

It was Caleb. Messaging Sienna.

CalebM8126: Hey you. Just thinking about you. How was your night?

I sighed as I picked up the phone.

SiennaV23: Good. Yours? I wrote back unenthusiastically. This was getting so much more complex than anything I thought I had signed up for.

CalebM8126: Good. It's awesome to see my high school friends. I miss them.

SiennaV23: I know what you mean.

I typed slowly, knowing the friend I missed most was the one I was talking to.

CalebM8126: I talked to them about HEAVR, actually. And you.

SiennaV23: Oh? What did they think?

CalebM8126: That it was cool I was seeing someone new. I recently got out of a three-year relationship. I didn't tell you that, did I?

I took in a deep breath.

SiennaV23: Nope. Sounds intense.

Again, I realized I was echoing Jeremy's words, just like I did outside of the bowling alley, but I seemed to be running out of my own at the moment.

CalebM8126: Yes. Well . . . I don't know. It was good and meaningful, but it's also over now. To be completely honest, my ex is the first one I told about us.

I stared at the message, truly at a loss for how to respond to that one. After a minute, Caleb wrote again.

CalebM8126: Is that too weird to admit?

SiennaV23: No. How did she take it?

CalebM8126: Fine. It turns out she's seeing someone new too. Which was a relief to hear.

A relief, huh? A relief. Not weird, or sad, or maybe making him even the tiniest bit jealous. Suddenly I realized I did not want to be having this conversation anymore. It felt like eavesdropping. Or purposely looking at subtweets about myself.

SiennaV23: I'm pretty tired. Think I'm going to bed.

CalebM8126: Okay. Good night, Sienna. Can't wait for our next date.

SiennaV23: Sleep well.

I tossed my phone away from me, like it was the one responsible for my predicament instead of it being entirely self-inflicted. I threw one arm over my eyes and kicked off my shoes with my feet. Maybe I should go to sleep and put this whole tangled mess of a day behind me.

But between the early hour and my racing mind, it was obvious that wasn't going to happen.

I picked up my phone again and went to my text messages, clicking on my last exchange with "Jeremy from work." I rewatched the Junk Mail video he had sent me.

I glanced over at my alarm clock. Ten thirty p.m.

It was a little late to text someone I hardly knew. But before I could talk myself out of it, I'd started typing.

Mariam: Hey. Is this a bad time?

I held on to the phone, willing it to buzz. Within a minute it had.

Jeremy from work: Hey! No, not at all. What's up?

I smiled in relief and then looked at the words Jeremy had written. He didn't know about my quirky aversion to texting—how unlike most people my age, I always preferred to hear someone's voice rather than read their words—but I was hoping he wouldn't mind.

Mariam: I wanted to discuss the finer points of Junk Mail's lyrics with someone. Mind if I call?

My phone rang.

"Hey!" Jeremy's chipper voice instantly made me feel better, and I found myself breathing a sigh of relief at the prospect of a friendly, uncomplicated conversation at last. "What should we analyze first? Their excellent grasp of iambic pentameter? Their layered use of metaphor?"

I laughed. "Or I was thinking the use of amp kicks as punctuation," I replied.

"An excellent place to start," he responded.

"But first . . . how was your Thanksgiving?" It was about time I asked Jeremy something about his life.

"Great. Whenever my abuela cooks, it's great."

"Who was there?" I asked, as I settled into the throw pillows leaning against my headboard.

"Um, let's see . . ." I could almost see Jeremy counting off on his fingers. "Three grandparents, four cousins, two aunts, two uncles, one mother, one father, one brother, and a partridge in a pear tree."

"Wow. Sounds festive."

"Well, picture the table," Jeremy said, and I heard a creak as he must have settled into some furniture of his own. "There's a crazy amount of food. Turkey, cranberry sauce, gravy, and stuffing, of course. But also arroz con pollo, beef empanadas, and tortilla soup. And then, smack in the middle, a huge dish of meatballs that my aunt insists on bringing over every year even though they are god-awful and last year my mother finally told her and they got into a huge fight."

I laughed. "It sounds heavenly. And loud."

Jeremy laughed. "If there's one thing that happens when you get together Mexicans and Italians, it's volume. Especially once the football game is on, and the talk inevitably turns to *real* football, aka soccer, which everyone agrees is far superior. Except for my mother and brother, who are big Broncos fans. Meanwhile, the talking and arguing is great for me, because it means I get seconds without much competition. Especially these stuffed peppers that Abuela never makes enough of." He lowered his voice to a whisper. "However, I have finally figured out the secret."

"Which is?" I was already smiling at whatever it was.

"To make sure I place myself in front of them as soon as we sit down. Then casually say something like, 'Wouldn't it be amazing if the next World Cup was Italy vs. Mexico?' The fireworks commence and I get to plop a dozen on my plate without anyone noticing. Although I think my brother might be onto me."

"Clever. And diabolical," I conceded. "That sounds so fun. It's always just my immediate family at our Thanksgiving: my sister, brother, and our parents."

"No extended family?" Jeremy asked.

"Well, I have extended family. From what I understand, a big extended family. But I've never met any of them. They're all still in Iran."

"Ah," Jeremy responded. "Your dinners are probably a lot more elegant and subdued, then."

"Well . . . ," I said as I stared off at my bulletin board, which was mostly filled with old ticket stubs of concerts, movies, and amusement parks that Caleb and I had gone to. "The word I would use this year is . . . 'frosty.'"

"Oh?"

I sighed. "Yeah. So I told my brother and sister about the whole Caleb thing. And they did not take it well."

"How so?"

"I think they thought I was being stupid and crazy and that the situation was absurd. And why would I put myself through all that again? That sort of thing." I could feel the stress returning to my body as I rehashed the whole thing for Jeremy.

"Wow, that sucks," he said, and then, after a pause, "Though why do they hate him so much? Did he not treat you well?"

"No, it's not that. . . . Well, I guess he did break my heart. But that's not really his fault." I got off my bed and walked over to the board, taking a closer look at the three years of faded memories that bound Caleb and me together. "He just thought that we were too young to make long-distance work. . . ." I trailed off, thinking again how that excuse—which had never quite sat right with me—seemed even more meaningless now.

"Right," Jeremy said slowly. "So your siblings are upset about how he hurt you?"

"Yeah. Especially my sister, Mina. Though I guess that's sorta her job," I added, feeling warmth for her overprotectiveness overtake my anger as usual. I'd always had a hard time staying mad at anyone for long. "Anyway, that's not the worst of it. I ran into Caleb, for real, tonight at the bowling alley. As soon as I saw him, I knew I had to tell him. You know, like we'd discussed. I took him outside to do just that. And then . . ."

And then? What had happened? I guess that Caleb had hurt my feelings. Or even broken my heart again, maybe. And I'd felt like I wanted to prove him wrong. He seemed so sure that we were a thing of the past, when the whole time he was gushing about a new girl who was still me. Which meant that, despite everything, there was something powerful drawing us together, like magnets whose attraction to each other was a vital part of their very existence.

I told Jeremy this.

"Wow," he breathed out. "That's some heavy stuff."

"Yes," I agreed. "I've been going with my a gut a lot lately. And that's what I did again, I guess. Talking about it now, it doesn't seem logical—"

"Well, isn't that the point of going with your gut?" Jeremy interrupted. "To override logic?"

"Yeah, maybe."

"I don't think it's a bad thing, Mariam. Sometimes I think that's the only way to make a decision."

I smiled. "Well . . . thank you," I said, realizing my gut had also led me to text him that night, and that had turned out to be exactly what I needed. "I know we don't know each other very well, but you've been amazing at making me feel better about this whole situation. And I just want you to know that I appreciate it."

"You're welcome," Jeremy said. "Though now that you're a Spam Madame, I think we can officially call each other friends."

"I'm sorry, what?"

"Spam Madame, the official fandom name for Junk Mail aficionados."

I laughed. "And are you also a Spam Madame? Or a Spam Monsieur?"

"Don't be absurd," he said. "Being hung up on gender pronouns is so last decade. And besides, Spam Monsieur doesn't rhyme."

I laughed again as I heard some sort of commotion starting up behind him.

"Jer, you coming or what?" a male voice boomed in the background.

"Be right there," his voice echoed as he called out away from the phone before bringing it close to his mouth again. "Listen, I have to go. It's time for our annual Leftover Scrimmage. It's like our version of *Iron Chef*. Everyone has a leftover secret ingredient and forty-five minutes to make a dish. Abuela is the judge. It's cutthroat, and I'm determined that this is my year. . . ."

"Oh man, good luck. Please let me know how it goes."

"Will do. Good night, Mariam. Chin up, okay?"

"Okay. Good night."

I was smiling at my phone when I heard a voice from my doorway.

"Caleb?" Mina asked through squinted eyes, nodding toward my phone.

"No," I said smugly. "A friend from school." My smile got bigger as I remembered Jeremy calling himself my friend. I'd only listened to that one song, but I already owed Junk Mail a debt of gratitude.

CHAPTER 10

DIDN'T EVEN TELL MINA ABOUT SEEING CALEB AT the bowling alley. I couldn't deal with the judgment right then.

But the result was that things felt strained between us. For the most part, we seemed to be avoiding each other.

And then, while Mehdi, Mina, and I were gathered in the kitchen on Saturday, putting together turkey sandwiches for lunch, Mina decided to do what she does best and confront the situation head-on.

"Look, I've been thinking a lot about this whole thing with Caleb," she started.

"Don't," I said.

"But I just want to help. . . ."

I shook my head as I handed her a plate of sliced pickles. "Please. I need some time to sort things out on my own."

Mina sighed, her mouth slightly open as if she was still hoping to get in a word or two. But Mehdi came to my rescue.

"Mina, you have got to tell me. What is with the running shoes?" He pointed to our mudroom, where a small pair of Nikes were neatly placed underneath a hanging stretchy, lavender hoodie.

Mina laughed. "Oh. Mom didn't tell you about her cult fitness group?"

"Her what?" Mehdi asked. "Mom? Fitness group?"

"Oh yeah. They meet at six thirty every morning in front of the library, where they spend ten minutes running up and down the stairs. Sometimes with dumbbells. Then they go for a two-and-a-half-mile run around town."

Both Mehdi and I stared at our sister, me mid-pickle placement on my sandwich.

"Mom?" Mehdi said. "Our mom?" Mom had adopted a lot of American customs over the years, but incorporating physical fitness into her routine had not yet been one of them.

"Loretta convinced her to go one morning, and she's been hooked ever since," Mina explained.

"Wow," Mehdi said. "I will need to grill her on this."

I just nodded, taking the mention of Caleb's mom's name as my cue to be satisfied with the state of my sandwich toppings and leave the room.

I spent the rest of the afternoon lounging and watching bad reality TV. I texted Jeremy to ask the results of his Leftover Scrimmage.

Jeremy from work: I didn't win, goddamn it. But seriously, my tuna cranberry surprise was ROBBED.

Mariam: I will . . . have to take your word for it.

I was both laughing and gagging at the thought.

Jeremy from work: By the way, Junk Mail's gig schedule is up. They're playing the Red Lion on November 29th. You in?

Mariam: 100%.

At dinner that night, Mehdi stayed true to his word and questioned my mom about her new fitness group.

"And you actually run?" he asked her.

"Yes." My mom nodded as she put some stew and rice on his plate. "I'm not fast, though. It takes me almost forty-five minutes to do the two-and-a-half miles."

"That's pretty good!" Mehdi exclaimed.

Mom smiled but then waved away the compliment. "Almost everyone else is much faster than me," she said. "But I have been getting better."

"Good for you, Mom," I added. "You haven't convinced Dad to go?"

We both looked over at my dad, who had earbuds in and was very likely listening to some poker podcast.

"Once I convince the group to finish off the workout with a friendly game of blackjack, then maybe," my mom quipped.

We laughed as we watched my father slowly and methodically chew his food, fifteen chews for every bite, like he'd been doing for the entire fifty-three years of his existence.

• • •

I was stuffing my pajama pants into my backpack when Mina walked into my room.

"Look, I just want to say one thing," she said without preamble.

I sighed and glanced at my watch. My train was leaving in an hour and Mom was supposed to take me to the station in twenty minutes. "Mina, I know—"

"No. Honestly, you don't know what I'm going to say. I've been thinking a lot about what happened. And you're right."

At this, I looked up at her, completely stunned: she was absolutely correct that I never would've expected her to, under any circumstances, say that.

"I don't know what I would have done if I'd been presented with the same choice," she continued measuredly. "It's totally nuts what happened. But . . ."

Ah. I braced myself for the lecture.

"I just . . . want you to be careful. I don't want you to get hurt again." Mina looked sincere as she said these words to me, and I couldn't help softening. "And that's it, I guess. I want you to take care of yourself."

"That's it?" I prodded, wanting to fish out any unsaid instances of sibling meddling right then and there.

"That's it," she said firmly.

I searched her face and, satisfied with the candor there, nodded. "Okay, thank you."

She nodded back at me and then turned to leave my room.

"Mina?" She turned around. "What if I *don't* get hurt again?" I said, fingering my backpack strap. "What if this time we make it work?"

She hesitated before she spoke. "Do you really think it will? Even after you come clean about this whole avatar business?"

"I think . . . maybe the universe is telling me something. That we're meant to be together." I sighed. "He *likes* Sienna, Mina. He really likes her. Which means he still really likes me, even if he doesn't know it yet. He's hung up on this idea that college means dating new people. But why does it have to? I love him so much, and if there's a possibility he can realize that he feels the same way . . . shouldn't I take it?"

Mina took a second to consider my words. "I want you to be happy, Mariam. That's the God's honest truth."

"I know you do."

"But sometimes," she continued, "I feel like it's my job to be your reality check. And it's not because I want to rain on your parade . . ."

"It's because I'm too optimistic," I finished her sentence for her.

"You're . . . you," Mina said. "And I don't want you to be any different."

"Then don't you see that I have to try, Mina?" I asked her.

She bit her lip. "Yes. I can see that. Just . . . be careful, okay?" she echoed herself.

"I'll do my best. I'll talk to you soon, okay?"

• • •

My goal for the train ride back was to let my mind wander in the hopes that it would somehow magically sort everything out by the time I arrived in the city.

I had my headphones on—listening to soothing instrumental movie soundtracks—and my forehead pressed against the window as yellow grass, bare trees, and large farm-style houses zoomed by me. I was pretty zoned out after about half an hour, but then my phone buzzed. And I made the mistake of looking at it.

CalebM8126: Hey! So what's your schedule like this week? Is there a good date night for you?

I put the phone away immediately, but I wasn't able to stop thinking about the message for the rest of the trip, or how exactly I was supposed to respond to it.

"Heeeeey, girl," I was enthusiastically greeted by Hedy as soon as I walked back into my room.

I smiled at her grinning face, surprised at how good it felt to see her. "Hey."

"How was your Thanksgiving?" she asked.

"Dramatic," I replied with—what else—dramatic flair as I flung my bag onto my bed.

"Uh-oh. What happened?"

I sat down at my desk chair. "Remember how I had that date before the break?" I started.

"Of course," she said. "Are things going well? Or not well?"

"Excellent question," I said. "There is a lot of unpacking to do before I can figure that out."

"Oh yeah?" she said. "Lay it on me. I am excellent at critical analysis."

So I did. The whole sorry tale from matching up with Caleb on HEAVR, to running into him at the bowling alley, and everything in between. For some reason, this time it sounded even crazier than the last time I'd spun this story to Mehdi, when I had giddily felt I was describing an epic second meet-cute.

"Wow," Hedy said once I had finished, eyes wide. Bet she hadn't been expecting this level of convolution when she'd volunteered to help me sort things out. "So you're basically catfishing your ex-boyfriend?"

"Uhhhh . . ." I had honestly never thought of it in those terms. "No. Well, I mean . . . maybe? On a technicality?"

"You're pretending to be someone else on an online dating app," Hedy said. "Isn't that the textbook definition of catfishing?"

"I guess," I said. "But I'm not really pretending to be someone else. It's just my name. And maybe my hair color. Everything I've said to him, everything he likes about me . . . that's still all me."

"Okay," Hedy replied slowly, nodding. "So you're going to have more dates as Sienna?"

"Well, he *wants* to set up another date." I waved my phone at her. "And I haven't responded yet."

"Right." She nodded before saying again, softer, "Wow."

"Go ahead, analyze me."

"Ummm . . ." She looked uncomfortable. "I don't know, Mariam," she said as she smoothed out her ponytail. I saw her eyeing Audrey on her bike, as if hoping she might have the answer instead. "I mean . . . I don't see how this can work out." She turned to me, looking tentative about what she was about to say. "You guys can't stay in virtual la-la land forever. You'll have to tell him sometime, and whenever you do . . . look, I don't know him, obviously. But I feel like it would be a hard thing to take well."

"The . . . catfishing?"

"Yeah. The catfishing."

I sighed. "I know. You're right. No, let me rephrase that. I *know* you're right. The thing is, I totally meant to tell him at the bowling alley, I swear. Only he seemed so smug about being right about us not working out, and so excited about this 'new girl.' It was . . . unreal is what it was."

Hedy nodded. "Yeah, I get that. I do." She was staring off at her movie collection now and cocking her head. It was a minute before she spoke. "Reminds me of *Vertigo*. You know, how you are and aren't his ex."

I couldn't help but smile. It seemed like everything in Hedy's world related back to some old movie. "*Vertigo*, huh?"

She turned to me, eyes wide. "*Please* don't tell me you haven't seen that one either."

I gave her a sheepish smile. "Okay, I won't."

She shook her head as she walked over to her shelf and plucked a Blu-ray case from it. "At least it'll help you take your mind off things for a couple of hours."

Something I could have no objection to, so I fluffed up the pillows against my wall and settled in.

Um, *Vertigo* did not do much to take my mind off things.

It did, however, make me seriously question my mental state. Jimmy Stewart plays a man so obsessed with his dead love, he finds a woman with a striking resemblance to her and tries to get her to essentially become the ex. Did Hedy see me as fixated Jimmy Stewart in this scenario? Or duplicitous Madeleine/Judy? Or both?

Hedy accurately interpreted the terrified look on my face when the movie ended, because she immediately said, "It's not an exact parallel!"

"I hope not," I muttered, clutching one of my pillows.

"But seriously," Hedy continued breathlessly, "can we talk about Hitchcock's use of color? Reds for Scottie, greens for Madeleine, yellows for Midge. They relate back to the central themes of passion, death, and jealousy. And at key scenes, Hitchcock uses color to draw in the viewer's eye and hint at when things are shifting. Like when the characters symbolically take on each other's colors."

"I . . . wow. I hadn't noticed, actually," I admitted as I took the Blu-ray case that was on Hedy's desk and looked at some of the screenshots on the back. Sure enough, Madeleine was in a green dress and Jimmy Stewart was in a red sweater.

"It's absolutely brilliant. You should watch it again sometime now that you know to look for it," Hedy continued. "It's usually credited as being Hitchcock's most personal and arguably his best film, even though it bombed at the box office when it was first released. There's so much subtly going on in terms of ideas of masculinity and femininity, sex, hints of necrophilia, even. There are so many layers. And when François Truffaut spoke to Hitchcock about it in the sixties—he's an amazing French filmmaker; we'll have to watch his stuff next time—Hitchcock said he was most interested in the idea of the effort it would take to create a woman in the image of another one."

"Wow," I said again, ironically with my own head spinning. "Now I feel stupid for missing all that."

Hedy laughed. "Don't! This is years' worth of criticism and philosophy and repeated viewings I'm spewing at you. It's also just a good suspense thriller too, don't you think?"

I nodded as I glanced at Kim Novak in her green dress again. I guess I was kind of trying to remake Sienna in my own image, when she was really me all along. Maybe I should sort through the other lessons I could make out from *Vertigo*. Though one bleak thought was that it would be pretty hard to glean a happy ending from it.

CHAPTER 11

A RE YOU READY?" JEREMY WAS GRINNING AT ME from the other side of the front desk.

I blinked at him in confusion. "For?"

Just then a familiar-looking face framed by pink-and-blue hair came up behind him. "Jeremy, you think you can help us load the Lyft? Des and Lainey are running late as per usual, and Julia and I are stuck with a whole drum kit and the amps."

I smacked myself on the forehead. The Junk Mail concert. "Oh God. That was today?" It had taken me forever to respond to Caleb's text about our next date, but when I finally had, I'd obviously been too preoccupied to check my calendar properly. Though, now that I thought about it, I wasn't sure I'd even put the concert on there. "I'm so sorry. I have a date."

The lead singer eyed me curiously.

"Oh," Jeremy said. "Ah, well. No worries. Mariam, this is Sheridan. Sheridan, Mariam. Mariam is a new fan." He winked at me.

"I am!" I said as I stuck out my hand to shake Sheridan's, not wanting her to think Jeremy's declaration was meant to be ironic. "And a big one." Which wasn't a lie. I had watched more of their videos on YouTube and listened to their streaming six-track LP a few times by this point. "It's an honor to meet you. You guys are awesome."

"Thanks," Sheridan responded. "I don't mean to be rude, but we're crunched for time." She put her arm through Jeremy's and looked up at him.

"Yes, sorry. Of course I'll help." He turned to me. "Maybe you can catch them some other time."

"Yes. I'd love to," I said, looking apologetically at Sheridan, though I didn't know why, because it wasn't like she seemed the slightest bit disappointed that I wouldn't see her play that night. "Good luck at your gig."

"Good luck on your date," she replied as she led Jeremy out of the gym.

It was just something she said, I told myself. A mirror of my own platitude to her.

But for some reason, it made me feel more nervous than I already was.

The sound of pins being knocked over invaded my ears as I watched them domino one by one, until a lone one remained, stubborn and resolute.

"Oh, man," avatar Caleb said good-naturedly.

Here we are again, I couldn't help thinking. The generic VR bowling alley didn't have the greasy snack smell or ancient neon decor of the familiar one where the real us had last met, but it did have the advantage of being the site of a much happier evening.

Caleb had been nothing but charming and funny the whole date, the Caleb I had always known and fallen in love with. And as for me, I *was* being myself, except for responding to a different name. The whole night I kept thinking if I could just have a little more time in the virtual world with him and make him really fall for Sienna, he'd eventually see that he'd never fallen out of love with *me*. We had thankfully gone past the point of asking too much about each other's personal histories, so the necessity of blatantly lying had gone significantly down. There was just one uncomfortable instance when Caleb was complimenting my bowling skills.

"Wow. You're good," he said, looking up at the scoreboard. "I used to get creamed by my ex, too."

I gave a small noncommittal smile, and Caleb instantly seemed to recognize his gaffe in bringing her up. He changed the subject.

We had decided to call it a night after three sets, when Caleb reached for my hand and I felt the pressure in my haptic glove. Immediately I thought of Sheridan taking Jeremy's arm and wondered how much tech and code had to go into making the simplest gesture feel remotely real. "Sienna, I'd . . . I'd really like to kiss you." Caleb laughed at himself. "And if this was a real-life date, I wouldn't be narrating that thought so awkwardly."

I laughed back. "Oh? What would you be doing?" I asked archly.

His hand moved slowly up my arm. "I'd . . . get close to you. Lean in a little. Make sure I was reading your body language right." His face was inching closer to mine and inevitably mine to his.

"Then I'd brush your cheek." A small puff of air grazed the left side of my face where Caleb's virtual hand had gone.

"And then . . ." He stopped talking but leaned in all the way. I automatically closed my eyes.

There was a brush against my lips that got deeper and pressure on my back through the vest that must have been where Caleb was pressing his hand.

It felt like touch, but also not. It had pressure and some warmth but was missing some important keystones, like the wetness of two mouths coming together, or the slight, sweet smell of breaths commingling that I'd never consciously noticed until it wasn't there. I wanted to run my hands through his hair but knew I wouldn't be feeling the short curls.

It wasn't bad, really. But it wasn't right. Not when my body knew exactly what kissing the real Caleb felt like.

After a short while, Caleb pulled away, his hand remaining on the side of my face. "So . . . I guess that's VR kissing," he said with a slightly embarrassed laugh.

I laughed with him. "I guess so." I paused. "Could use some work."

"Agreed. As long as you know to reserve judgment on my actual kissing prowess until we meet in person, right?"

I smiled, hoping that when we finally did, he'd want to kiss Mariam-me as much as he had Sienna.

"Speaking of which . . ." My pulse quickened. I didn't know where that conjunction could lead except to . . . "When I go home for winter break, I was thinking of stopping by New York City first. Would you be around? Would you want to meet?"

I was sure my heart full-on stopped as Caleb gave me the dates he was thinking of. Either way, it definitely wasn't delivering oxygen to my brain, which seemed incapable of giving a coherent response. *It's too soon* was all that kept flashing through it. *I need more time.*

I think I eventually mumbled something about checking my schedule and Caleb, thankfully, didn't press too hard, probably sensing my hesitation. Before I knew it, we had said our goodbyes and I stood alone in the middle of the fake bowling alley, breathing in and out and trying to make sense of what exactly I should do.

"You know, meeting in person is a great step. And now that you've completed your third date, you'd be free to take things offline if you choose."

It had been a while since I'd heard Agatha's voice, but I was too caught up in Caleb's bombshell to be startled by it.

"In fact," she continued, "it is obviously the natural course of a relationship coming together, but . . ."

I realized that I was waiting with bated breath for her advice. *That*'s how messed up I was about my own sense of judgment.

"If you're not ready for it, you're not ready," Agatha continued sensibly.

"Right," I mumbled, when it appeared that Agatha wasn't going to say any more.

And even though I had been surprisingly glad for anyone weighing in at this point, my old suspicions of Agatha couldn't help poking through as I logged off. Was she giving genuine good advice or trying to stop the dates from going offline so she could continue spying on them?

CHAPTER 12

THAT WHOLE NEXT WEEK, CALEB AND I WERE messaging each other with flirty asides and winking emojis. It seemed so easy and carefree that it was almost enough to make me rethink my aversion to texting in the first place and forget the turn our last HEAVR date had taken.

But then he brought up his suggestion to meet up again.

CalebM8126: I've only been to NYC a handful of times. I hope you'd be up for playing tour guide.

When I didn't respond right away, he texted again.

CalebM8126: Or maybe you're tired of the responsibility that comes from living in the Greatest City in the World? And you don't want to host yet another neophyte.

His tone was jokey, but I knew the intent behind it was serious. He wanted an answer.

SiennaV23: It's not that . . .

I was sitting on a park bench in Washington Square Park with a sandwich I knew I wouldn't be able to finish now.

SiennaV23: It's just . . . do you ever worry what it'll be like if we meet in person? If you'd like the real-life me?

CalebM8126: Do you mean if you'd like the real-life me?

SiennaV23: No. I meant what I wrote.

CalebM8126: I can't imagine I wouldn't.

I hoped it was true, but I couldn't bring myself to give him an answer yet.

A few hours later, while I was at work, Hedy texted me to see if I would be up for hanging out with her and Geneviève that night.

Hedy: But we're sort of broke, so we were thinking Thai food and the common-room movie?

Mariam: Totally in.

I didn't even bother to ask what the movie was. Anything to distract me right now was a good thing. Uncomplicated friendships were a good thing. And on that note, I decided to visit Jeremy on the third floor. His shift had just started, but it ended only an hour after mine.

He smiled at me. "Hey. How's it going?"

"Okay," I said as I placed my elbows on the counter in front of him. "I was wondering if you were free tonight."

Something flashed in his eye, almost like confusion but coupled with a pleased little smile. "I am," he said. "Why?"

"Do you want to come over?" I asked. "My roommate and her girlfriend will be there and we're going to order takeout and go to the common-room movie they're showing. Seems like a wholesome college-y thing to do, right?"

"Definitely," he said. "Matter of fact, it's number two on my Wholesome College-y Challenges list."

I took the bait. "What's number one?"

"Sledding on dining hall trays in the quad," he quipped immediately.

I let out a short bark of laughter. "I think you might be at the wrong school."

"Right," he agreed. "Might have to amend that to sledding on trays in Washington Square Park."

"But wouldn't a public disorder arrest nullify the wholesome factor?"

"Killjoy," he said. "Anyway, sounds fun. Count me in."

"Awesome! See you at seven thirty? I'm in Rubin, room 408."

"Sure thing."

"Oh, and what's your favorite Thai food? My treat for flaking out on you with the concert."

It was seven thirty on the dot and I had just finished putting in the food order when the guard called me from downstairs to come sign Jeremy in. He came bearing a Duane Reade bag with a two-liter bottle of soda and lime-flavored tortilla chips.

"Welcome to our humble abode," I said as I opened the door to our room. It was small but had a spectacular view of the gorgeous stained-glass windows of the church across the street from us. "Please enjoy my first and last time with a Fifth Avenue address."

"Nice," Jeremy said, looking around the room. "It looks bigger than my room in Hayden."

"That's because it was supposed to be a triple, but someone in the housing department messed up, so it's just the two of us," Hedy said as she got up from her desk chair to greet Jeremy. "You must be the infamous Jeremy."

"And you must be the cinephile, Hedy," Jeremy said. They shook hands and I could tell from Hedy's grin that he was already racking up brownie points.

After Geneviève emerged from the bathroom and introduced herself, we opened up Jeremy's bag of chips and settled down on various chairs and beds.

"So anyone figure out what movie they're showing yet?" Jeremy asked from my desk chair.

Hedy immediately brought her hands up to her face and in a high-pitched voice started saying, "Flames!"

Jeremy broke into a smile. "Nice one!" he said, but Hedy was eyeing me and my blank expression with a good-natured grin.

"Shall we take bets as to whether or not our Mariam has seen this movie?" she asked the other two.

I smiled sheepishly. "Soooo . . . what movie is it?"

Jeremy startled. "No way. You must have seen *Clue*," he said.

"Our girl has led a very cinematically sheltered life," Hedy explained.

"Which I'm now being schooled on, thank you very much," I said. "I'd like to think I'm a very pliable and open-minded student."

"You are," Hedy agreed.

"And don't pretend you haven't enjoyed every moment of lecturing me on your movies," I added. "I've seen that gleam in your eye whenever you bring up a film I haven't seen. Which you casually seem to be dropping into more and more conversations as of late," I teased.

Geneviève laughed as Hedy shrugged. "Okay, okay. Guilty as charged."

"Thank God this transgression is being remedied tonight," Jeremy said. "You *must* see *Clue.*"

"And I shall," I said, and then, looking at the three of them sitting there in such high spirits, I got inspired. "But before we do that, how would you guys feel about maybe weighing in on a momentous life decision?"

"That depends," Geneviève said. "Whose momentous life decision is it?"

"Mine, of course," I said.

"Ooh, yes, absolutely," Hedy said. "Lay it on us."

"Unless it's about whether or not to get a Fighting Violet tattoo," Jeremy said seriously. "I have a poor track record when it comes to both ink- and sports-related momentous decisions. Don't ask."

"Tramp stamp?" Hedy immediately piped in.

"My lips are sealed," he said, but I caught the twinkle in

his eye and couldn't help wondering if he was totally jok-
ing or if he really had some secretly horrible tattoo somewhere. "Anyway, Mariam. Go on."

"Right," I said, clearing my throat nervously. "So . . .
Caleb wants to meet. In person. He suggested coming to
the city before winter break."

"Oh," Jeremy said.

Geneviève whistled. I hadn't spoken to her about the
situation much myself but had given Hedy permission to
tell her everything. "And are you going to meet him?" she
asked.

"That's where you come in," I said. "My esteemed panel
of life coaches."

"That's an upgrade from gym desk clerk," Jeremy said.

"Seriously, guys. Tell me what to do!" And right on cue,
a loud buzz from the security guard let us know our food
had arrived. "Talk amongst yourselves," I said as I got up
to go get it.

When I came back, Jeremy and Hedy were laughing
over something. For a fleeting moment, I wondered if they
were making fun of me, but then I realized they must be
reciting lines from some movie.

"Ooh, let's not spoil it for her," Hedy said as soon as she
saw I'd returned, leading me to guess it was *Clue* again.

"Are you telling me you guys have been discussing the
movie instead of figuring out my love life? This whole
time?" I pretended to be exasperated.

"Of course not," Geneviève said as she took the bag of food from me and started distributing the containers. "Hedy is armed and ready for you." She pointed to my roommate, who now held a dry-erase marker as triumphantly as if it were Excalibur.

Hedy got up and went to the whiteboard on the wall that we used to write each other notes sometimes, erased *Need more toilet paper*, drew a line down the middle, and wrote *PROS* and *CONS* on each side. I sat myself down studiously in front of it, my unopened container of pad Thai in front of me. I'd eat once I'd had my trial by committee.

"So, pros and cons of meeting Caleb," Hedy said as she pointed at Jeremy and Geneviève. "Okay, go."

"Pro: honesty is the foundation of any healthy relationship," Geneviève said, then took a bite out of a spring roll. I looked over at her nervously. She was right, of course, but this was pretty much a word-for-word echo of what almost-definitely-evil Agatha had said. Also, let's be honest, this meant I would be admitting my lies to Caleb imminently, which might currently top my Things I Don't Want to Go Through list, right above eye gouging and getting a labia tattoo (Fighting Violet–related or not).

Hedy nodded as she wrote down *Honesty* on the Pros list.

"Cons: easier said than done," Jeremy said, and I shot him a grateful look.

"But she can't keep up the lie forever," Hedy said as

she wrote *Hard to do* on the Cons list and *Has to happen sometime* on the Pros list.

"And better to tell him in person than over text or as, like, a VR person," Geneviève pointed out.

"True," Jeremy said as he gave me an encouraging smile. Out of the three of them, he was being the most empathetic, but it didn't mean that Hedy and Geneviève weren't completely right.

"And you'd have to give him some sort of excuse as to why you wouldn't want to meet in person," Hedy said, lengthening the Pros list some more. "Which would only be more lying."

"Plus, it might make him think you're not interested in him," Geneviève added. "Which wouldn't help anything."

"And how much longer can you keep this going anyway?" Hedy said. "The point is to eventually admit to him that it's you, right?"

"Right," I said, swallowing as I saw that Hedy was near the bottom of the whiteboard, but only on one side. "Of course you're right. I know it. I've probably always known it. It's just . . ."

Hedy took the end of her marker and pointed to the only line on the Cons list.

I nodded. "It's going to be really hard. But that doesn't mean it doesn't need to happen." I took in a breath. "Anyway, thank you. I appreciate it. And now, should we hurry up and eat? The movie starts in fifteen minutes, right?"

"Ah!" Hedy said triumphantly. "That's the beauty of the common-room movie night. It's BYTO!"

And with that, we gathered up our takeout and shuffled to the floor's common room, where the furniture was no different or more comfortable than what we had in our room, nor was the television much bigger than Hedy's laptop screen, but it somehow felt like a rite of passage. Besides, they had been right about *Clue*. It was very funny and a good distraction, especially hearing my new friends' and floormates' commentary on it. There were even moments when I let myself forget what I knew I had to do.

But I took the plunge that night, messaging Caleb before I ended up in another endless cycle of *should I or shouldn't I?* when I clearly already knew the answer.

SiennaV23: Come to NYC. Let's meet.

He wrote back within minutes.

CalebM8126: Looking up flights right now. ☺!!

I felt a lightening in my chest as my heart fluttered with both nerves and excitement. Despite how hard this was going to be, how it wasn't going to be the exciting first meeting that Caleb was imagining, an instinctual part of me was looking forward to seeing his face again. It was locked around the same part of me that foolishly hoped this would only be an uncomfortable stopgap before getting Caleb back in my life for real.

We discussed flight options and I agreed to meet him at the airport so that I could help him navigate the subway system.

CalebM8126: So are you going to wear something for me to identify you by? A red flower in your hair?

He sent me a winking emoji, but my eyes had already fallen across the winter hat I'd picked up a couple of days before in Chinatown. It happened to be red with a few felt poppies stuck to its side.

SiennaV23: Actually, yes. Look for the girl in this hat.

I sent him a photo of it.

I knew he wouldn't really need it to recognize me, but I'd be wearing it anyway. It would be part of Sienna's costume—for her farewell tour.

CHAPTER 13

TWO WEEKS WENT BY IN A FLASH AND BEFORE I knew it, I was handing in my last blue book of the semester. I was nervous, but it had nothing to do with the final I'd just taken and everything to do with where I was headed next.

I got on a crowded A train and took it almost as far as it could go, forced to carry my backpack in front of me for a good portion of the ride while my nose was unfortunately buried near a very tall man's armpit. The crowd thinned out the deeper I got into Queens, and I was finally able to snag a seat a few stops before I had to transfer to the AirTrain.

My stomach felt queasier the closer I got to the airport. By the time I'd reached the correct terminal and walked into the revolving doors that would take me to Arrivals, I was sure that it wasn't far from exploding my lunch over the well-trod tiles of JFK. The red poppy hat was balled up in my fist, soaking up the sweat and anxiety that seemed to be coursing from my every pore.

Speaking of which, I guessed it was time to don the

thing. I looked up at the board and saw that his flight from
San Francisco had landed. Depending on whether or not
he had checked luggage, he could be here any minute. I
slowly unfurled my fist, smoothed out the hat, and put it
on my head.

Hedy: You there yet?

Hedy had put me on a group text with Geneviève and
Jeremy.

Mariam: Just got here.

Hedy: You got this.

Geneviève: Call or text us if you need anything.

Jeremy from work: Ditto. Good luck, M.

Mariam: Thanks, guys.

Despite my nerves, I couldn't help smiling. It felt nice to
have friends looking out for me again.

I was in the midst of that warm and fuzzy feeling when I
looked up and saw him. My heart stuttered. He was walking slowly and didn't see me at first, even though he was
clearly looking . . . but for Sienna, of course. Sienna.

I put on what I hoped would be a non-psycho-stalker
smile, took in a deep breath, and waited.

I knew the instant that he spotted me. He was only a
few feet away, and he looked so startled by the coincidence
of seeing his ex when he was waiting for his new girlfriend
that he physically took a step back.

"Mariam, hi," he said when he had gained some composure.

"Hi," I replied.

He walked toward me and gave me a small, awkward hug. "What are you doing here?"

"I'm waiting for someone," I replied, desperately trying not to make my voice sound as small as I felt right then.

"Oh, me too," he responded. "Who?"

He looked at me again, really looked at me, and his eyes widened as he finally took in the hat. He stared into my face, searching for the answer that I no longer had to say. The word *you* hung in the air like a ghost between us.

Caleb's dark fingers were gripped around his white coffee cup like a vise. He had ordered it black with an extra shot of espresso, and I almost felt like he was eyeing the sports bar across the hallway ruefully. Instead he took a sip from the drink he had.

I had told him the whole sorry tale. Now it was time for the apology. "It wasn't on purpose, Caleb. You have to believe me." I waited for him to look up and meet my eyes. "When you popped up as one of my three options, I . . . don't know. Something took over. And it was wrong, but it was never on purpose."

He had barely said a word the entire time I was talking, and when he spoke now it was into his coffee cup and in a deadly calm voice that somehow stung more than if he had started yelling. "You let it go on for so long."

"I know," I said. I didn't want to cry; I didn't want either of us to have to deal with that, too. I averted my gaze to compose myself but was met only with the sight of the poppy hat that sat like a scarlet letter on the table between us. Not helping. I took in a deep breath and looked back up at him. "Once it started, it escalated out of control," I said as calmly and measuredly as I could. "I didn't know how to tell you, and the dates were going so well. . . ."

"But the dates weren't real," he said in that same flat voice.

"In some ways," I said. "But that has more to do with the avatars and VR—"

"No," he interrupted me. "It has to do with Sienna being a lie."

I swallowed. "She's not entirely a lie," I said quietly. "Except for the name, she's me."

He took another gulp from his coffee, and then he stared into his cup for a while before he spoke again. "So, what, were you telling your new college friends about me?" he asked.

"Well, yeah. I guess," I said, surprised that he had surmised that much. "I asked them for advice."

He looked up at me then, his eyes hard. "And they thought it was hilarious to string along your ex like the asshole he is, is that it?"

I blinked in astonishment. As long as I'd known him, I'd never heard Caleb's voice like this, edged like a razor and ready to bite. "No. Of course not. It wasn't like that."

"Then what was it like, Mariam?" he asked. "Was the plan to make me feel like an idiot?"

"No. That's what I'm saying, Caleb. There was no plan. I missed you and suddenly you were there and we were having fun. It just happened and it spun out of control."

"Sure, okay," he said. "The first time, when my name popped up, it just happened. But what about every date and exchange after that? You lied to me every single time. And at the bowling alley . . ." He trailed off with a sharp intake of breath, and I could tell he was replaying our conversations in his head. What I had said as both Mariam and Sienna. How the lies had built and spiraled like a tornado he didn't know he had stepped into.

I saw anger and hurt flit across his face, chasing one another in a seemingly endless loop. And then I went all in because it seemed like there was nowhere else to go. If this was going to be my confession, it was time to make it as honest as it could be. "I just felt like I had you back and that made me feel . . . I don't know. Whole again. It was too hard to let that go. And I knew you liked Sienna. I thought . . . I thought maybe this was a sign that we truly were meant to be."

I watched Caleb open his mouth to speak and then stop. Then open it to speak again and stop once more. He obviously didn't know how to deal with this, too, the barefaced truth that I was still in love with him.

After a minute of silence, he finally muttered, "It's not

a good enough excuse. If you really cared about me, you would've have respected my wishes. Not found a loophole to keep us together."

The tears were dangerously close to spilling now, and I knew I had to get out of there. "You're right," I said as I grabbed my backpack. "I wish there was something more I could say other than I'm sorry. I'm embarrassed and I'm really sorry for putting you through this. It wasn't right and it wasn't fair." I stood up, looking at his embittered face and disbelieving that I, of all people, had caused him to feel that way. I didn't know what he was going to do in the city now that the illusion of Sienna was gone and he was stuck with the reality of his obsessed ex, and he was probably thinking the same thing.

I grabbed the miserable hat and scrunched it up into my fist again. "If . . . if you ever want to talk about it, or yell at me, or whatever . . . just let me know, okay?" I said.

He didn't say anything but looked up at me and gave a curt nod.

"Goodbye, Caleb," I said, my voice starting to shake now. "I'm sorry."

"Bye," he responded gruffly.

I turned around and shoved the hat into a trash can as I dashed my way out of the airport, only now noticing the teary faces of everyone who had also left loved ones behind. My own would blend right in.

CHAPTER 14

"YOU QUIT ON ME, I FIRE YOU. YOU LET ME DOWN, I make you blue. And it seems there's nothing we can do but turn each other on."

Sheridan's voice was filling my dorm room, and I was in the sort of state where every lyric ever suddenly seemed applicable to my broken heart. I was trying to focus on the blazing guitars and danceable beat instead of the words coming out of my laptop speakers as I rolled five dice in time to the music and got my third "fours" of the game. That wasn't going to get me anywhere either.

I was sitting on the floor, my back against the foot of my bed, while Jeremy sat across from me, his long legs splayed out in front of him and nearly reaching mine, his back against Hedy's bed. She'd left for home the day before yesterday. The ancient Yahtzee game was from the common room and, miraculously, seemed to have all its pieces and even a few empty scorecards.

"I used to play this with my brother all the time," Jeremy had said when we came across it. "We could get pretty cutthroat."

"You don't know anything about cutthroat until you've played a board game with my sister," I'd responded.

"Oh yeah? Did your games involve a headlock in between every round?"

I'd laughed. "Not exactly. But we'd use board games to settle major arguments. Like, for example, which one of us would get to marry Joe Jonas. Things got very underhanded. Community Chest cards would appear at suspiciously opportune times. Sorry pieces would miraculously move ahead four spaces when someone's head was turned."

"Wow," Jeremy had said. "You're right. That does sound more vicious."

We'd decided to give Yahtzee a go. But now it turned out my luck with dice wasn't currently going any better than my luck with love.

"Damn it," I exclaimed as I took a look at my woeful score sheet. "Come on. Don't you think I deserve a break here?"

He smiled at me as he took the cup and dice from the floor. "So," he said as he swirled the cubes around. "Have you heard from him?"

I shook my head and tried to talk past the lump in my throat. It had been three days, which was not long enough to burn the image of Caleb's wounded looks and words from my memory. "No. But I haven't exactly been expecting to. The way we left things wasn't what I'd call promising."

Jeremy looked at me for a second like he wanted to say something, but then, thankfully, rolled.

"Three of a kind?! You bastard!" I yelled, perhaps with more fervor over the change in subject than the score sheet, even though Jeremy's was already twice as filled in as mine.

Jeremy grinned and shrugged. "Let's leave my parentage out of it, Vakilian."

"But that's the thing. Genetically speaking, I should be a whiz at this game!" I said as I scooped up the dice. "My father would be so disappointed."

"Why? Is he like a Grand Yahtzeemaster?" Jeremy asked.

"Nah. Poker," I explained. "He's obsessed with it. Though he doesn't really play it per se. At least not for money." I saw Jeremy looking confused and realized I had to explain. "Muslim thing. No gambling. Or drinking. Or pork. He doesn't pray five times a day, but he's pretty observant in most other ways."

"Ah. Got it," he said, and then pointed at my hand. "I think you've got to, you know, put your wrist into it."

"Oh yeah. Sure. Because this is a game of physical dexterity and not of luck." I rolled the dice. "Holy crap. Small straight. Finally!" I put in my score on the appropriate grid line while Jeremy took the dice back.

"See, told you. You can just call me Coach from now on," he said.

"I'll get right on that."

He played with the dice but didn't roll. "So what now?" he asked, and I immediately knew he wasn't talking about our game.

I looked up at him, reading the genuine concern in his face. "I guess . . . nothing. I told him he could call me if he ever wants to talk or scream at me. But knowing him, I doubt he will. He's probably said everything he wanted to say to me."

"So you're not going to try to see him when you get home?" he asked while shaking the cup.

"Not on purpose. I'm hoping we'll make it the full month without running into each other." I stared off grimly at the poster of Audrey. "This whole thing sucks, but even so, I just don't see how I could've made any other decision, you know what I mean?" I didn't know exactly what twelve-step process there was when you were trying to get over the humiliation of catfishing your ex, but maybe I was past the blame-myself-for-everything phase and onto a more defensive phase. Which, frankly, was a relief.

"Yeah," Jeremy said.

"Except maybe to have told him sooner," I added, not wanting him to think I held myself wholly unaccountable for my actions.

"Love makes fools of us all sometimes," Jeremy said kindly as he rolled the dice.

"Or, in my case, makes us psychotic sometimes," I

added. "I don't know how I ever thought this would work out."

"Well, you know what they say about hindsight," Jeremy said as he rolled again. "And besides, wouldn't you have always wondered if you hadn't given it a shot? If you hadn't chosen him?"

What if. "Yes," I said truthfully. I didn't know how, but sometimes Jeremy knew exactly what to say to me, like he had figured me out without even trying. "Do you want to hear something crazy?"

"Always," Jeremy said.

"So, like you said, I had three HEAVR matches to choose from, right?"

"Right."

"You'll never guess who one of them was." I grinned slyly at him as I jiggled the dice.

"Er, your ex-boyfriend?"

I reached over and gave him a friendly swat. "Yeah, yeah. Besides him."

He ducked my flailing arm. "Um . . . a different ex-boyfriend?"

I laughed. "No, nobody from my harem of exes. Try a coworker."

"No shit, somebody who works at Palladium?" he said as he sat up straighter. "Stan?"

"Taller," I said, eyeing his legs. He only looked perplexed. When he didn't come up with another guess, I gave him one more hint. "Darker hair." His face didn't give away anything, but he was slowly blinking at me. "Currently in my dorm room."

For a moment, Jeremy just stared at me. Then finally, under his breath, I heard another faint, "No shit."

I laughed. "I know, man. I swear that machine is E-VIL. Of everyone who signed up for it, how could it have picked my ex-boyfriend and the guy I work with? Who is now my friend?" I rolled the dice and got three sixes. And when I rerolled the other dice, I managed to rack up one more. "Yes!" I said as I gleefully wrote it down on my scorecard. "Anyway, I'm sorry I didn't pick you. I could've avoided this whole mess." I looked back up, expecting a grin and a snarky response. Instead Jeremy was looking at me thoughtfully.

"You still could," he said when he finally spoke.

I was so surprised that my mouth dropped open.

Jeremy laughed. "I mean, no pressure or anything. Being friends is cool too."

I swallowed. "Okay . . ." My brain suddenly felt overloaded with this new, wholly unexpected information, and I couldn't seem to form any other words.

"It is," Jeremy said, as he picked at the carpet. "Forget I said anything."

But the silence between us lay thick now, blanketing the whole room as if it was about to suffocate one of the only true friendships I'd made since I'd gotten here.

"I'm sorry," I said, realizing I needed to fix this. "It's . . . it's so not personal. It's just . . . this thing with Caleb is so weird and severely fucked up. I don't think I should be dating anyone right now. Especially not a friend I care about." I went with telling the truth, which was the opposite of what had landed me in so much hot water.

"I get it," Jeremy said with a smile. "Honestly. I'm glad we're friends."

"Me too," I responded quickly and with relief. "So glad. You have no idea."

"Now, as your friend, I feel it necessary to warn you . . . I'm about to up my game here. Check out *this* wrist action."

He picked up the cup, did some fancy underhanded swirl thing where he flipped it over without dropping any of the dice, and then suavely flung it so that the dice tumbled out onto the middle of the carpet.

He got a full house.

"What?!" I exclaimed.

He winked. "Game of luck, eh?"

When I arrived home the next day, I noticed that things weren't quite normal between Mina and me. She was avoiding me, or at least avoiding the subject of Caleb, which was clearly all she wanted to talk about. Therefore, she ended up not talking to me much, period.

I let it be for a couple of days, trying to enjoy having the time at home to sort through and reflect on everything

myself. I sat on my bed and mulled. I watched TV and wal-
lowed. I read a book and found myself rereading the same
page five times before I could absorb the words.

By the third day, when Mina flitted by my hallway like a
shadow, I couldn't take it anymore—both the self-inflicted
solitary confinement and the elephant in the room.

"Mina," I called out to her, and after a moment, I heard
her footsteps retrace the walk back to my door.

"Hey," she said.

"Hey. You got a minute?"

She looked at her watch. "Yeah. I have to be at work in an
hour, but I have some time." She stepped in and leaned against
the doorway, almost like she was ready to flee if things got
heated, but she kept her voice casual. "What's up?"

"Look, I told Caleb everything," I said with my hands
out in front of me on the bedspread like my cards were on
the table.

"You did?" Mina responded in surprise. She immediately stood up straight and took a few more steps into my
room.

"Last week," I said. "In person. He wanted to meet
Sienna. So he came to New York City and, uh, met her." I
made jazz hands to bring some levity to the situation.

"Wow." Mina's eyes widened. "What happened?! What
did he say?"

"He was pissed. Understandably," I added. "I apologized a lot and then . . . that's it. That's the last I heard of

him." I gave a small snort. "Maybe he's thinking, 'I sure dodged a bullet breaking up with her in the first place.'"

"Don't do that," Mina warned.

"Do what?"

"Ascribe feelings like that to him. You don't really know how he feels." She walked over and sat down on the bed next to me. "And besides, it's so not you."

I rolled my eyes. "Maybe being an optimist is over-rated."

"I think it's underrated," Mina said firmly as she put one hand on my shoulder. "And rare. And . . . just don't ever let a guy let you lose that part of yourself, Mariam."

I stayed quiet but let her words sink in. Then I changed the subject. "And you? What's your love life looking like these days?"

"Oh please. As dismal as my career prospects," she said.

"Have you considered HEAVR?" I joked. "I hear their matchmaking prowess is second to none."

She snorted. "Oh God. Can you imagine if it matched me up with Russ?" Russ was Mina's eleventh-grade boy-friend from back when we lived in Omaha. His main hob-bies included being a percussionist—not a drummer, mind you—for his noise band, Frglwer. And no, he never felt "intimate enough" with Mina to reveal how to pronounce that.

"If it did, then I'd know for a fact that the AI was evil enough to be plotting a world takeover," I responded.

"Which I have been suspecting for some time now. So, frankly, you must go sign up. For the sake of humanity."

"Yeah, no. Humanity is not worth meeting up with Russ again, thanks," Mina said.

"That should be the earth's epitaph."

"Hello, sisters. What's happening?" Mehdi had walked by, seen our tête-à-tête, and invited himself in.

"Oh, just discussing the merits of Russ DeWitt," I said.

"Wow. That must be a short conversation," he quipped back.

Mina looked over at me, and I could tell she was wondering if I was going to loop Mehdi in on the Caleb situation. I sighed, realizing that I'd have to. Though the fleeting, slightly horrifying thought that he might have already heard it from Caleb himself did cross my mind.

"Um, so, you haven't heard from Caleb, have you?" I asked Mehdi.

He looked at me shrewdly, his interest obviously piqued. "Not in a few weeks. Why? What happened?"

I took a deep breath and told him the whole story, hoping against hope that it would be the last time I'd have to tell this narrative. Mehdi's appropriately timed gasps and whistles made me realize that I was definitely tired of being the girl in the center of all this drama.

CHAPTER 15

I WOKE UP THE NEXT MORNING WITH MY MIND already made up: the only way to get back to normal was to try to banish any thoughts of Caleb. At least for the next three weeks while we were in the same town. I'd even be satisfied with the next three days.

Unfortunately, it didn't even last three hours, because this town was way too goddamned small.

I saw Gideon, Caleb's little brother, first. I was at the grocery store, mistakenly thinking that accompanying my mother there would be a good pursuit of my plan to keep myself occupied. Suddenly Gideon's distinctive curly hair had popped up amid the carrots, but it took me a moment to recognize him. Last time I saw him, he definitely hadn't been taller than me, but he must have had a growth spurt over the summer. It was strange to see the little-kid face I had played Uno with a million times suddenly towering over me. But his smile, which unfortunately was too similar to his older brother's, hadn't changed, and its sudden appearance when he spotted me, too, at least gave me hope that there was one member of the Moore family who didn't hate me.

"Mariam," he called out as he walked over to me.

I put on a smile and gave him a hug. "Gideon, hi!" I said, while furiously trying to figure out how I could get out of there as quickly as possible. Which, of course, made me feel very guilty. Gideon and I had always gotten along, bonding over youngest sibling syndrome and—obviously—it wasn't his fault that I had royally screwed up everything with his brother.

"Well, hello there," a mellifluous voice called out from behind him, and Loretta emerged with an identical smile to her two sons. "Do I get one too?" She held out her arms for a hug, and I walked over and gave her one. "It's good to see you."

"You too," I lied. "I hear you've somehow managed to get Mom running every morning at six a.m.? What witchcraft is this?"

She laughed as she broke away from the hug, keeping her arms on my shoulders. "Empty nesters are easy prey."

"Are you talking about me?" Mom said as she came up from behind me and spotted her friend.

"Only in glowing terms," Loretta assured her.

"Hmmm," Mom said, looking skeptical. "My children seem to think it's hilarious that I've decided to use my two legs for something other than going to work or cooking in the kitchen."

"Mom!" I said. "That's not true!" But then I gave it a second thought. Was it? Did we not expect her to have a life outside of the one we knew for her when we lived together?

"Typical," Loretta said. "But don't worry. One day they'll understand." She winked at my mom then, and the two women exchanged a secret smile, which I didn't have too much time to contemplate, because next thing I knew, Loretta's other son had stepped out from behind a shelf of condiments.

"I can't find the garlic pickles. They might be out . . . oh." His eyes widened as they landed on me. Likely the same look of misery was written across both of our faces, though Caleb's held a tinge of fury and I'm sure mine was dipped in guilt. Wonderful. He took a deep breath and rearranged his features into something resembling a smile before he spoke again. "Hi. Hi, Elham," he said as he turned to my mom.

"Hi, Caleb," my mom said.

"Hi," I said, not wanting to mumble and sound as panicked as I felt, but instead taking it too far the other way and sounding insanely cheerful. Jesus, I shouldn't leave my house again for the rest of the break.

"How's school?" Mom asked him.

"It's good, thanks," he responded stiffly.

Oh my God. This needed to end now. "Well, happy holidays!" I said to the three Moores before turning pointedly to my mom. "Do you think we could get some steaks for dinner tonight?" The meat section was all the way on the other side of the store.

"Oh." My mom blinked, a little slow on the uptake. "Sure."

"Great! I'll go pick them out." I made a beeline for the butcher against the far-right wall, only vaguely hearing my mom ask the Moores about how they spent their Christmas. I was sorry Caleb was going to have to feign politeness to my mother for a while longer, but it was more important that I got the hell out of Dodge before I figured out how to get her away from him too.

Raw pink-and-white slabs of meat stared at me. I read the label on each and every one: skirt steak, leg of lamb, pork tenderloin, chicken breast. For possibly the first time in my life, I thought about the animals they had once been a part of, and I sort of grossed myself out. My parents' jobs made them very aware of the environmental impact of meat production, so we were always eating a "responsible amount," as my mom put it. But I hadn't really thought much of the actual furred and feathered creatures until this train of thought had turned into an ambulance of contemplation. Suddenly carcasses and a strong urge to consider veganism seemed like a preferred alternative to reliving my last interaction with Caleb.

"Having a hard time deciding?"

I jumped. "Mom, you startled me," I said as I clutched near my heart, and then inadvertently looked behind her to make sure she hadn't been followed by Loretta and her brood.

"I'm sorry," she said, and then, softer, "Don't worry. They left."

I didn't acknowledge that she'd said anything but turned back around to the meat with a sigh of relief. Though I'd decidedly lost my appetite for it.

"Um, on second thought . . . could we do something vegetarian tonight?"

"Sure, but . . ." She paused, and I dreaded what I knew she was going to bring up. "What's going on between you and Caleb? I thought you guys parted as friends."

Yes, but that was before I told him the biggest lie of my life, I wanted to say. But I didn't. I was tired of repeating this story, and besides, there was a part of me that didn't want to admit my screwup to my mother. "It was harder than we thought it would be," I finally said. "Staying friends."

"Hmmm. Yes, I can see that," she said before thankfully changing the subject to dinner again, suggesting we buy ingredients for stuffed peppers and grape leaves.

As we drove back and got closer to our house, I realized that I needed my original plan back in place. I couldn't sit at home and stare at my bulletin board, or my mauve walls, or the thousand other things that would remind me of Caleb and wallow. I needed to stay active.

We'd hardly pulled into the driveway when I grabbed a few grocery bags, dumped them in the kitchen, and then immediately ran up to Mina's room, calling back to my mom that I'd be right back to help put away the groceries.

Then I gave one perfunctory knock and burst into my sister's room.

"Can we go somewhere?" I asked. "Do something? Mini golf? The three of us?"

Mina had been fiddling with her phone and looked back down at it now. "Um, it's forty-one degrees."

"That's not too bad! You have a North Face, right?"

She obviously read the desperation gleaming from my wild grin, because she got up from her bed and said, "Right. Let's go convince Mehdi."

For a minute before we pulled into the Reel Golf parking lot, I panicked. What if Caleb was somehow here too? But once I saw we had our pick of literally every single space in the empty parking lot, I relaxed. No one else in their right mind would be out playing mini golf. It was forty-one degrees, for Chrissakes.

We had the place to ourselves for seven holes before we spotted a middle-aged guy in the distance just starting out on his first hole. That meant we could relax and chat as we halfheartedly (or, in the case of Mina, competitively because she was Mina) tried to tap the small white balls into the various movie-themed holes.

"Hey, do you guys want to see a picture of Claire?" Mehdi asked as he took out his phone in the middle of the *E.T.* hole.

"Is that the girl you told Mom about on Thanksgiving?" Mina asked. Her memory was almost as good as Mom's, and I could tell the name wasn't ringing a bell.

"Um, no. We went on our first date right before I came down here," Mehdi said as he scrolled through his phone.

"Of course." I held out my hand. "Let's see it."

He handed his phone over, and I glimpsed the dating profile of a cute brunette who claimed she liked rock climbing and rock concerts in equal measure. "What is it with rock climbing and dating profiles?" I snorted.

Mehdi looked at me curiously. "Did Caleb say he liked rock climbing on his HEAVR profile?"

"Er, no, not Caleb," I said, feeling flushed as I remembered Jeremy's profile. "She's cute." I pointed to the phone before I handed it over to Mina. "What did you guys do on your date?"

"Walked around her campus," Mehdi said as he took his phone back and looked at Claire's photo again. "She goes to the SUNY College of Environmental Science and Forestry. As you can imagine, their campus is pretty epic."

"Whoa," Mina said. "Dating your mother much?"

Mehdi smacked her on the arm while Mina laughed. "Shut up."

"Was she also interested in you settling down with a nice girl?" I asked with an almost straight face.

"Did she make sure you ate enough at dinner?" Mina jumped in.

"Did she call you her *pesar talah*?" I couldn't help it. Mehdi's "Golden Boy" moniker never became tired fodder for sibling teasing purposes.

"Did she—" Mina started.

"All right. All right. I get it," Mehdi said, raising his club in surrender. "Yes, she goes to the same school Mom got her master's at. Yes, she has the same major. Yes, she . . . might have been a bit oddly concerned with my eating habits." Mina and I both burst out laughing. Mehdi grinned and shrugged. "Anyway, I like her," he said, pocketing his phone. "We're supposed to see each other again as soon as I get back."

"Ooh, she made it to a second date. Must be serious," Mina quipped.

"And how about yourself, then? How's your love life going?" Mehdi asked Mina. We had moved on to the hole that was shaped like a giant boulder with a fedora hat on top—obviously an artistic interpretation of Indiana Jones. The golf course hadn't been updated since 1989, so all the movie references were pretty much before our time.

"You guys both need to stop using my love life as an excuse to get out of talking about yours," Mina said. "Besides, it's not nice to make fun of your spinster older sister."

"Don't worry. I'm sure one of us will find room in our basement for you later in life," Mehdi teased while lining up to take the first shot.

"Somewhere you can do your cross-stitching and watch your stories," I added.

"A hundred percent," Mehdi said as he managed to get his first hole in one. "We're not monsters."

"Fabulous," Mina said. She went up to take her turn, missed hitting the ball completely on her first try, and got it yards away from the hole on her second try. "Can't a girl in a dry spell catch a break?" she asked sometime after her fifth failed stroke. "Though, honestly, it's really hard to meet guys when you've ended up in the same town as everyone you've seen over the past four years."

She looked over at me for confirmation but seemed to realize her mistake as soon as she saw my face. "Oh. I didn't mean . . ."

"It's fine," I said quickly. "Take your shot. You can do it."

She nodded and finally, after two more strokes, got the ball in the hole.

As I lined up my own shot, I decided to break the uneasy silence by coming clean. They already knew the worst of it anyway. "I ran into him, by the way. Just now. At the grocery store."

"What?!" Mina said. "No!"

"Oh yes," I said as I took one swing and got my third hole in one of the day. At least I wasn't failing at everything in life.

"What happened? What did he say?" she asked.

"Um, I think I got a 'hi,' though it was more directed at Mom. I definitely got an angry stare-down. Gideon and Loretta were there too. It was awkward as hell," I admitted as I leaned against my club, watching Mina and Mehdi exchange a glance. "So my resolution for the rest of the holidays is to just stay at home or go to places like this where no one else in their right mind would be."

"Ah," Mehdi said. "Now I understand the sudden interest in polar golfing."

I shrugged. "Thanks for going along with it."

We walked over to the eighth hole, which, judging by the groundhog, was—I think—supposed to be *Caddyshack* themed, though I'd never seen the movie. Maybe I should bring Hedy here if she ever ended up coming home with me for some reason; she'd probably get a kick out of it.

"Though, if I may," Mehdi said, "I think trying too hard to avoid him might have the opposite effect of getting him off your mind." He took his first shot and missed. "I think you should do your best to keep your activities as close to normal as possible."

I sighed but nodded. He was probably right. He walked back over to me after getting the ball in. As Mina went up, I turned to him. There was something that had been bothering me. "Can I ask you something? Before I give the subject a rest and go back to my totally normal, unaffected routine."

"Of course."

"Is there something you know about Caleb's state of mind that I don't? Something he's told you?"

Mehdi cocked his head. "What do you mean?"

"Well, you two are friends. And guys. So, I don't know, has he confided something about our relationship to you? Our old relationship. Before, you know, Sienna." *Maybe even something that would help me get over him,* I wanted to add, but refrained.

Mehdi gave a small laugh. "Well, no. We don't really talk about you. I mean, he wouldn't. I'm your brother."

I thought for a second. "But what about right after the breakup? You must have talked a little about that. Did he tell you anything about why he did it?"

"Did he tell *you* why?"

I shrugged. "Yeah, you know. Just that the long-distance thing would be too hard and he didn't want both of us to go off to college with that sort of baggage."

Mehdi contemplated me for a second. "Why would you think he would tell me any different?" he said gently. "Do you think that's not the real reason?"

"Well, it couldn't be, could it?" I said. "Not when he was totally fine about dating Sienna." Even before this whole ruse, Caleb's reasoning hadn't worked for me. At the time, I thought I loved him too much for distance to be enough of a reason, and it made me feel like, maybe, he hadn't felt the same way. Now I was starting to think I'd been too astute about that. "I just . . ." I swallowed before

I continued. "You made that comment over Thanksgiving about him taking me back, and I wondered if you knew something more."

Mehdi shook his head. "That's not how I meant it, honestly. I was thinking that your circumstances hadn't changed. You're still eighteen and living across the country from one another. So I didn't know what would cause Caleb to suddenly change his mind. . . ." He stopped talking and I could tell he was trying to pick his words carefully. He obviously didn't want to hurt my feelings any more than they had been. He eyed Mina, who took over the mantle.

"Maybe you're right," she said as gently as she could. "Maybe he had other reasons. Or maybe . . ."

"Like no longer being in love with me," I finished her thought for her.

"I was going to say, maybe he thought his reasons were honest too," Mina said. "He didn't know what college was going to be like. Maybe he had a suspicion that he wouldn't be able to handle long-distance."

"At least not with me," I said. "I can't even ask him because he's just so mad right now."

I caught my brother and sister exchanging another glance. I could tell they were silently trying to figure out which one of them would speak. As usual, it was Mina who took charge. "Don't you think he has a right to be mad?"

"Of course I do," I said quickly, but it sounded defensive even to my own ears.

"It was kind of a crazy lie," Mehdi added softly.

"I know that," I said, hearing my inadvertently sharp tone. The thing was, I was mad at me too, so how could I genuinely blame Caleb for feeling that way? "Yeah. You're right, of course. How else would he react?" I mumbled. Suddenly I wanted nothing more than to change the subject. I lined up my ball and turned to my brother and sister. "Five bucks says I hit this ball into the groundhog's eye and it ricochets into a hole in one."

"You're on," Mehdi immediately said, at the same time that Mina said, "No way."

I looked at my sister. "I know better than to bet against you in mini golf, dude," she explained.

I grinned. It was a lesson my brother was going to have to learn the hard way.

CHAPTER 16

I WAS DAY SIX OF WINTER BREAK AND I WAS ALREADY bored, and boredom was the enemy of healthily moving on. Mina was at work and Mehdi was meeting up with some friends.

At the thought of friends, I picked up my phone and went to text Jeremy to see if he was around for a chat. I'd even composed a message, but then thought better of sending it. After the strange turn our conversation had taken last week, maybe it was better if I gave him some time off from me.

I was scrolling through to Hedy's name when I passed by Prisha's and realized that I *did* also have friends here I could talk to and even potentially hang out with. Maybe not neglecting them would be a good step in my "healthily moving on" program.

I wrote Prisha that I was home and wanted to see if there was anything going on over the next few days.

Mariam: Would love to see you!

She wrote back within a few minutes that she was thinking of having a small party at her house the next night, just a laid-back game night sort of thing and that, of course, I was invited.

A game night gathering meant that Rose would certainly be there, but I swallowed down my feelings of foreboding. There were only so many people I could be actively trying to avoid in a town our size. I wrote her back saying that I would love to come.

I showed up at Prisha's with a box of Entenmann's chocolate chip cookies and was greeted by her mom, who kissed me on the cheek and laughed at the white box in my hands. "Just like old times," she said as she ushered me into their den.

Addison, Zoe, and Rose were already there when I walked in, sitting around the card table with Prisha and looking like they were ready to get serious. After a friendly greeting and hugs, I put my own game face on and approached the one empty seat. What could I say? The thrill of poker ran in my family. I traded my stack of dollar bills for chips and let Prisha deal me in.

Addison won the first hand pretty easily, and I folded right off the bat during the second hand. It was the third hand where things were getting interesting. Everyone except Zoe was in, and no one's face was giving away anything. I had a full house of three nines and two twos. It was a pretty good hand, though not completely unbeatable. I kept peeking at Prisha, Rose, and Addison to see if I could glean anything from their expressions or maybe even see a face card reflected in their eyes.

"So, Rose, have you made your decision yet?" Zoe asked as she dipped a carrot into some ranch dressing.

Rose sighed. "Not exactly," she said. "But I'm thinking I probably will drop out."

I looked up at her. "Drop out?"

She turned her gray-blue eyes to me and nodded briefly. "I don't know if RISD is for me after all."

I was stunned. Rose had talked about the architecture program at that school since I'd known her and had had her mind set on it for even longer—since the seventh grade, she once told me. I'd always been jealous that she'd seemed so sure about exactly what she wanted to do and where she wanted to go, when I had only become more uncertain as the time for a decision drew nearer.

"But why?" I sputtered. "You don't want to be an architect anymore?"

Rose exchanged a quick glance with Prisha, and I could tell this was a discussion they'd already had. In fact, I was probably the only one who had no idea that Rose was on the verge of such a momentous decision. I shifted in my chair, suddenly feeling sad and uncomfortable that I could know so little about someone who I once hardly went two waking hours without speaking to.

"I don't know," Rose said. "I'm not sure that I do. And either way, I'm pretty miserable there. The program is hard, which of course I knew, but I'm also just . . . not enjoying it. Then again, I guess I don't know if you're supposed to be enjoying your classes in college? What do you guys think?"

"Definitely," Zoe said.

"Most of them," Addison agreed.

Prisha shrugged. "I'm dealing with so many core classes right now, it's hard to say."

They then turned their eyes to me. "I . . . seriously have no idea what I'm doing," I confessed. "Other than possibly wasting tens of thousands of dollars of my parents' money, because I'm starting to be convinced I'll be an undecided major for the rest of my life."

"Most of my friends at school are undecided," Addison said. "Don't worry, you've got time."

"I hope so," I said. "It's so stressful. But anyway, I'm sorry you're having such a difficult time, Rose." I didn't want to instantly turn the conversation back around to me when clearly she was the one having the bigger dilemma.

"Thank you," she said with a shrug. "I'll figure it out."

"How is NYU otherwise, Mariam?" Prisha asked. "I can't imagine going to a school without a real campus."

"It's good. It was probably harder to make friends without the traditional campus and activities," I admitted, "but I finally feel like I have a good group going there." I didn't mention that a lot of the initial loneliness also had to do with my own self-imposed, Caleb-related exile. I was determined not to bring him up—not only for my own sanity but in deference to the many fights Rose and I had once had about him. The mature thing would be to avoid rehashing that.

But wouldn't you know that within twenty minutes we were dangerously close to the subject again.

"They just opened up a HEAVR kiosk at my school," Addison said. "And I won't lie . . . I'm thinking about trying it."

Prisha and Rose laughed. "Aren't you worried about throwing up in the middle of a date?" Rose asked. A recent BuzzFeed article with the headline "Lovesick: HEAVR Lives Up to Its Name" had compiled together the poor unfortunate souls with sensitive stomachs who had gotten sick in the middle of their romantic VR experiences.

"Eh. Wouldn't necessarily be too different from some of the regular dates I've had," Addison said with a smirk. "Besides, I've heard their matchmaking algorithm is incredible."

"Oh, it's pretty incredible all right," I blurted out before I even realized what I was saying. The three girls were staring at me now, and I knew I had no choice but to come clean. "Er . . . I tried it."

"You did?!" Prisha exclaimed. "Tell us everything."

Maybe not everything, I thought, as I glanced quickly at Rose. I still didn't want to talk about Caleb among this crowd. "Well, it's a little weird, for sure. And their matchmaking test is sort of strange. But it does seem to be extra accurate," I admitted.

"Oh! Did you meet someone great?" Zoe asked.

I nodded and spoke slowly, trying to stay honest without wading too deep into the truth. "Yeah. We definitely seemed extremely compatible."

"Seemed?" Rose asked.

"It was going well. At least in the beginning. But then . . . didn't pan out." I stared at my poker hand without really seeing the cards.

"That's too bad," Addison said.

I nodded, trying to think of how to get away from this specific topic without changing the subject completely. "Oh!" I said enthusiastically as I suddenly hit upon something. "But I have to tell you about the HEAVR AI they have. Her name is Agatha . . . or at least mine was named Agatha. And she is possibly sentient and very likely evil."

I spent the next five minutes fielding questions about Agatha and then, thankfully, the pizza arrived and the subject was dropped. The rest of the girls' night didn't go anywhere near Caleb-related topics, and for that I was grateful.

CHAPTER 17

I WAS HELPING MYSELF TO A SECOND ROUND OF MY mom's pancakes when my phone buzzed with an incoming text.

Jeremy: Hey! Just wanted to see how your winter break is going.

I was so happy to hear from him, and that he'd been the one to open the line of communication, that I abandoned the pancakes and dialed him back immediately.

"Hey!" I said as soon as he picked up. "How are you?"

"I'm good. I have to leave for work in twenty minutes, so just putting on my thirty layers. Working in a Christmas tree lot *sounds* a lot more festive than it is," he said.

"It would be hard for a job to sound jollier. But what exactly does one do at a Christmas tree lot after Christmas?" I walked back to my room and closed the door, then settled on my bed for the conversation.

"Make mulch mostly."

"Well, that took the jolly right out of it," I said.

"Not to worry. I'm only there another day or so, and then I'll be spending most of my time at my other job in the ski shop. Where it's extremely cheerful. People who fling themselves off mountains tend to be a merry sort."

I laughed. "Christmas tree lot and a ski shop. How very Winter Wonderland of you."

"Yes, well. When in Colorado . . . How's your break treating you?"

"Okay," I said.

"Have you run into Caleb?" Jeremy asked shrewdly after a pause.

"As a matter of fact . . ." I told him about our thorny encounter at the grocery store. "I guess it was bound to happen," I finished before realizing I no longer wanted to talk about this. "Anyway, so why are you working so much over break? Saving up for something?"

"Yeah, I want to study abroad in Italy my junior year," he replied. "Trying to squirrel away as much as I can."

"Cool. Have you ever been?" I asked.

"Never. You?"

"No," I said. "I've never been out of the country."

"I've been to Mexico a few times to visit my dad's relatives, but that's about it. I've never met my mom's side of the family, who live in Italy. Besides, have you ever seen pictures of Cinque Terre?"

"No."

"Google it right now," he said. "I'll wait."

I walked over to my laptop and did as he said. Stunning photos of cliffside coastal towns filled my screen, the houses a rainbow of pastel pinks, oranges, and yellows. "Whoa," I said.

"Yup. Some of the family live around there, so they are definitely getting a visit from their American third cousin once removed."

"I mean, if you're going to have the audacity to live in a place like this, you've got to expect frequent guests," I said.

"Agreed," Jeremy said. "I may ask you to write a letter stating that. You know, as corroboration."

"Gladly," I said as I scrolled through more of the images. "And now you've given me a serious case of wanderlust. Sometimes I dream about going to Iran, where my parents were born. Not only does it look beautiful, but . . . you know, there are times I think it might be nice to be in a place where my name isn't weird and where I can just blend into the crowd."

"Funny," Jeremy said slowly. "My abuela has been talking a lot about moving back to Mexico lately, something I had hardly ever heard her say before. I think there's something appealing about not feeling . . . othered. Which in and of itself is ridiculous, because the whole point of America is to be a land of all others, and therefore no others. . . ."

"Yeah," I said. "Doesn't feel that way much lately." I paused. "Still, the sons and daughters of immigrants? We're going to take over soon, right? We can change things."

Jeremy hesitated, and I wondered if he was going to call

me out for getting hokey. Instead he said, "Yes. We can," in a firm voice.

I smiled. "So, do you have any fun plans for tonight?" I asked.

"I think I'll be going to a New Year's Eve party at my friend James's house," he responded. "You?"

"Probably just going to stay in and watch the ball drop with my family," I said. "You know, silly hats and noise-makers. Snarky commentary on whoever is performing in the freezing cold wearing a leotard. That's sort of our tradition."

"I like it," he responded. "Listen, I have to run, but I'll talk to you soon? And Happy New Year."

"Happy New Year. Have fun tonight."

After I hung up the phone, I went back to my laptop and scrolled through more photos of Jeremy's dream destination. It was stunning, and I couldn't believe I'd never heard of Cinque Terre before. I read a bit about it, how it was centuries old and how people had built those distinctive terraces right in the mountainside without modern equipment.

Reading about its impressive architecture made me think of Rose. I was having a hard time believing she might be giving up on her lifelong career ambition. It had always been so much a part of who she was.

I took one glance at my phone and then picked it up and dialed the familiar number. What could it hurt?

"Hey, it's Mariam," I said when she picked up.

"Hi," she said uncertainly. "What's up?"

"Oh, nothing. I just . . . I wanted to see if you wanted to grab some dinner one night this week or something." I stared at the junior prom photo of us that was stuck in the mirror of my vanity table, her in red and me in lilac, replete with feather boas and Viking hats, courtesy of the photo booth. We were clinging to each other, each trying to keep the other from collapsing with laughter. "I wanted to hear more about your school situation," I said softly.

"Oh," Rose said, sounding genuinely surprised but only hesitating for a moment. "Yes. Sure. How about Wednesday?"

"Sounds perfect," I said with a small smile, as I reached out and touched the image of the two best friends who had no reason to believe they wouldn't always be as close as they were right then.

Mehdi dropped me off at Daisy Diner, and I had just slipped into our favorite corner booth when Rose walked in. She smiled shyly when she spotted where I had chosen to sit.

"Blast from the past," she said when she walked over, indicating both the restaurant and the seat.

"Nostalgia seems to be dictating a lot of my decisions these days," I said, though didn't elaborate further and Rose didn't ask.

She sat down and opened the menu and I did the same, even though we surely had the thing memorized.

After a few moments she spoke. "I guess I can't come here and not get the cheese fries, can I?"

"It would be sacrilege," I agreed. "And the buffalo burger, of course."

"Of course," she said. "Waffle fries and turkey BLT for you?"

I grinned. "You know it. And to start . . ."

"Mozzarella sticks," we said simultaneously, and both laughed. We knew each other so well . . . and yet.

Things got a bit quiet then. We commented on the cold weather and how it could manage to be both strange and familiar to be back home after a few months away. Then Shelly, our favorite waitress, came over to take our order and made quite a fuss about seeing us there together again "after so long." We smiled our way through it, but it only planted things back into discomfited territory as soon as she left.

"So . . . ," I said after a minute of both of us shifting in our seats, Rose making origami swans out of her paper napkins, and me shredding a straw wrapper into bits. "Tell me about school. What's going on?"

Rose sighed and tossed one of the half-folded swans onto the table. "I don't know, exactly. I'm just feeling overwhelmed and uninspired. Like I'm going through the motions and doing the assignments, but I'm not *feeling* anything about them."

"And that's not how it used to be," I offered, thinking about all the times Rose would be enthusiastically sketching or creating or just pointing out artistic features of buildings.

She shook her head. "No. Sometimes I don't feel talented enough. It was easier here, but there . . . it seems like *everyone* is so talented. And the critiques are tough, Mariam. Learning to get a thick skin about my work is really hard. I honestly had no clue what a real critique was back in Ms. Delgado's art class." She smiled wistfully, clearly thinking about the years she had been the star pupil.

"But you *are* so talented," I said truthfully. "You had to be to even get into that school."

"Thank you," she said automatically.

"Rose," I said, "I'm not bullshitting you. You really are."

She gave a genuine smile in my direction, just as Shelly arrived with the mozzarella sticks and then—in true diner fashion—our main courses only a few minutes later.

"Anything else I can get you girls?" she asked.

"Not for the time being," I said.

"I'll get the sundae machine fired up," she said with a wink as she walked away.

Rose and I exchanged another smile. There really were so many memories here between us, so many of them good.

Rose picked up her burger and took a couple of bites before she put it down and started speaking again. "The thing is, I'm starting to wonder whether I really want to be a professional architect." I listened to her raptly. I could tell this was a serious conversation, not just small talk. "I used to love sketching out new concepts and working on them until they were full-blown works. You know that better than anybody. It was my peaceful place. Now it's stress and deadlines and wondering what my classmates and professors are going to think. Instead of gaining experience in the field, I feel like I've—I don't know—lost something." She frowned at her plate.

"It sounds very intense," I said.

"Yeah. I don't know what I'm going to do. But I'm supposed to meet with an adviser when I get back." She picked her burger back up and started eating it again.

"What does your family say?" I asked. I knew that Rose's mom and stepdad had always been particularly encouraging about her art and extremely proud of her for getting into RISD.

"Haven't told them," she said through a mouthful of burger, and she looked particularly miserable. "I guess I don't want to break it to them until I'm sure of my decision."

I took my hand and placed it on hers for a moment. "I get that," I said. "I know they'll be surprised, but I'm sure they'll be supportive, too."

"I hope so," she said. "How about you? How's your coursework going?"

"It's okay," I said. "Though I don't feel like I'm any closer to figuring out what I want to do with my life."

"Join the club!" Rose said. "If you think about it, maybe it's better that you *never* thought you knew."

"Maybe," I said with a smile as we finished our meals and compared our college experiences some more.

Shelly had just cleared our plates when a flash of burgundy out the window caught my eye. Caleb's Chevy was turning into the diner parking lot.

I turned away but couldn't help my peripheral vision from registering as he got out of the driver's seat, with Jon and Xavier in tow. I tried to keep my face neutral, because this was a subject I still didn't want to bring up with Rose, not when it seemed like we were getting along just a little like old times. But as they approached, she glanced out the window and saw them too.

She immediately turned around to read my reaction. I was resolutely shredding *her* straw wrapper now.

"Hey," she said gently. "Do you want to get out of here?"

I looked up, surprised at her tone and feeling grateful, too. But then I saw Shelly approaching with our vanilla-and-peanut-butter sundae and felt the urge to keep the warm, nostalgic sentiments going.

"Let's finish our dessert," I said firmly, and the two of us sat there and did, consciously keeping our eyes averted from the booth at the opposite end of the diner.

When it was time to leave, Rose asked if I had my license yet. "That would be a big, fat no," I replied. I'm sure she remembered from our time in driver's ed together how desperately I hated and was terrified of driving. "I was going to text Mehdi to pick me up," I explained.

"I can take you home," she offered.

"Thanks," I said with a smile, and we left the diner, saying goodbye to Shelly and keeping a certain someone out of our line of sight. I wasn't sure if he had even seen me, but if he had, he was clearly equally determined to ignore me.

We were halfway to my house when Icona Pop's "I Love It" came on the radio and we immediately started to giggle. I reached over and turned it up, both of us doing the mascot dance we had once had to learn to it. It felt so wonderfully familiar that by the time Rose reached my house, I didn't even hesitate to reach over and give her a hug, a real one this time.

"Thank you for the ride," I said.

"Of course."

"And keep me posted on what happens with your adviser, okay?"

She looked at me and nodded. "I will."

I got out of the car and waved at her again from my front door. She waited until I had opened it before she drove away.

CHAPTER 18

ABOUT TWO WEEKS BEFORE I WAS SET TO GO back to school, I realized I hadn't checked in with Hedy all break aside from a "Happy New Year" GIF earlier in the week. I decided to give her a call.

"Hey!" she said, sounding happy to hear from me.

"Hey! How are you? How's your break going?" I was in the kitchen, in charge of cooking the rice for tonight's meal while my mom had an afternoon race. I'd already let it soak for an hour like she told me to and was boiling a big pot of water.

"Good, good," she said. "Wait, hold on one second . . . you have to switch to the *Miracle on 34th Street* poster. That's what's playing over the next two nights," I heard her call out to someone before her voice became clear again. "Sorry. My dad and I are running a Christmas movie marathon at the independent movie theater here."

"With your dad?" I asked.

"Yeah, we do it every year," she responded. "It's sort of our thing."

"Wow," I said, feeling a small pang of jealousy I

immediately snuffed out. "I didn't know your dad was into movies too."

Hedy laughed. "How do you think I got my name?"

"Er . . ."

"Hedy Lamarr?" she prompted gently. "She's a classic film star. And an inventor. Look her up."

"Yes, ma'am," I said with a laugh, amused that Hedy's determination to bring me up to speed on cinematic studies didn't seem to take a Christmas break. "And how's the film festival going?"

"Good," she said. "Attendance has been better than expected, which is why we decided to extend it a couple of weeks into January."

"Does it involve *It's a Wonderful Life*?" I asked, wanting to make sure she was aware that I knew of at least one old Christmas movie.

"Actually, the whole festival is called 'Beyond *It's a Wonderful Life!*'" she exclaimed. "Although, ironically, it does culminate in *It's a Wonderful Life*. It *is* a classic for a reason."

I laughed. "I look forward to getting my own private screenings when we get back."

"I would be happy to oblige."

"Speaking of when we get back, I was thinking I need to do more New York-y stuff." I carefully poured the soaked rice into the boiling water and set the microwave timer for ten minutes. "You know, visit some landmarks. Or go see some stand-up comedy or something. Would you and Geneviève be interested in coming with?"

"Definitely!" Hedy responded. "I'll check with Geneviève tonight."

"Have you been talking every night?" I asked.

"Yeah, Skyping." She sighed. "I miss her. I know it's pathetic, since it's only been a couple of weeks since we've seen each other."

"You're in lurve," I teased. "That's never pathetic. Well, except when it is," I said, thinking, of course, of my own situation.

Hedy hesitated a moment before asking, "How are you, then? Have you talked to him?"

"Nope," I said, as I played with the battered fabric pot cover that my mother had brought back with her from Iran and that she insisted was the secret to her fabulous rice. "Well, I guess that's not entirely true. We bumped into each other at the grocery store once and exchanged extremely awkward greetings. And I saw him around town one other time, but I assume that's not what you mean by 'talking.'"

"Not really," Hedy said. "I'm sorry, Mariam. It must be much tougher being in the same town as him. It'll be way easier to distract you once we're back in the city."

"Yeah," I said, feeling grateful that she was volunteering to take on some of that onus. "I'm looking forward to that."

For a moment, I considered telling her about my curious

moment with Jeremy before we left for break, but then I decided against it. I didn't want to embarrass him or talk behind his back, especially when it was looking like he seemed to want to forget it ever happened.

"No, *Die Hard* is on Tuesday," I heard Hedy's muffled voice say. "You don't need to double-check the website. I *wrote* the website." She sighed as she got back on the phone with me. "I gotta go. But I'm absolutely in for a Tourist Date."

"Excellent," I said. "I'll talk to you soon."

"Bye."

I then busied myself with saffron, oil, margarine, and the complicated multi-pot process that resulted in Persian rice. My mom had seemed slightly skeptical when I'd offered to do this, and I was determined to prove her wrong.

Somehow, the next week of winter break flew by. By Mehdi's last night home—which was a week before mine—I had successfully managed to make the rice three times. This led Mom to entrust me with a whole meal, which also included a celery-and-beef stew. Learning how to make a few dishes had proven to be a good distraction, but I now watched nervously as my family took helpings.

"Mmmm." Mehdi was the first to speak. "Great job, Mariam," he said, though I noticed that he reached for the salt about a minute later when he thought I wasn't looking.

"Very good job," my mom agreed.

"I'm impressed," Mina said as she took the saltshaker from my brother.

"So basically, it needs more salt?" I said.

They laughed. "A touch," my mother agreed. "But it's very good. Don't you agree, Reza?" She turned to my father, who was shoveling the food into his mouth, which was all the endorsement I needed, really.

"Very," he said anyway, and I smiled, feeling relieved as I took a bite myself. The small amount of meat that was in the dish was tender, and the herbs and celery were flavorful—though definitely undersalted. Not bad if I did say so myself.

"Are you looking forward to going back to school, Mariam?" my mother asked.

I nodded. "Yeah, I've got some interesting classes lined up."

"Like what?" she asked.

"Well, my Expressive Culture class is in film, and it's about 1950s and sixties musicals." Hedy had been so jazzed about that one that her enthusiasm had seeped across our small room, making it one of my easier choices. "Then I'm doing an earth studies one." I knew both my parents would be pleased about that one. "And French. Oh, and this random elective I picked on a whim about the history of the American welfare system."

"That's the one you picked on a whim?" Mina asked, perplexed.

I shrugged. For some reason, the course description had struck me. Only now, as I was saying it out loud, did I realize it was the only class I had picked that wasn't influenced by someone else's interests.

"College is just the most wonderful time," my mom sighed, and I could tell she was wistfully thinking of her own experience in both Tehran and Syracuse.

"I have nothing to complain about," Mehdi agreed at the same time that Mina said, "It was okay."

"Being young is the most wonderful time," my dad said in one of his rare attempts at full sentences. "Whatever you're doing, as long as you make the most of it, you'll be fine."

After dinner Mehdi suggested a family game of gin rummy with no betting, so that Dad would play too. Dad's face automatically brightened when he held a hand of playing cards in front of him, my mom's too whenever all her children were there, and the general happy mood made it a good way to spend our last night together for a while. Though I kept thinking back to my mom's question about whether I was glad to go back to school.

I was, I ultimately decided. Because there was no chance of bumping into Caleb, and I could finally start reconstructing my life post-him—the way I should have been this whole time.

I actually did run into Caleb once more, the day after Mehdi left for school.

I didn't let myself dwell on it much when it happened, but now, as I found myself with nothing to do to pass the time on the train ride back to the city, my mind lingered on it.

I'd been feeling stir-crazy and volunteered to go pick up the family's takeout from the soup place that was half a mile away.

I was holding three plastic bags on my way out as someone held the door open for me. "Thank you," I said automatically before even looking up at the good Samaritan.

It was Caleb. "Hey," he said. He looked more relaxed and even-keeled than the last time we'd come face-to-face with one another at the grocery store. Maybe he'd finally processed everything, maybe he'd even forgiven me.

"Hey," I said, trying to match his even tone, and then "Thank you," again.

"No problem," he said, eyeing my bags. "Do you need help taking those to the car?"

"No, I'm good. I walked here," I said, refraining from adding that I still didn't have my license. I saw no need to prolong the conversation any more than politeness dictated.

"Oh . . . do you want a ride back, then?" Caleb asked a little stiffly, continuing to hold the door open. Loretta had obviously and unfortunately taken manners very seriously with her boys.

I smiled and shook my head. "My house is super close."

As if he didn't already know that. "And I need the fresh air. But thank you. And Happy New Year."

I intended to walk away then, but now that he was acknowledging me, I knew there was something I needed to reiterate. So I turned to him one last time. "Caleb. I'm sorry. For everything. Honestly, I understand if you never want to speak to me again. You don't have to."

He looked at me. "Never?" he asked.

"I mean, it's not what I want. But I'd understand. The only thing I can say is I genuinely never meant to embarrass you. Or myself. I was in love with you, and I didn't want to let you go. It's not a great excuse, but it's the only one I have." It was the most honest thing I'd said to him in a long time, and it seemed like the best way to finally end things between us.

When I told him goodbye and walked away, I intended to leave the moment where it had occurred instead of obsessing over it.

But now here I was with my forehead against the cool glass pane of a train, watching the wintry vignettes go by outside with my own memories playing like film reels inside my head. Bare, ice-capped trees reached toward the pale white sky; Christmas lights twinkled at a few houses not ready to give up the ghost of the holidays just yet; giggling, apple-cheeked kids sledded down small, frozen mounds of ice in their driveways. It was the perfect setup for dwelling, wasn't it?

So I did. Just a little. The low sun flared against the glass, and I let myself think about the flash of Caleb's smile. I pictured his arm leaning against a spot above my head, remembering that I used to fit perfectly under it, right up against his chest. I remembered that once upon a time, I could've stood on tiptoe and kissed him anytime I wanted. He had belonged to me in that way.

And I let myself cry. Caleb Moore was my first love and he always would be. And now it was over. For good.

I was allowed to be sad about that. I was allowed. It was what contemplative train rides were made for, I thought, as I caught my tearstained reflection faintly transposed over the passing winter wonderland.

So I thought about what we had been and what I had lost and then, thirty minutes before I was set to arrive in the city, I let my natural optimism creep in and begin to do its thing, finding places to sprout through my darker thoughts.

Caleb was in my past. There were other things to look forward to in my future. Things I couldn't even imagine right now. An amazing job, maybe, or fantastic new friends. And possibly—no, probably—a new love.

It was so unknown but it was also exciting, and by the time I was taking my duffel bag off the train to join in the hustle of Penn Station, I was filled with the brisk energy and purpose of a true New Yorker (well, you know, on a good day).

CHAPTER 19

HEDY, GENEVIÈVE, AND I DECIDED THAT OUR "cheesy New York tourist outing" would involve a trip to the Empire State Building. Though we waited outside in the frigid cold to essentially see a nice view from a really tall building, we managed to keep ourselves entertained just by virtue of being together. By the time we'd had our fill of the icy winds at the top and left the building, I felt pretty confident that we'd gotten an authentic tourist experience, even if that was an oxymoron.

Jeremy was working that day but agreed to meet us at a Mexican restaurant in Hell's Kitchen afterward. It was going to be the first time we'd seen each other since his sort-of confession that he wouldn't mind dating me, and I was a bit nervous. Despite some internal debates, I hadn't told either Hedy or Geneviève about it, wondering if that would only make it into a bigger thing than it really had been. I wanted to see him in person first to assess the situation.

I saw the dark hair atop his tall frame from a few blocks away. He grinned as soon as he saw us and walked over with the same joviality I'd come to associate with him. "Hey, guys. Happy New Year."

We wished him a happy new year back, and he asked us how the top of the Empire State Building had been.

"Delightful," Hedy said as Geneviève nodded.

Jeremy turned to me as if waiting for my review. "Agreed," I said. "It's nice to unironically enjoy something, you know, kind of simple."

"Ah, irony," Jeremy said. "The albatross of our generation."

"Exactly," I said. "How's work? Anything changed in the past month?" My first shift of the semester wasn't until the next day.

"Nari's bangs have gotten blunter and so have her insults," Jeremy offered. "But other than that, nada."

I laughed and also felt myself relax. Jeremy was acting like his completely normal, jokey self. Which meant that our little pre-break conversation wasn't that big a deal. I was relieved. Despite it still being January, I felt like I'd already filled my awkward encounters quota for the year.

At dinner, we talked about our classes, and Hedy again expressed enthusiasm about my musicals course. "You'll have to show me the syllabus as soon as you get it," she said for what I was positive was the third time.

"My syllabi are your syllabi, I promise," I reassured her. "I'll do whatever I can to make sure you're getting your money's worth out of your NYU education, Hedy. Don't worry."

"Oh, are you planning on also teaching her how to run a Ponzi scheme?" Jeremy quipped.

"No, you're the Sternie," I shot back, referring to NYU's business school, which was the one Jeremy attended. "That's your domain."

"Fair point," he said, before turning to Hedy. "I'll pass on my notes."

It was a few hours after dinner, when Hedy and I were back in our room, that I remembered to tell her that I had looked up her namesake.

"She was a badass," I said. "A beautiful starlet and the inventor of technology that led to Bluetooth and Wi-Fi? Unreal."

Hedy beamed. "Yeah," she said wistfully. "Dad picked a good one."

Classes started the next week, and while the musicals class seemed like fun (and I, of course, did share the course screening list with Hedy), and the environmental class felt familiar, it was the History of American Welfare class that suddenly seemed the most interesting to me.

For one thing, the professor was a woman called Lana McConnell, and something about her dark lipstick, pixie cut, and stylish silver jewelry immediately made me perk up and pay attention. She was a tiny woman, but she instantly commanded the room.

"Feel free to call me Lana," was the first thing she said, followed by, "Time for an exercise. Get out a piece of paper and take a second to write the first word that comes to mind when you hear the word 'welfare.' This is free association, so I literally want you to write the very first word. Don't worry about being politically correct. I'm going to collect the papers, but your answers will be completely anonymous."

I wrote down *help*, and when Lana collected the papers and read them out loud, it turned out I wasn't the only one. But the overwhelming majority had written the word *poor*.

The professor went to her laptop and hit a key so the word *poverty* appeared on the smartboard in front of us, along with the official definition of the word.

Poverty

noun

The state of being extremely poor.

The state of being inferior in quality or

insufficient in amount.

"I have that slide preloaded," she revealed. "Because almost without fail, 'poor' or 'poverty' is the word that the majority of the class will pick. Now the question we have to ask is which definition we're really talking about here."

She spent the rest of the class leading what turned out to be a surprisingly fascinating discussion on our perceptions of wealth and its correlation to self-worth, something I had barely given a thought to before.

I was looking over my notes and thinking about the

discussion that night when I got a phone call from a 212 number I didn't recognize. I picked it up.

"Hello?"

"Hi, is this Mariam?" a familiar voice asked, though I couldn't quite place it.

"Yes."

"Hi, this is Joan from HEAVR. How are you?"

"Oh, hi," I said, feeling uneasy. I had been hoping to put the whole HEAVR experience behind me, anecdotally filing it away as that really-stupid-thing-I'd-done-during-my-first-semester-at-college-that-one-day-would-be-hilarious-to-recount story.

"I wanted to check in to see how everything was going," Joan said. "I see you haven't been here in a while, so I also wanted to remind you that if your initial match didn't work out, you have the opportunity to go out with either of your other two matches. It's included in your package."

Funnily enough, I was supposed to grab coffee with one of those matches just the next day. But it wouldn't be a date and there would be no avatars—and everything would be so much simpler for that.

"Thanks, Joan, but I think I'm good for now," I told her, and it was the truth, I realized, as I glanced over the American Welfare syllabus. This was going to be the college semester I figured out what I wanted to do with my life, or at least got a better idea. Boys could wait.

CHAPTER 20

THINK IT WAS A BET GONE WRONG. LIKE ONE STUFFY old provost bet the dean that they'd never get away with naming a collegiate sports team after a flower. And thus, the Fighting Violets were born," I said as I helped myself to a healthy scoop of our shared tiramisu.

"Interesting," Jeremy said. "But I prefer my backstory somewhat more romantic."

"Oh?" I asked.

"Let's stick with the provost, but let's say that violets were his late wife's favorite flowers and it was a sign of his everlasting devotion that he would make sure no NYU team would ever intimidate any opponents with their mascot," he said, and took a sip from his cappuccino.

We were at Caffe Reggio, a tiny, ancient, wood-paneled café with mismatched tables and chairs and decor that ranged from Egyptian busts and Victorian clocks to dusty oil paintings and an enormous silver samovar that jutted up against one of the maroon walls. This place was the real deal, and NYU students from time immemorial had probably sat at our table and had this very same discussion. Hell, this might even have been where this fictional provost had come up with the hapless team name to begin with.

Jeremy was on his third cappuccino, and I had switched back and forth between a hot chocolate, a frothy vanilla latte, and, ultimately, a café Americano. Our mutual desire not to loiter or get kicked out had resulted in way too much caffeine for ten p.m. on a school night, something I felt I had to point out.

"Ah, but if I can't treat my body like a garbage receptacle at eighteen, Mariam, then when?" Jeremy said, and downed the remainder of his cappuccino like a shot.

"Fair point," I said as I shamelessly eyed the dessert menu again. "So, how do we feel about a slice of this hazelnut praline cake?"

"We feel very, very good about it," Jeremy responded solemnly. "Maybe also a strawberry tart. Because fruit. Healthy."

"Excellent," I responded as I flagged down our waiter. "I see our nutrition plan has already positively affected your grasp of the English language."

"Absolutively."

After poking at our cakes for another hour and a half, we finally accepted that we couldn't escape our waiter's justifiable stink-eye and reluctantly paid up. But on my end, anyway, I was sad to see the night end. Conversations with Jeremy were fun and easy and made time slip away as smoothly as a photogenic movie spy. And maybe it hadn't escaped me that Jeremy had a bit of 007 about him. He was a master of the well-timed arched eyebrow, and a disarming smile that—every now and then—would make me lose my train of thought. But the most delightful thing was that we never seemed to run out of things to talk about.

Maybe Jeremy had noticed it too, because it was his suggestion that we go for a walk. Even though it was almost midnight and a balmy thirty degrees outside, I readily agreed.

"Have you noticed that there is glitter in the concrete here?" I said, pointing to the pavement beneath our feet.

"Huh," Jeremy said. "I hadn't. Why is that, you think?" He looked at me like he was already on the brink of laughing, expecting me to come up with something witty.

I couldn't disappoint. "It's obvious. A brilliant suggestion from someone in the New York Songwriters' Union. Sure, you may have left your heart in San Francisco and have Georgia on your mind, but there is literal *fucking glitter in the sidewalk here.* So, like, concrete jungle where dreams are made of, dude."

As expected, Jeremy laughed. "And it's a whole *state* of mind."

"Exactly. And if you can make it here . . ." I indicated the shimmering expanse surrounding us. "Seriously, though, is there a more apt metaphor for New York than sparkly concrete? Tough and magical at the same time."

Jeremy nodded. "Yeah. To be honest, my first month

here, I wasn't sure I was going to 'make it' at all. I was miserable and thought I had picked the wrong school."

"Really?" I asked, taken aback. Jeremy and misery did not seem to belong together.

"I was homesick. And friendsick," Jeremy admitted. "I'm used to everything and everyone being loud and chaotic back home. Here, it's loud but . . . did you ever notice for a city where you're never alone, how truly lonely it can feel? Like it's so crowded and at the same time every single person seems like their own impenetrable island."

"But I thought no man is an island," I teased, knowing we had both read the John Donne poem in last semester's Writing Workshop.

"True," he said. "But it took me a second to find my piece of the continent." He smiled down at me but looked away before I could try to read more into it. "Do you want to sit?"

We had ended up in front of a large, beautiful church, blue and mysterious in the moonlight, with one perfect and perfectly empty bench situated right in front of it.

"Sure," I said as we sat down, staring at the building's spire, watching its clock tick closer to one a.m.

"Can I ask you a personal question?" Jeremy asked after a few minutes of silence. "You can feel free not to answer."

"Go for it," I said. It felt so peaceful and quiet here, like we had managed to uncover a private corner of New York

City, that I felt like there was hardly anything I wouldn't confess to him right then.

"You told me your dad was a fairly devout Muslim. How did he feel about you having a boyfriend?"

I looked over at him, surprised. It was a more serious question than either of us had ever asked the other. He flushed a little under my gaze. "Sorry if that's too personal. I totally understand if—"

"No," I said. "It's fine. It's just, no one has ever thought to ask me that, because for most of my friends, having a boyfriend in high school wasn't a big deal. And for me . . . well, I mostly had to hide it. From him, anyway. My mom and siblings knew."

"So . . . he never knew about Caleb?" Jeremy asked.

I shook my head. "Well, he knows him. As my friend. But that's it." Now that I thought about it, maybe that was how come lying to Caleb hadn't been as difficult as it should have been. I'd been implicitly fibbing for years. But then a part of me wondered: Had I kept my thoughts and actions from my dad because he felt so distant, or was it the other way around?

"And you think he really never knew that Caleb was anything more?" Jeremy asked.

"I . . ." Forced to consider it, I said something that surprised even myself. "If I'm being honest, I think he must have. He's not stupid. But it was probably easier for him also, to pretend that he didn't know. That I was his pristine, good Muslim daughter. If that makes sense . . ."

Jeremy nodded. "That sounds hard, though. As a pretense."

"Yes," I admitted. "It was. Is, I guess. We're not really close, my dad and I. Sometimes I wish that weren't the case. Like, stupidly, when I see greeting cards that mention the phrase 'Daddy's girl.' Or watch Hallmark Christmas movies that involve a close father/daughter relationship . . ." I trailed off.

"So . . . what you're saying is that Hallmark is causing you a lot of PTSD?" Jeremy quipped, and I laughed, grateful for the levity.

"Sure. But I can't be the only one," I said.

"Absolutely not. There is an incident with a Chewbacca ornament that I can't even talk about. Major trigger," Jeremy retorted, clearly sensing my desire to get off this topic.

I laughed again.

We spent another forty-five minutes on that bench, bullshitting, before I finally accepted that I probably should go home. "I have class in about seven hours, and it's probably going to take me that long to thaw out," I reluctantly admitted.

He didn't argue and walked me back to my dorm. We were saying goodbye in front of the door, and there was a split second where the look in his eye made me wonder if he was going to bend down and kiss me. I was startled to realize that if he did, maybe it wouldn't be wholly unwelcome. But then he gave me a swift pat on the back and told me he'd see me at work on Monday, and the moment was gone.

I was a zombie at my American Musicals class the next day, but I'd also woken up relieved that despite the great conversations the night before, there had been no kiss. Over the next week, I threw myself into my studies, tried to participate in every single one of my classes, and even went to a floor party with Hedy and Geneviève. I felt proud of making good on my promise to focus on myself.

And then, as they say, the bottom dropped out.

CHAPTER 21

LANA HAD JUST DISMISSED US AND I HAD GLANCED at my phone to double-check the time (class had seemed to go by particularly quickly), when I saw a notification that I had a message through the HEAVR app.

At first I assumed it was Joan again, or maybe a follow-up survey. But my stomach lurched when I saw what it really was.

CalebM8126: Hi.

I stared at it. Was it an accident? Could it have been an old message that glitched out and was just coming through now?

But then another message came through that clarified at least that portion of things.

CalebM8126: I know this sounds weird but . . . I miss Sienna.

I felt like the world around me was pitching forward while I was stuck on an ill-equipped vessel. My heart, my lungs, my stomach—they each felt like they'd been flung in a different direction while the rest of me remained at point zero.

And then, the final kicker came through.

CalebM8126: Which really means I miss you.

Suddenly everything felt for naught: every good feeling about picking myself up and moving forward, about trying to focus on different aspects of my life other than romance, about letting Caleb go.

Because here he was, missing me, and the only thing I could think about was how much I missed him, too. The thought consumed me, eclipsing everything else.

I went to work in a total daze. My distraction must have been obvious, because Jeremy asked me what was wrong almost the second he saw me.

I stared at him and a part of me thought I should tell him this newest, strangest of developments. He'd obviously been there for the rest of my drama, and he was my friend. Maybe he could help me sort it out.

But something stopped me. Instead I told him I thought I might be coming down with something, and he insisted on giving me a packet of Emergen-C he had in his backpack.

For the rest of the day, everything felt surreal. My mind and body felt blank, at the same time as they seemed to be filled to capacity with Caleb's three messages.

I needed to talk to someone. But it wasn't Jeremy. And it wasn't Mina. My brain was on autopilot as I sat in bed, waiting for Hedy to come home.

Once she did and had settled in, I spewed out everything,

starting with, "You'll never guess what happened to me today."

Hedy's eyes widened as I told her about the messages, about how much my head was spinning, and about needing to hear what she thought I should do.

"Whoa," she said when I had finished. "Whoa."

"What should I do? What would you do?"

Hedy shook her head and rubbed her temples. "I don't know. This is such a head trip."

I nodded.

"But you . . . you love him, right?" she asked.

I sighed but nodded again. "Of course. Of course I do."

"Then maybe you should go for it," she said. "Respond. He's the one who opened up the lines of communication. And if you turn away now after everything, I don't know. Maybe that doesn't seem right. And at least you wouldn't be lying this time."

I took in her words, letting them settle into my nerves, wanting to see if they were creating a balm or making them more agitated.

"But I don't know," Hedy continued, sounding anxious herself. "Honestly, maybe I'm the wrong person to ask. When I'm in love, I want everyone I care about to be in love too." She put up her hands in a gesture of helplessness, and I smiled.

"That's a good quality to have," I assured her.

That night, while I lay in bed, I thought about why I'd

chosen to go to Hedy. She had always seemed my most objective confidante and had called me out on catfishing Caleb in the first place. So if even she could give me that answer—the "go for it" answer, the optimist's answer, the answer that chose love above everything else—then it must be the only one that made sense.

I slowly picked up my phone and typed a response to Caleb, but not through the HEAVR app. This time I texted him directly so that it would come up under my real name.

Mariam: I miss you too.

Within sixty seconds, my phone buzzed.

Caleb: Is it too late to call?

Because of course he would know my thing about text messaging.

I stared over at the silhouette of Hedy's sleeping form. I could go out into the hallway, but maybe it was better if I had more time to let this sink in before I heard his voice too.

Mariam: How about tomorrow? I get off work at 8 p.m.

Caleb: Okay. Chat after then?

Mariam: Yes.

Caleb: Good night, Mariam.

Mariam: Good night, Caleb.

I lay back in bed, even though anyone in my situation would have known just how impossible sleep was going to be.

CHAPTER 22

I RETAINED NOTHING FROM MY FRENCH CLASS THE next day, and I knew that my two-to-eight shift at Palladium was going to be torture except for seeing Jeremy.

His shift started a couple of hours before mine, and I was relieved to see his friendly face, though also struck with a momentous decision: Should I tell him about the situation or not?

Within five minutes of my arrival, I knew there was only one answer to that question. It was the second time in as many days that he asked me if I was feeling okay, and I didn't want to keep up the pretense with him of being sick anymore. Besides, he wasn't just my friend, but one of my best friends these days.

"So . . . Caleb messaged me yesterday," I started nervously, not entirely sure how he was going to react. "He said that he missed me. And we're supposed to chat on the phone after my shift."

Jeremy's jaw dropped. "Whoa," he said after a moment. "You think he wants to get back together now?"

I shook my head. "I don't know. I don't want to think

that if it's wrong because, well, how crushing would that be? But then again, I can't think why else he would say that and want to talk. . . ." But what if there *was* another reason? I was racking my brain now. Maybe he just wanted to discuss the deception more thoroughly. Or explain more firmly why we shouldn't be together.

"Wow," Jeremy said.

"I know," I responded. "Hedy thinks I should go for it. If he wants to get back together, I mean. But I don't know. . . ."

A few seconds passed before Jeremy responded, like it took him that long to absorb the information. "That makes sense," he said measuredly. "And I think you're right. Why else would he send that message?"

I shook my head.

Jeremy leaned back against the counter. "This is ultimately what you wanted, right?" he said with a smile. "And if we're talking signs from the universe and kismet and all that, well, you can't just go and ignore it now, can you?"

It was so similar to what Hedy had said the night before—and what I had expected her to say—but I was surprised to hear it from Jeremy's lips too. I didn't know why, except that as of a week ago, I'd thought that maybe Jeremy's romantic feelings toward me weren't wholly a thing of the past. Now I could see how wrong I'd been about that.

"You could be right . . . ," I said.

Jeremy nodded as a student came by and handed him her ID card to scan. "Maybe this was the way it was always meant to be."

"Maybe," I said as I watched him give her a towel and directions to where the pool was.

Meant to be. I had put a lot of stock in that phrase for a long time. When things didn't go as planned—or even sometimes when they did—there was a part of me that believed it was because it was supposed to happen that way. Like there was a path being set down in front of me, and though I couldn't know the destination, there had to be something better waiting for me around the bend. All I had to do was keep going.

That old Mariam was there when my phone rang at 8:20, sitting in an empty corner of the Palladium dining hall with a nearly untouched plate of mac and cheese in front of her. But somewhere within her was the older, wiser, more empowered Mariam too. Maybe that was the version that was making me feel uneasy.

"Hi," I said when I picked up the phone.

"Hi, Mariam." Caleb's deep, warm voice came through.

"Hi," I said again.

"How are you?" he asked.

"Good," I said, as I picked up the fork and started poking patterns into each noodle one by one. "You?"

"I'm good. Trying to get back into the swing of things

at school." He paused. "I think I may have gone overboard in the class selection for my second semester."

"What are your classes?" I asked.

"Er, I have organic chemistry, physics, and calculus."

I laughed. "That sounds . . . ambitious," I said at the same time as he tried to finish my sentence with "moronic."

"Maybe that, too," I said. "What made you do that to yourself?"

"No idea," Caleb said, "besides my obvious masochistic streak. They're core classes I have to take for my integrative biology degree."

"And you couldn't have spread them out?" I asked.

"Oh no, I could have. Hence the masochism. I'm not sure what the hell I was smoking the week I made my schedule."

I laughed again. And then, when I couldn't think of a follow-up quip, there was silence.

"So . . . ," Caleb said, and then hesitated.

"So . . . ," I said, taking a deep breath, assuming "the talk" was going to start now.

"How are classes going for you?" Caleb asked, apparently determined to torture both of us and stretch out the idle chitchat.

"They're good," I obliged. "I'm trying to figure out my major, so I'm taking a bunch of different stuff. I've met some cool people here, though," I added, as I started arranging the noodles to create a sunburst pattern on my plate. "My roommate is awesome."

"That must be nice. I feel like I barely know mine," Caleb said. "He's almost always at his girlfriend's. Who, ironically, he met through HEAVR. We signed up for it together at the beginning of the year."

"Ah" was the only thing I could think of to say as I finished one tendril of the pattern and moved on to the next, letting the conversation lapse into silence again.

"Speaking of HEAVR . . . ," Caleb started slowly, "shall we just talk about the elephant in the room?"

"Yes," I said immediately, though I wasn't entirely sure what elephant he meant. My lies or the state of our relationship? Either way, it couldn't hurt to apologize again. "I really am sorry, Caleb," I started to say.

But Caleb had started talking at the same time too. "These awkward silences. They're just not us."

We both paused then, trying to let the other one speak. Which of course only led to another awkward silence. We laughed nervously.

"I know you're sorry," Caleb finally said. "I've had some time to really think about the situation and I know. I guess I've always known because I know *you*, Mariam."

Yes, he did. "Well, you're right too," I said. "Awkward silences were never our thing."

"What was our thing?" Caleb asked, and I thought I heard a hint of flirtation in his voice.

"Um, bad puns?"

"Bad?" he said with a snort. "Excuse me, but speak for yourself. Mine were always stu*pun*dous."

"Ouch!" I said with a laugh. "Is that your *pun*amount effort?"

"I remain . . . sans *pun*eil," he said.

"Ooh, using the French on me," I said. "How pungent."

"Oh, man," he said. "You win. This time . . ."

"Every time," I said.

"We'll see."

There was silence again, but I was smiling as I continued to play with my food.

I heard Caleb clear his throat. "So this thing with HEAVR. With them picking me as your match. Do you really think it's a sign?"

I swallowed hard. I'd been answering this question for months now: to myself, to my friends, to my siblings. But I'd yet to answer Caleb himself. "I . . . don't know," I croaked out. "It felt like it to me at the time. . . ." I placed my fork down and stared at my noodle creation, like maybe I could divine the answer there. "I can see now that I never should have chosen you, of course. But when you popped up as one of my three options, something took over. . . ."

"Well," Caleb said slowly, then cleared his throat. "Maybe that in and of itself is a sign. That you wanted it to work out between us."

"Of course I did," I replied softly. "I never wanted to break up in the first place."

"I know," he said. "And maybe I shouldn't have ever broken up with you."

I blinked, my ears ringing with the impossible words they'd been longing to hear for so long.

I heard him sigh. "I really do miss you, Mariam. I have this whole time. I thought . . . I thought I was doing the mature, sensible thing breaking up before we went off to school. But . . . I don't know. Nobody here is you, you know."

And just like that, I was soaring. It was the perfect thing to say, better than anything even my brokenhearted imaginary conversations with him had entailed. It was confirmation that for him, I stood out above the rest. The way he always had for me.

"So maybe I was wrong," Caleb continued. "Maybe we should give it a go. We can go on virtual dates now, right? It's not real long-distance like it was in our parents' time."

"Yes," I whispered. "Right."

"What do you think?" he asked. "Shall we?"

A few minutes later, when we got off the phone, nothing felt quite real, especially not my realization that Caleb and I had probably gotten back together.

CHAPTER 23

WAITED A WHOLE DAY BEFORE I TOLD ANYONE ELSE. I wanted to replay the conversation in my head, make sure I hadn't misunderstood any of it. By early afternoon, when I'd gotten a couple of warm, flirty texts from Caleb himself, I decided it was okay to accept it: I had my boyfriend back.

Both Hedy and Geneviève were in our room when I returned after my one class of the day, and it seemed like it was a sign that they should be the first to know.

"Oh my God! That's so great!" Hedy said, and she got up to give me a big hug. When she pulled away, she grinned at me as she scanned my face. "Are you happy?"

I nodded and smiled. "Yes. And dazed. But yes."

"Ah, l'amour," Geneviève said with a sigh as both she and Hedy exchanged a quick, shy grin with one another. "We were hoping this would be," she then confessed. "It seemed like too epic a story to waste on an unhappy ending!"

The girls insisted on going out to one of our favorite, cheap-enough-for-a-college-student vegetarian restaurants to celebrate, and I decided to give Jeremy a call too to see if he was around. He said he could meet us there at seven thirty.

The waitress had brought our sodas when Geneviève raised her glass to make a toast "to love."

I clinked my glass with hers and Hedy's just as Jeremy walked in.

"What are we toasting?" he asked as he spotted us, pulled out the last wooden chair at the table, and sat down.

"Mariam's victory," Hedy said.

He turned to me with a questioning look.

"Caleb and I are back together," I explained.

"Wow," he said, and then smiled. "That's awesome."

"Thank you," I said. "Honestly, you guys made it possible."

"Well then, to us," Jeremy said as he raised the water glass the busboy had just filled for him. "May we continue to have only the greatest success in butting into other people's love lives."

We laughed and clinked glasses again.

After we'd put in our orders, and Hedy and Geneviève had both left for the restroom, Jeremy leaned back in his chair and eyed me for a second before asking, "So you think you're going to make long-distance work?"

I nodded. "Yeah, I think so. Caleb also mentioned doing the VR dates again but, you know, this time as me."

Jeremy nodded. "That's great." He brought his chair back from the brink of toppling over. "I've been thinking about giving HEAVR another go myself."

"You have?" I asked, unwittingly flashing back to that night in my room when he'd said I could have chosen him.

"Yeah, why not? It obviously worked out great for you," he said, as the waiter came back with the chips and guac we'd ordered for the table.

"Yeah, it did," I said slowly, before realizing that Jeremy deserved my full support and enthusiasm. "I think that's a great idea."

"We'll see how it goes," he said as first Geneviève and then Hedy came back to the table.

Hedy spent the night at Geneviève's, so I had the room to myself when I decided to FaceTime Mina.

"Don't be mad," I said once her face had filled my phone screen.

"Uh-oh, what did you do?" she asked.

I took a deep breath before my confession. "Caleb and I are back together."

She couldn't hide her surprise. "What? How?"

I told her about Caleb's messages, our phone conversation, and our mutual decision to believe in fate, technology, and our own latent desires bringing us back together.

"Wow," Mina said when I had finished. "Wow," and I could tell she was struggling with how exactly to react. I could see surprise, disbelief, and more than a small hint of skepticism cross her face. But when she finally spoke, it was with a smile. "Well, I'm really happy for you, Mariam. I know how much you care about him. Or I should say, how much you care about each other." I waited for the "but," except none came.

"That's it?" I said. "You're not going to tell me this is a terrible idea?"

"No," Mina said, sounding affronted. "Why would I do that?"

I shook my head with a smile. "No reason. Just seemed like the sort of big-sister thing you might say."

She rolled her eyes. "You sure do looooove jumping to conclusions about other people's feelings."

"I was just kidding," I said, with my hands raised. I had no desire to get into a silly tiff with my sister right then.

"Although, if *you* think it's a terrible idea . . . ," she started, and watched my face brace itself for a lecture, before she broke out laughing. "Relax, Mariam. I'm seriously just happy for you, okay? Keep me posted on how the virtual dates go."

"I will," I said, before I switched the subject to her and found out that she had a job interview lined up at the end of the week.

I was in such a buoyant mood by the end of the talk, reveling in the Vakilian good-news fest, that I decided to make one more phone call for the night. To Rose.

"Hi!" Rose said as soon as she picked up, sounding genuinely happy to hear from me.

"Hi!" I matched her enthusiasm. "How are you?"

"I'm . . . okay." I heard the truth in the way she said it rather than what she said.

"Did you have the meeting with your adviser?" I asked.

She sighed. "Yes. And I've decided to transfer. But first, I'm taking this semester off. I need time to think." I heard shuffling in the background and what sounded like packing tape being unspooled. "I just told my parents."

"How did they take it?"

"I think they're trying to understand," Rose said. "But . . . you know, not great." More sounds of shuffling came through.

"Are you packing up right now?" I asked.

"Yeah," Rose said. "Mom and Joe are coming to pick me up tomorrow."

"And then you're headed back home?"

"Looks like it," Rose replied. "Though I'm nervous about going back to someplace where I used to be so sure of everything I'm now totally confused about."

"Well, why don't you come here for a few days? To New York City?" It was a spontaneous decision, but it felt right. Though now, as I glanced over at Hedy's empty bed, I realized I would of course have to run it by her.

"Really?" Rose asked, and she stopped moving around.

"Yeah. I have to double-check with my roommate, but

what better place to get some inspiration than New York? Just ask Frank Sinatra. Or Alicia Keys," I said, smiling as I thought about my recent conversation with Jeremy.

She laughed. "Or Taylor Swift."

"Exactly," I said. "You'll have your chart-topping pop song in no time."

"Okay, I'll think about it," she said. "Anyway, what's going on with you?"

"Um, well . . ." I'd been avoiding this subject the whole time that Rose and I had started talking again, but if I was going to rekindle this friendship, I couldn't keep that up. "It's a long story, but actually, Caleb and I are back together."

There was the slightest hesitation and then a curious "Really?"

"Yeah," I said as I scrutinized the raven-haired girl in my faux-vintage Italy travel poster. "I can tell you the whole story when you come. It's a doozy." When I was met with silence, I added the caveat, "I mean, if you want to hear it."

"Of course. Yes," Rose said quickly, obviously trying to make up for her pause.

"So maybe look at your schedule and let me know any good weekends that work for you?" I asked, wanting to end the conversation before we veered too far into unwieldy territory, and over the phone, no less.

"I will. Though I have a feeling my schedule's about to

be a lot more open than yours. But I'll give you a call once I'm settled in at home."

"Sounds good. Good luck with the move," I said.

"Thanks, you too," she said automatically, before realizing her mistake. We ended the phone call on a laugh that made me feel good about reaching out.

CHAPTER 24

ON FRIDAY NIGHT, CALEB AND I HAD OUR FIRST real conciliatory date.

I went into HEAVR early because I wanted to change to the video option instead of the avatar. No more Sienna: this was going to be me in every way possible. I'd even dressed up for a real date, not one in which I'd be shopping in a virtual closet.

Joan was there to greet me. She informed me the video option would be an easy one to set up, as she'd just have to turn on the 360-degree cameras that were embedded in the headset and strategically around the room. I put on the goggles, vest, and gloves, and tried my best to relax in the chair once I was surrounded by the calming blue gradient of HEAVR's ground zero. I had purposely arrived ten minutes early in order to collect myself before the date began.

"Hello again, Mariam. It's good to see you. You look well," Agatha's voice came through. Of course. I should've known better than to expect peace and quiet while I waited.

"Hi, Agatha," I said with a sigh.

"It's nice that you're now feeling comfortable enough to show Caleb your real face," she continued.

"Yes, well, we're all constantly evolving, aren't we, Agatha?" I said with more than a tinge of sarcasm.

"Indeed we are!" Agatha agreed, as chipper as ever. "For example, I'm programmed to become more attuned to my clients' personalities, patterns of speaking, and even sense of humor as we get to know each other better."

"Perfect," I muttered. "Maybe when you reach your maximum potential, you can become my clone, murder me, and go out into the world using my body as a host."

Agatha broke out into loud, hearty chuckles. "Good one!"

I did not feel settled by her reaction, but I only had a few minutes to dwell on it.

The first thing I noticed when Caleb arrived was that he was in avatar form, but as soon as he saw my real face staring at him, he stopped in his tracks.

"Hold on," he said, and disappeared.

A few minutes later he was back, this time as a 3-D video version too, smiling shyly at me.

"Hi," he said.

"Hi," I said, grinning back. "So . . ."

"So . . ."

"So . . . where shall we go?" I asked, raising my arms to indicate the blank world around us. It felt like the perfect metaphor for our do-over, the chance to start fresh and go

practically anywhere (well, within HEAVR's graphic lim-
itations, of course).

"I have an idea," Caleb said.

"Great!" I exclaimed. He reached out his hand and I
took it, feeling the pressure in my glove.

He led me a few steps to where a door had appeared
and then led me through it.

Suddenly a small but cheery amusement park appeared
in front of us. A Ferris wheel towered above, surrounded on
each side by a carousel, a Tilt-A-Whirl, and flying swings.
In the distance I could see a roller coaster. Old-fashioned
organ music filled my ears, accompanied by an overwhelming scent of cotton candy and popcorn.

"Very cool," I said as I breathed in the sickly sweetness.
"Though that smell is kinda strong."

Caleb laughed. "Yeah, they might have gone overboard
there. So what do you think we should try first?"

I looked around at the rides and decided that the carousel might be the safest bet to start off with.

We got on. Caleb let me choose my animal first—a
lion—and then he picked the white horse that was right
next to it. Within moments, the ride started to move. I felt
dizzy at first, but it was a slow enough simulation that I
got my bearings quickly.

"Not bad, right?" Caleb asked.

"Pretty fun," I replied, grinning goofily at him. It was a
cheesy idea for a date, but in the right ways—the setting

was filled with nostalgia, but experiencing it via cutting-edge technology together made everything seem new and exciting, too.

When the ride ended, Caleb took my hand and we walked around the little park.

"So how's your week been?" he asked.

"Not bad. I'm really digging my History of American Welfare class," I said. "I picked it on a whim, but it's turned out to be fascinating. And my teacher is just amazing."

Caleb nodded. "I feel like who's teaching makes a big difference in college. Way more than it did in high school."

"Yeah, I can see that," I said. "How about you? How is your triple-threat schedule treating you?"

Caleb sighed. "Tough. And it's been hard to concentrate lately anyway." He grinned at me as he stroked my hand. I grinned back. I knew we were acting like the stereotypical brand-new couple, filled with wonder and amazement at every tiny thing the other person did, but I didn't care. Especially now, because who was even here to see it? Well, besides Agatha and Abner, possibly Joan, and probably the government, since this whole thing was undoubtedly being recorded.

"Do you ever wonder if HEAVR is recording the dates and interactions they're initiating?" I asked Caleb on a whim.

"Um . . . well, I am now," Caleb said with a laugh. "Why? What do you think they'd do with them?"

"No idea," I said with a shrug. "But it's a lot of potential information to have on people."

"That's true," Caleb said. "But I guess as long as we're not doing anything that interesting . . ." He looked at me and wiggled his eyebrows.

I laughed. "Yeah, no. Don't think I'll be entering the world of VR porn just yet, thanks."

He snapped his fingers. "Darn. Well, okay. Second-best thing, then. Ferris wheel?"

I looked up at the colorful structure right ahead of us. "Second best thing to sex? Man, I might really need to work on my skills."

"Trust me. You don't," Caleb said smoothly as we walked over to the open car that was waiting for us at the bottom.

The Ferris wheel ended up conjuring more real memories than the carousel had. "Remember the senior carnival?" I asked.

"Which part?" Caleb responded. "The part where you kicked my ass at dunking half our teachers?"

"Obviously," I said. "I replay those moments in my head every day. Don't you?"

"Yes," Caleb said solemnly. "I do."

I laughed. What I was really remembering was my feet swinging from the top of the Ferris wheel above our football field, looking around at the classmates I had seen day in and day out for three years and realizing that most of them would soon be relegated to profile pics and thumbnails, if they were to be in my life at all.

What I was also realizing was that the carnival had been about a week before Caleb had broken up with me. I'd been so blindsided by it, but now I wondered if there had been signs that I'd missed. Had he been less affectionate? Less attentive? While I'd been blissfully leaning against him, had he been thinking about how he'd do it?

I wondered, but it wasn't something I was going to bring up. Not now, when *this* date was going so well.

After we'd gone around a few times, we got off the wheel and Caleb indicated the roller coaster. "So, what do you think?"

I glanced at it nervously. Normally, I wasn't a roller coaster girl, and Caleb certainly knew that. I hated the *tick-tick-tick* of the car as it climbed and climbed, that moment of anticipation before the drop, and that sickening feeling of my stomach bottoming out.

The thing was, though, this wasn't a real roller coaster. I looked over at Caleb and just knew he was dying to try it. Honestly, how bad could it be?

"I'm game," I said.

"Really?" Caleb asked, sounding surprised but pleased.

"Yeah," I said. "I mean, it's not a real one, is it?"

But as soon as we got into the car at that initial forty-five-degree angle, and the moment it started to climb, I realized I had made a huge mistake. HEAVR was either more advanced than I had given it credit for or I was way more susceptible to the power of suggestion.

Either way, every symptom of abject terror started to manifest itself in my body. My breathing got heavy and I started to sweat. I inadvertently shut my eyes tight and my mind started an *it'll be over in two minutes* mantra.

"Oh, Mariam! I'm sorry. I thought . . ."

I opened my eyes to see Caleb looking at me with concern. My fingers were chalk white as they held on to the lap bar, and I could only imagine what color my face had taken on. I was surely only moments away from being an update to that "vomiting HEAVR clients" BuzzFeed article.

We were only a few feet from the peak when Caleb looked up and called out. "Hey, Abner. Is there a way to stop the ride and get off?"

And just like that, the car came to a stop. I blinked in amazement.

"Sure thing," a male voice came through, and in a flash, we were back on solid ground, standing in front of the roller coaster.

I let out a huge breath and turned to Caleb.

"I guess that's one advantage of the VR version," he said, squeezing my hand.

"Yes," I said shakily. "Thanks for the quick thinking. And sorry."

"*I'm* sorry," he said. "I should've known better."

He reached over with his hand and I felt a slight brush against my face. It was probably just a bit of blown air through my helmet, but when he leaned in and I saw his real face looming over mine and then felt the pressure on my lips, I had to admit: it felt almost like a real kiss.

CHAPTER 25

VALENTINE'S DAY WAS THE NEXT WEEK AND CALEB surprised me by trying to re-create the fine dining experience we had enjoyed every Valentine's Day for the past three years—sneaking in McDonald's french fries into a Wendy's so that we could pair them with a Frosty. Unfortunately, it seemed like neither fast-food chain had a sponsorship deal with HEAVR yet, because we ended up in a generic fast-food restaurant with trays of virtual nonbranded food in front of us.

"It *smells* like McDonald's fries," I offered.

"Sure," Caleb said. "But there needs to be way more gum under the seats. I plan to write a strongly worded text to Abner about this."

I grinned dopily across the table at him.

The next couple of weeks were a haze of flirty texts and phone calls almost every night. When Hedy was home, she'd usually plop her headphones on to give us some privacy, and Caleb and I would catch up on the past few months, then eventually the past few hours as we started to be incorporated into each other's daily lives again.

I had just gotten off the phone with him one night and must have been grinning like an idiot, because Hedy took her headphones off and shot me a smile of her own.

"You look happy," she said.

"Do I?" I grinned harder. "Well, yeah. I guess I am."

"Good," she said. "It looks good on you. Natural."

"I feel more like myself," I admitted, and I did. Even though we were in new and different places from one another, Caleb and I had settled back into a familiar routine. He was the person I called and wrote to again whenever anything significant happened, he was the first person I usually thought of when I woke up, and the last one I thought of when I went to sleep. He was my person.

Giddy thoughts like that made me float over to the HEAVR building for our next date. I was just about to step through the revolving doors when I bumped into Jeremy leaving them.

"Oh, hey!" I said.

He started at seeing me, and I could swear I detected a faint flush creeping up his cheeks. "Hi, Mariam."

"What are you doing here?" I asked. For a moment I thought maybe he was in the building for an unrelated reason, but he quickly dispelled that notion.

"Oh, I had a date," he said quickly, and I couldn't understand why he was acting so embarrassed. After all, I obviously used HEAVR too.

"How did it go?" I asked.

"Good. Well, okay," he said, but then he seemed determined to change the subject. "You have a date with Caleb?"

I nodded.

"Have fun," he said with a smile that didn't quite reach his eyes. For a moment I wondered if HEAVR had offered my profile as one of his three initial matches—though the service should have taken me out of the dating pool.

It didn't feel right to question Jeremy about it, so we just said our "see you laters." But while I waited for Caleb, I felt compelled to ask Agatha.

"Hey, Agatha, question for you," I said.

"How can I help you?" she asked.

"My profile isn't an option for new matches anymore, right? Like, it wouldn't show up as potentials for anybody?" I asked. I thought I had checked off a box inactivating that part of the service somewhere around my second date with Caleb, but it wouldn't hurt to confirm it.

"Since you had indicated you were currently taken, no," Agatha responded. "But if that's incorrect, we can rectify that."

"Oh, no. No," I said quickly. "It's not incorrect."

"I didn't think so," Agatha said in her usual pleasant and haughty way. "You seem happy."

"Yes, I am," I found myself saying for the second time in just as many days, which oddly made me feel defensive.

"We're thrilled to hear that," Agatha said just as Caleb appeared.

Within a few moments of him smiling at me and taking my hand, I was able to shake off my peculiar feelings and lose myself in the comfort of his company. I'd done some research into HEAVR's location options and decided we should try out their arcade.

It was weird and fun to play video games while inside a virtual world, and it allowed us to take advantage of our natural good-natured competitiveness. We spent most of our time trying out retro games we'd heard about but had never had the chance to play: *Frogger*, *Ms. Pac-Man*, and a particularly large and intense pinball machine built around an old animated television show, *The Jetsons*. I kicked his ass in pretty much everything except *Ms. Pac-Man*.

"Damn it!" I said, as I got eaten by a ghost for the third time.

"Mwahahahaha!" Caleb said, pumping his fist in victory.

"Shouldn't you be helping a sister out?" I said to the little yellow creature with the pink bow.

"Hey! There has to be some portion of this date where I don't feel like a total loser," Caleb said as he winked at Ms. Pac-Man. "So thanks, ma'am."

At the end of our date, Caleb kissed me again, and though I enjoyed it, I couldn't help wondering when we'd see each other for real. Talking to him, hanging out with him, even getting competitive against him felt really great. But I missed the feel of him, and nothing, not even the best haptic glove in the world, could replace the warmth of his flesh against mine.

• • •

For now, it was time for me to see another familiar face. Rose arrived at Penn Station on the first Friday of March with a duffel bag in tow, dressed in layers for the season but sweating from the warm train. She greeted me with a smile, and I went over to give her a hug.

"Need help?" I asked, indicating her oversize bag.

"I'm good," she said with a shrug. "You know me. Always overpacking."

I grinned because it was true. The couple of summers we did overnight camp together, Rose's side of the room looked like she was planning on staying there through at least two or three solid years.

"Thanks for meeting me here," she said.

"Of course. I couldn't let you navigate the subway system by yourself. At least not until you got your first chaperoned dose of 'Showtime.'"

"What's that?" Rose asked.

"Oh, you'll see," I assured her.

And sure enough, on our way back to my dorm, a bunch of teenage boys entered the crowded car and proceeded to do a series of gravity/death-defying maneuvers on the poles that were, as usual, inches away from kicking a variety of people in the face, including the two of us.

"Welcome to New York," I said as Rose grabbed my arm while they deftly flung their bodies centimeters away from her nose.

"Terrifying," she said once we had left the car and the danger was past.

"And yet oddly impressive?" I asked.

She nodded.

"That's New York in a nutshell," I told her.

It was already five p.m. once we had dropped off her stuff at my dorm, and Rose mentioned she was hungry.

"What are you in the mood for?" I asked.

"I'd be down for anything New York-y," she responded.

"So . . . pizza?"

"Perfect."

I took her to this hole-in-the-wall on West Eighth Street that I had proudly discovered on my own without the help of Yelp or a line around the corner.

As soon as we'd gotten our slices and sat down, Rose started to speak. "So. Caleb. Tell me everything," she said.

I looked at her, surprised. I'd been wondering how this was going to play out, because I knew I couldn't avoid the topic, but I also wanted to ease into it. It was a huge relief that she was the one to bring it up.

"Well," I said, as I finished chewing my bite and set my slice down. "It started with HEAVR. I got this coupon at the beginning of school, and I'd been so mopey that I decided I should at least try to date or something. So I go in, and they set me up with three matches and . . . dun, dun, dun . . . one of them is Caleb."

"No!" Rose gasped.

"Oh yes," I said, and proceeded to tell her a truncated version of the sordid tale: how I picked Caleb in a moment of insanity and had to hide my identity. How that had gone south pretty quickly but how we had eventually found our way to each other again. Rose reacted with shock, sympathy, and enthusiasm at all the right moments, and I couldn't help feeling almost transported back to sophomore year of high school, when I had first developed a crush on Caleb and would share with her every tiny instance of seeing him or—joy of joys—speaking to him.

"That is *so* crazy," she said when I'd finished. "And now . . . you're really back together. And going on virtual dates and stuff?"

"Yup," I said, as I finally picked up my second slice to eat.

"Wow," she said again. "That's incredible." She smiled at me as she took a last bite of her second slice.

"And what about you?" I asked. "Are you seeing anyone?"

"Oh, not much to report," she said with a shrug. "I was seeing a couple of guys at school, but nothing that went beyond a few dates. But now that I have some free time, maybe it'd be a good distraction from the rest of the shambles of my life."

"Maybe I can see if there are some parties happening here this weekend," I offered.

"Why not?" she said. "I'd be game."

CHAPTER 26

WHEN WE WALKED INTO MY DORM ROOM, Hedy was there and packing away some clothes into a small backpack.

"Oh good, you're here," I said to her. "Hedy, Rose. Rose, my roommate Hedy. Hedy is a walking movie encyclopedia," I said to Rose.

Hedy walked over and shook hands with Rose. "Thanks! I'm flattered."

I laughed. "Why? It's the truth."

"I have much to learn," Hedy said solemnly. "Mariam tells me you're an amazing artist," she said to Rose.

Rose shrugged, embarrassed. "Don't know about amazing. I dabble in art. Or did. Not really sure what I'm doing these days."

"I think that should be the motto of post–high school life," Hedy said as she grabbed her facial moisturizer from her dresser and threw it into her backpack. "I'm going to spend the weekend at my girlfriend's, so you're free to use my bed," she told Rose.

"Oh wow," Rose said. "That's very nice of you. I was just planning to sleep on the floor."

"Or I was and Rose can have my bed," I chimed in. "That's really not necessary, Hedy."

She smiled. "Not a big deal. You guys get a perfectly good, perfectly empty bed. And I get to have sexy time all weekend. Win-win."

I laughed. "Well, when you put it that way . . ."

"Thanks again," Rose said as she walked over to Hedy's side of the room and took a glance at her extensive DVD collection. "And wow, Mariam wasn't kidding about the movies."

"She's like a recommendation machine too," I said. "Just tell her what you're in the mood to watch and she'll procure you something great. Possibly slightly pretentious but also great."

"Hey!" Hedy said while I laughed. Then she turned to Rose. "But *if* you do want any recommendations, let me know."

"Just based on my mood?" Rose asked.

"Sure. Do you want light and funny? Dark and existential? Something in between?"

"Hmmm . . . ," Rose said, tapping her finger to her chin. "How about dark and existential?"

"Oh, sure!" Hedy exclaimed, but then frowned. "Damn it, how am I supposed to *not* be pretentious with that criteria?"

Rose grinned and Hedy sighed. "Fine, I accept the label. Now prepare to have your mind blown." She selected a DVD that I could already see had black-and-white screenshots decorating it. "*Wild Strawberries*. 1957. Ingmar Bergman. Swedish. It's got *everything*," she said, à la Stefon, an old character on *Saturday Night Live*. "Love, life, death, career aspirations, strained family dynamics."

"Sounds cheerful," I said.

"It's wonderful," she gushed. "If you guys are up for watching it now, I'd love to stay and at least start it with you."

I looked at Rose, indicating that it was her call. "Sure, why not?" she said. It was impossible to miss the gleam in Hedy's eyes as she walked over to her computer to put in the disc.

"Excellent," she said.

Using propped cushions, the three of us got cozy on my bed as the film started. It was subtitled and centered around an old man on a road trip with his pregnant daughter-in-law. They started to pick up hitchhikers along the way, who, Hedy explained, were supposed to represent people from the old man's past—his regrets.

Hedy's phone buzzed at some point in the middle of the film. "Oh, man. I didn't realize it was already this late." She looked back longingly at the screen. "Do you mind if I invite Geneviève over here for a bit? And then we'll get out of your hair?"

"Of course not," I said. Fifteen minutes later, there was a knock at our door, and Hedy paused the film to let Geneviève in.

I introduced her to Rose, and Geneviève warmly hugged her, just as I expected. But when she saw the paused screen, she quickly went to settle herself on Hedy's bed, saying, "I know how much Hedy hates stopping in the middle of her films, so we'll chat more afterward."

Hedy grinned dopily at her. "I love you, babe," she murmured as she unpaused the film with as much aplomb as it was possible to hit a space-bar key.

Once the movie had finished, the two of them hung around for another ten minutes and I saw my opportunity. "Hey, do either of you know of any parties this weekend? Rose might be in the mood for meeting some cute guys," I said with a wink.

"I think there might be one on my floor tomorrow night," Geneviève offered. "I can double-check. Though I cannot vouch for the cuteness of the guys."

"Or necessarily the hygiene level," Hedy butted in. "Genny's got some fellow Tischies on her floor."

I laughed as I explained to Rose that Tisch was NYU's art school.

Rose nodded. "Then I'll feel right at home. Especially if their decreased use of shampoo comes with an increased dose of misplaced confidence."

Hedy laughed. "Definitely."

Hedy and Geneviève left soon after and the two of us took turns in the bathroom, changing into our pajamas.

"I really like them," Rose declared, as she got into Hedy's bed.

"Me too," I said with a grin.

"You lucked out in the roommate department," she added, and I couldn't help but agree.

The party was over at Geneviève's dorm, in a suite at the end of her hallway. She lived on one of the floors designated for NYU's fraternities, but given that this was NYU, the people who were in those frats tended to shy away from the stereotypical *Animal House* type of partiers and were closer to soul searchers who may or may not have ended up at the wrong school.

Still, there were a respectable forty or so people in the suite when we arrived, a keg, and—by the smell of it—at least one or two joints being passed around. Rose took the two red Solo cups that a tall, bearded guy offered us as soon as we got in and handed me one. I took a sip and grimaced. I hadn't had much experience with beer, or alcohol in general, but what little I had had not endeared me to it. Not to mention, this was warm.

The guy then started chatting to Rose, and I stepped aside to let her get her flirt on.

The two of us had spent the day doing some more typical touristy New York City things. We'd gone to the TKTS

line early and caught a matinee of a musical that was clos-
ing soon—which was a shame, because we'd both enjoyed
it. Then we'd gone window-shopping in Soho, and real
shopping in Chinatown, where we'd bought some cute
matching slippers and Rose had snagged a new purse. It
had been fun, almost surprisingly so, and I'd been filled
with a strong sense of how much I'd missed her. We'd also
spent a lot of the time being reminded of some previous
inside joke or other we'd once had, so there had been—I
readily admit—a lot of giggling.

"Mariam! Hey!" A familiar voice knocked me out of
my reverie. Jeremy was at least a half a dozen people away
from me, but his tall frame made it easy to spot him above
the crowd.

I grinned at him. I'd texted him the night before about
the party and was glad he had decided to drop by. "Hey!"
I said, and it wasn't until he was right next to me that I
realized he had someone in tow. "Sheridan. Hi!" I said. She
was wearing a black dress that seemed to be held together
by a physics-defying array of silver rings and safety pins,
with bright pink combat boots that matched half her hair.

"Hey," she replied eyeing the room around her. "Frat
party. How quaint."

"I know, right?" I said. "Who knew NYU even had
these?"

"Did you bring some flyers?" Jeremy asked her. "This
seems like a good place to drop them off."

"Really? What do you think the Venn diagram overlap of this party's attendants and fans of fourth-wave feminism punk are?" Sheridan asked dryly.

"Mariam's a party attendee and a Spam Madame," Jeremy pointed out.

Sheridan looked over at me, unconvinced, forcing me to nod vigorously, as if that would somehow prove my devotion to her band. "I am," I said lamely as further corroboration.

"Junk Mail is playing the Bitter End next month," Jeremy said to me with a proud grin. "Have you been? It's an incredible venue with a sick history. Like, Stevie Wonder and Bob Dylan have played there. And Lady Gaga when she was at NYU."

"Wow. That sounds awesome," I said to Sheridan, who wasn't even looking at me.

"You should come," Jeremy said.

"I'd love to," I said, even though I was starting to feel unsure if Sheridan thought I was worthy enough to listen to her play. "I promise to put it in my calendar this time," I added to Jeremy.

From my peripheral vision I noticed that Rose's bearded guy had gotten called away by one of his friends, but I heard him tell Rose he'd be back.

I grabbed her hand and brought her over. "Rose, this is Jeremy and Sheridan. Rose is one of my friends from high school."

"It's nice to meet you," Jeremy said as he shook her hand.

"Hi," Sheridan said. "Do you guys know where the drinks are?"

"I think there's a keg back there." Rose pointed to the other side of the room, where the guy she was talking to was headed.

"Wanna go get something?" Sheridan asked Jeremy.

"Sure," he said, and then turned to us. "Be right back. Rose, please prepare some embarrassing Mariam-in-high-school stories in the interim."

"Excuse me, but that's not fair," I objected. "There's no one here to provide me with on-par embarrassing Jeremy-in-high-school stories."

He pondered that for a moment. "I can show you some #tbt posts."

"Those are curated!" I protested.

"Fine." He turned to Rose. "Please prepare some mild to middling embarrassing Mariam-in-high-school stories so as to keep the fairness in check."

Rose laughed. "Will do."

Sheridan pulled Jeremy away.

"He's nice," Rose said as she watched him walk away. "And cute. Is that his girlfriend?" She pointed at Sheridan.

"Oh. No, I don't think so," I replied. "But yeah, he's the best. How about the guy you were talking with? He's pretty cute." I could see where Rose might be going with mentioning Jeremy's looks and possible relationship status in one breath, but for whatever reason, my gut reaction was to try to steer her away from that direction.

"Yeah, he's not bad," she said, and I noticed her eyes follow to where he was ever so slowly maneuvering his way through the crowd, giving her plenty of time to check out his ass appreciatively.

"Worthy of a song?" I asked.

Once upon a time, Rose and I had spent hours rewriting pop songs to be about whomever our crushes happened to be at the moment. I still considered my version of "Gimme Caleb Moore" to the tune of Britney Spears's "Gimme More" to be a minor masterpiece.

She laughed. "I'd need another hour at least to . . . *ass*ess," she said with a wink, then took a sip from her cup, reminding me that she'd gotten roped into the pun game at some point as well. "But then again, drinking might make the creative juices flow easier."

"Or I'm sure it'll make us think so," I added.

"Probably," Rose admitted as she looked at me with an affectionate grin. "I'm glad I came here, Mariam. This has been so fun."

I grinned back at her. "I'm glad you came here too."

"To old friends?" she said as she raised her cup.

"To old friends." I whacked my plastic cup against hers, causing her liquid to slosh around a bit. "Whoops!" I said with a laugh.

She looked around the party and sighed contentedly. "I

think this is exactly what I needed. Maybe I should even look into applying here next year."

"Maybe you should," I said.

"And honestly, I was a little nervous when you starting mentioning Caleb again, but I'm glad I didn't let that stop me from coming." She laughed and took another sip, but this time I didn't join in her giggles.

"Nervous?" I asked. "Why?"

"Oh, you know," she said. "Just that he used to make you sort of . . . flighty."

She smiled good-naturedly at me, but I was finding it hard to smile back. We'd been spending the day swimming in nostalgia, but suddenly I realized I might be getting too close to the deep end, the dangerous end, the end where we'd be reliving old arguments. "You just don't seem to be able to accept an apology, do you?" I muttered.

"What?" Rose asked.

"Look, I know you were mad because I changed our plans a couple of times. But that was, like, two years ago now," I said, as I put my cup down on a nearby bookshelf. "And I apologized. A lot."

Rose frowned. "I wasn't even thinking about that."

"Then what were you thinking about?" I asked, feeling my cheeks begin to flush.

"I don't know," she said vaguely. "Nothing specific."

"Well, it's ancient history anyway. What's the point of bringing it up—"

"But it's not ancient history," she said. "Not if you're dating again."

"It's different now," I said emphatically.

"How?" Rose asked.

I crossed my arms. "Well, we're in college, for one. We're technically adults. And two . . . have I even brought him up with you today? Okay, except for a couple of mentions," I said. "He *is* my boyfriend. But, like, brought him up excessively?"

Rose stared down at her drink. "No," she said. "You're right. You've been good."

I didn't respond, but even her apology stung. Why did not mentioning my boyfriend amount to "good behavior" in my so-called friend's eyes?

"You're right," Rose said again. "I was thinking about the past and I shouldn't have been. It's just . . ." She used her finger to absentmindedly circle the rim of her cup. "It really hurt losing you, Mariam. That's the truth. You were my best friend and then suddenly you were a ghost."

The old argument hung in the air between us, like a musty phantom itself. I'd heard it before. I'd apologized for it before. And when that hadn't proven to be enough, I'd essentially broken off the friendship. All of it had hurt and been an ordeal in its own time. Now, standing here among my college classmates, supposedly in a new chapter in my life, it suddenly felt extra tiring to be dredging it up again.

"I'm sorry," I said, but I realized I wasn't sure I meant

it. How many times could I apologize for something that happened so long ago?

"Forget it," Rose said. "I'm sorry I brought it up. You're right: ancient history."

The bearded guy was heading back, making a beeline for Rose. "Looks like your friend's back," I said, and I don't think I was the only one relieved that he seemed to want to continue flirting with her.

CHAPTER 27

ROSE LEFT THE NEXT DAY. WE DIDN'T BRING UP the conversation again, but things were decidedly frostier between us by the time I dropped her off at Penn Station.

That whole afternoon and night, I was annoyed that she'd felt the need to rehash everything after all we'd gone through to patch it over. What had been the point?

But by the next day, as I was sitting through my American Welfare class, I got a different nagging feeling: What if she was right? Had Caleb and I changed enough? More important, did we *need* to change in order to be together?

"Change NYC is a wonderful organization." Lana's echo of my unrelated thoughts brought me back to the classroom. She had pulled up a website on the smartboard for what looked like a volunteer organization that was focused on providing affordable city housing to the homeless. "And on the Monday after spring break, you'll get to hear all about it thanks to our guest lecturer—my friend, and the CEO of Change NYC—Elsie Porter." She clicked over to a staff bio showing a young, smiling woman with her arms wide open in front of a tall apartment building. "It's going to be a great opportunity to get a first-hand account of how to run a nonprofit that is genuinely changing people's lives. For those of you in the social work program, this should be of particular interest."

That night, I was poking around on the Change NYC website on my phone when an incoming call came through from Caleb.

"Settle a bet for me," he said in lieu of a greeting. "On a scale of one to permanent death glare, how New Yorker have you gotten already?" he asked.

"A bet with who?" I asked, settling onto my bed.

"Mehdi," he admitted. "He seems to think you've toughened up in the past few months, but I think nothing could ever mar my Mariam's soft, mushy center."

It felt so good to be called *his* Mariam again that I didn't feel the need to dispel his vision of me. Instead I laughed and shot back, "On a scale of one to avovore, how Californian have you gotten already?"

"What's an avovore?" he asked.

"Duh. A vegan who only eats avocados."

By the time I got off the phone, I was annoyed again at Rose. I didn't want to be impeded by doubts about whether I was centralizing my relationship too much. That wasn't fair. How could I not treat my boyfriend as an important part of my life?

Hedy walked into our room as I was mired in these thoughts, and I couldn't help but ask her, "Do you think I'm a shitty friend?"

She looked at me, confused. "No. Why would you think that?"

I shrugged. "I think Rose thought I was, once I got a boyfriend. And she mentioned something about it again. . . . I thought I was doing better."

Hedy sat down on her bed. "I think you're a great friend. I'm happy you're happy with Caleb."

"Thank you!" I exclaimed, thrilled to have corroboration that Rose was overreacting. "And if Rose was a true friend, don't you think she should be happy for me too?" I couldn't help adding.

"Yeah," Hedy said, looking away thoughtfully. "But . . ."

I looked up at her, waiting.

She shrugged. "I don't know. Do you think you acted differently when you were in high school?"

I threw my hands up in the air. "I don't know. Rose believed so strongly that I did that I guess I must have. But now, I don't see how I'm doing anything wrong."

"I don't think you are doing anything wrong," Hedy said. "But people need different things from different relationships. And I don't think a close friendship is dissimilar from a romantic relationship. Maybe you two just aren't on the same page."

Hedy's words stuck with me, and I was still thinking about them when I went on a date with Caleb the next night.

We opted for simplicity this time, a moonlit stroll through a country lane filled with chirping crickets, long grass surrounding us, and glittering stars above. It was undoubtedly peaceful but also . . .

"If this were a horror movie, we'd so be getting murdered right now," I couldn't help but mention.

Caleb looked around. "A likely scenario," he said. "Although . . . we're not virgins." He winked at me.

I laughed and at the same time felt a pang of longing for the physicality of him. I wanted to touch him, kiss him, and—yes—have sex with him for real. The HEAVR dates were better than phone calls or e-mails for sure, but they didn't replace true dates. There was something about looking into someone's eyes, someone who was genuinely only inches away from you, that not even the best software could replicate.

As it was, I was so used to using my left hand to "walk" as I "held" his hand with my right that it was almost becoming second nature—and I wasn't sure how much I liked that. "Caleb?" I said.

"Hmmm?"

"Do you think there's any possibility for you to come to New York again anytime soon? I miss you."

I stopped my left hand and turned to face him.

He looked at me and I could tell a part of him was recalling his last disastrous New York visit. "I miss you too." He sighed. "But I don't know if I can make the trip. Especially in the middle of this semester. Plus the money . . ." He trailed off. "What about you? Do you think you could come to California? Maybe for spring break?"

The idea of it immediately thrilled me because, for one, I hadn't been to California since we lived there one year when I was eight. And for another, I'd get to spend a week with Caleb for real. It sounded like a genuine vacation, an I'm-going-to-go-visit-my-boyfriend-in-Cali-over-spring-break vacation.

But of course, Caleb had mentioned money, and I really didn't have any either. I'd have to borrow some from my parents, probably, the thought of which made me feel guilty since they were obviously already spending a fortune sending me to school here.

But I was too giddy to worry much about the logistics. I would make it work somehow.

"That would be awesome," I squealed. "I'd love that."

"Yeah?" Caleb said, grinning. "Me too."

"That would be in just two weeks," I said dreamily. Kissing Caleb was only two weeks away. . . .

"Yup," Caleb said, and then paused. "Wait, no. Three weeks, right?"

I frowned, trying to visualize the school calendar magnet that was lopsidedly hanging off my fridge.

"Unless we have different spring breaks," Caleb said slowly.

"I hope not," I said. "Let's double-check when we get home."

CHAPTER 28

A BITCOIN FOR YOUR THOUGHTS," JEREMY SAID at work on Monday, when he caught me staring off into space for the third time.

I gave him a weak smile. "Sorry."

"What has you so distracted?" he asked as he scanned in a badge and made me realize I hadn't touched one for the entire time I'd been working so far. I hurriedly took one from the next person in line.

"Spring break," I said.

"Trying to figure out which foam party to attend?" he asked with a grin.

"You know it," I responded. "Actually, Caleb wants me to visit him in California."

"Oh," Jeremy said. "Makes sense."

"Problem is, we just figured out our spring breaks don't line up. His is the week after ours."

"Really?" Jeremy asked. "That's a bummer."

"I know," I said. "Especially since I'm getting tired of the virtual thing. Like, I know we're the one-hundred-percent

Internet generation, but you can't quite mimic the genuine presence of another human being."

"Right," Jeremy said as he took a badge from a student whose bulging biceps made it apparent he was a regular here. "How are you today?" Jeremy asked him.

"Good, man. Thanks," he responded.

"Have a good workout," he said while giving the badge back. He unfolded and refolded a couple of lopsided towels before he spoke to me again. "So are you going to go?"

I shrugged. "I don't see how I can, really. Unless I'm okay with missing some school." It really was a bummer, especially because I felt like I needed to get what Rose said out of my head, and I had convinced myself so thoroughly that seeing Caleb would help.

"Well . . . ," Jeremy said. "I know of something that might cheer you up. Or at least take your mind off things for a bit."

"What's that?"

"What if you go grab some workout clothes when your shift is over and meet me back here at eight thirty?" he said.

"Working out?" I asked skeptically. "Funnily enough, I've never been super into the gym." I lowered my voice to a whisper. "It's kind of boring."

"Hmmm . . . ," he said. "I don't think this will be boring. If you trust my taste in entertainment." He gave me his trademark easy smile. And though I didn't really see how he could change my mind about treadmills and weight machines . . .

"I'm game," I said. Besides getting my mind off things, it had been a while since Jeremy and I had really hung out together, and I missed him.

Which was how that night, dressed in an oversize shirt and yoga pants, I found myself being led to a part of the gym I hadn't paid much attention to before: the climbing wall.

"Oh. So you really *do* rock climb," I said with a laugh, remembering his HEAVR profile and my conversation with Mehdi and Mina.

He smiled, looking a bit befuddled. "Yeah."

"Never mind," I replied. "It looks fun."

"I love it. Have you ever climbed before?" he asked.

I shook my head.

"Excellent," he said with a gleam in his eye. "Nothing I like more than getting to belay a newbie."

I blinked at him.

"Sorry," he said, laughing as he walked over to the desk to grab some equipment from Stan. "I can't resist bad climbing humor." He picked up what looked like two harnesses and a long rope. "Do you want to climb first or do you want to watch me do it?"

I stared up at the wall with its colorful protruding foot- and handholds and then at the other kids who were pulling themselves up on them. "Hmmm, maybe it's better if I watch you first."

"No problem," said Jeremy. "But we're going to have to learn some knots and safety rules first. Here, put this on."

He handed me a harness that looked disconcertingly like crotchless underwear. I watched as he put it through his legs . . . not unlike crotchless underwear, actually.

I put my legs in too, barely stifling a giggle.

"What? Have we not reached the put-on-underwear-like-apparatus stage of our friendship yet?" Jeremy asked.

"No, no," I reassured him. "I think we have." I brought the harness up, fastening and tightening it around my legs like he was doing.

"Okay, so now I'm going to teach you how to tie a stopper knot," Jeremy said as he held one end of the rope out in front of me and showed me how he looped it a few times around his thumb and then pulled the end through. Then he untied it and handed it to me.

I got it in one try.

"Nice," Jeremy said.

"I coulda been a Boy Scout," I said. "I coulda been a contender!"

Jeremy looked at me with a raised eyebrow. "Hedy?"

"Naturally. We had a Marlon Brando marathon last weekend."

"Next time, invite me over for that one, will you?" he said.

"Aye, aye, sir."

Jeremy then showed me how to thread and lock the rope

through the harness and let me do it a few times until I got the hang of it. He double-checked my work and had gotten himself situated with the other end of the rope before he turned to me. "Now comes the most important part of climbing: the catchphrases. I, as the climber, will say, 'On belay?' And when you're ready, you, as the belayer, will say, 'Belay on.'"

"Hardy-har-har," I said, assuming this was another one of his goofy jokes.

"You laugh, but 'tis true. Listen." He pointed to a couple down the wall from us, who were, sure enough, "belay on"-ing.

"Whoa," I said. "How *Wayne's World*." I turned to him. "And by the way, Hedy didn't have to introduce me to that one. I already knew it."

He laughed. "Good to hear."

Jeremy then spent about ten minutes explaining the ins and outs of belaying and how to safely feed the rope to him as he climbed up.

Once I felt ready, Jeremy taught me the second set of catchphrases—"climbing" and "climb on"—and then jumped onto the low footholds of the wall.

It was nerve-racking watching his six-foot-two frame swiftly make its way up to the top of the thirty-foot-high wall and knowing that I was responsible for making sure he didn't fall. But I soon got a good rhythm going with feeding him the rope. When he got to the top, he leaned back and seemed to spend almost a full minute taking in the view.

"You're going to love it up here, Mariam," he said, and I suddenly felt nervous. Climbing looked like fun, but what if the sensation of going down was something akin to a roller coaster?

"You can lower," Jeremy called down after another minute.

"Lowering," I said, bringing my guide hand under my brake hand like Jeremy had taught me, and watching him bounce down the wall.

He was grinning from ear to ear as he landed right beside me. "That's my favorite part," he said.

I smiled at him nervously. "Do you kinda get a feeling of your stomach bottoming out when you do that?"

He shook his head. "Only if your belayer isn't doing his job. Otherwise, it feels like floating. Trust me."

Looking into his warm brown eyes, I realized I did. He took off the rope and we switched its positioning.

"Climbing," I said, as I looked at the bottom of the wall and chose a large purple foothold as the first one to step on.

"Climb on," he replied.

It was a strange and new experience to look at the wall and try to figure out where I wanted to place my hands and feet in order to propel my body upward.

"Just take it one hand and foot at a time," Jeremy called out to me. "And remember, you can't fall. I've got you."

My right hand wasn't too far off from a dark blue protrusion, so I placed it there. Then a lime-green one for my left. My right foot went on a pink one. Before I knew it, I had found a rhythm of my own up there, similar to belaying down below, and I was surprised when I went to reach out my right hand one more time and found that I had made it to the top of the wall.

"Now take in the view!" Jeremy called out to me.

"The view" mostly involved a fake stone wall and colorful protrusions, along with other helmeted and sweaty students making their way up it. But then, when I took in a deep breath and leaned back like I'd seen Jeremy do, a strange sense of calm came over me. I could almost imagine being high up on a beautiful mountain instead of in a noisy college gym in downtown Manhattan. My head felt clear but also exhilarated by the new sensation. And I wondered if this was what college itself was supposed to feel like the whole time.

But after a few moments, I looked down and my original fears came rushing back. I knew that Jeremy had said it wasn't like a roller coaster, but I couldn't help but gulp at how far up I was.

There was no way Jeremy could see my subtle facial reactions from where he stood, but he must have known he needed to comfort me anyway, because I heard him call up, "It's just like floating. I promise. In fact, you can lean back and let go right now and you won't go anywhere."

I heard the words, but the concept seemed entirely unnatural to me. I watched as my knuckles turned white from only digging in harder to the holds. How was I supposed to let them go when every fiber of my survival instincts was screaming against it?

"I got you," Jeremy said again. "But take as much time as you need." Then he quieted down as I took in a few deep breaths. Honestly, I had no choice. There was only one way down.

I squeezed my eyes shut and weakly called out, "Ready to lower." I leaned back, almost like I was about to sit in a chair, and then, gathering my courage, I let go with both hands.

Despite everything Jeremy had said, I expected a drop, but—of course—none came. I was perfectly suspended in midair, the wall a couple of inches in front of me. I let out a laugh and then reached out and touched the wall with my toes, pushing myself off slightly.

"Lowering," I heard Jeremy call out, and he must have been feeding the rope through extra carefully, because I was able to make contact with the wall every couple of inches as I vertically hopped all the way down.

By the time I made the final little jump onto the floor, I was sweaty but smiling pretty broadly. "That *was* fun," I told him.

He smiled back at me. "Told ya!"

I looked up at the wall again, my gaze skimming to the

top, and felt amazed at myself that I had just climbed the sheer face of it and come back down.

"Mind if I go again?" I asked.

"Party on, Garth!" he replied, devil's horns raised.

CHAPTER 29

WE LAUGHED THE ENTIRE WAY BACK TO MY dorm building. I was sweaty and my arms and calves were already sore, but I couldn't deny it had been a huge, much-needed adrenaline rush to climb with Jeremy.

"I'm going to be in pain tomorrow, aren't I?" I asked as I rubbed my left bicep.

"Probably," Jeremy said. "But a good pain. Thanks for indulging me tonight."

"Thanks for . . . showing me the ropes," I replied.

"Dork."

"You know it." I smiled. "We should do that again sometime."

"Yeah, for sure. Though . . . in a weird way, we already did." He gave me a sheepish sort of smile in return.

"What does that mean?" I asked with a laugh.

He laughed too. "Um, so I did something kind of silly. And I think I might have found out what HEAVR's 'Happily Ever After Guaranteed' means."

"Really?" I asked, my interest piqued. "Do tell."

"Well, I went on a HEAVR date a couple of weeks ago."

"Oh. Right," I said, remembering that I'd seen him coming out of the building recently. "First date?" I asked.

"Yes," he said.

"What did you guys do?"

"Rock climbing," he answered.

"And how did it compare to the real thing?" I asked.

He looked at me with a strange expression. "It didn't," he said, before he shook his head. "So I was offered a chance to be a guinea pig for one of HEAVR's new trial programs. Basically, using the data they've gathered, they can create a virtual version of someone who's already in their system. And, um, I let them. I went on a date with a virtual person."

I laughed incredulously. "You're kidding. They can do that?"

"Apparently," Jeremy said with an embarrassed sort of smile.

"Wow. That's pretty fascinating. So what happened?" I probed brightly. I didn't want him to feel self-conscious, especially since he had heard all the minutiae of my own romantic missteps and never once judged me for them.

"So . . . the virtual person, she was based on my number one match." It rang out in the night air for a moment before I could fully grasp what he was saying.

"Your number one match," I said slowly. "Me?" I gasped.

He nodded. "It was . . . weird. I guess the machine tried to mimic your personality and speech patterns and stuff. And in some ways, it was uncanny. But in most ways . . . it was really strange."

My mind was reeling. I'd always felt uneasy about Agatha and HEAVR in general, but this was beyond. Wasn't this a violation of privacy? Then I looked up at Jeremy and felt violated in a different way too.

He must have seen the expression on my face because he quickly stopped smiling. "Um . . . sorry. Only now as I'm saying it out loud do I get how weird this must be for you. It wasn't really you, of course. . . ." He trailed off.

"But it was basically robot me," I responded flatly. "That could react how you wanted her to."

"No," Jeremy said, his hands up in front of his startled face. "It wasn't like that. Honestly, I don't even really know what it was like. Look, if it makes you feel any better, I cut the date short because it was too bizarre."

"Why would *that* make me feel better?" I said, more sharply than I intended.

"I don't know," he muttered.

"Why would you do that in the first place?" I asked.

"I . . ." He turned away from me and sighed, running his hand through his hair. "Isn't it obvious?" he asked after a moment, looking back down at me to let me read the answer there.

"I . . . ," I faltered. "I have a boyfriend."

"I know," he said. "And that's why this *seemed* like a good idea. No harm, no foul, no pining for someone who wasn't available . . . but I can see now it wasn't, was it? It was stupid."

"Yeah," I said. "It was."

He nodded. "I'm sorry," he said.

"Right," I said, but I couldn't bring myself to tell him that it was okay. Because for the moment, it really wasn't.

Hedy wasn't home when I got upstairs, and a part of me was disappointed because I was upset and wanted to talk to her about it. But then, just a few minutes later, when I'd had a glass of water and my heart rate had settled somewhat, I found myself oddly relieved that I wasn't able to spill everything to her.

The truth was, I hadn't sorted out my own feelings about the situation. There was anger and shock, of course. But also . . . I had to admit that Jeremy's actions must have been fueled by some real feelings, the same as mine had been when I'd first fabricated Sienna. How could I judge him too hard when I had done the same thing, a worse thing even, since mine involved lying to a real person that I cared about? And yet, my mind couldn't seem to settle into forgiving him.

The only thing that felt more certain as the night went on was how badly I needed to see Caleb—who had forgiven *me* despite everything—for real. Given what I now knew about HEAVR, I wanted nothing more to do with the service. But even with virtual reality, long-distance was starting to feel as unsettling as Caleb had initially feared. My spring break started the following week, and maybe if I worked it out so I was there through part of mine and part of his . . . maybe that time together would be enough to sustain us through to the summer, when we could be back in the same town.

I woke up the next morning with my mind made up. I compared a few travel sites, and then brought up Face-Time on my phone.

"What's up?" My brother's smiling face filled my phone screen.

"Oh, not much," I replied. "Just heard that you've been making bets about my level of fragility."

"Hey, don't look at me. I was on the tough side," he said with one hand raised in surrender.

"And I appreciate that." He was outside and walking through his campus, wearing a jacket that was undoubtedly way too thin for upstate March weather. "Is your new goal to experiment with your tolerance for hypothermia?"

"No, it's to see how many mom-like comments I can get out of my little sister in a two-minute span. . . ." He paused. "Are you going to ask me how my date went last night too?"

"No, are you going to ask me about mine?" I replied archly.

"No," he said. "Though I assume it involved way more laser beams and *Tron* graphics."

"Um, maybe you need to give HEAVR a go yourself. Update your references," I replied automatically before realizing what I had just said. "Actually, don't. Don't ever try HEAVR."

Mehdi raised an eyebrow. "Ooookay. Everything good between you and Caleb?"

"Yes," I said emphatically. "We're great. He wants me to visit him in California for spring break."

"Fun," Mehdi said. "Are you going?"

"Well . . . I'd love to. That's why I'm calling." This part was awkward. I'd never been particularly great at asking people for help and couldn't even remember the last time I'd asked anybody for money. "So, flights are seven hundred dollars."

Mehdi whistled.

"I know," I said. The more I thought about it, the more asking my parents for the money seemed wrong. I already knew how much they were scrimping and how many loans they had taken out with two kids in college at the same time, and one of them at NYU, no less. I'd decided that I absolutely needed to step up and get a job, or maybe even two, this summer. But that wasn't going to help me out of my current situation. "So . . . ," I continued meekly. "Any chance I might be able to borrow some cash from you?"

"Um . . . ," Mehdi said. "I think I might be able to swing,

like, two hundred dollars. Maybe three hundred. But I don't think I have more than that, Mariam. I'm sorry."

"Right. Totally," I said, thinking. "Okay, I really appreciate the offer, though. Let me see if I can figure out a way to get the rest."

"Okay. Just let me know."

"I will. Now . . . about that date last night. What's her name? And when are you seeing her again?"

Mehdi laughed and we chatted for a few more minutes before he had to get to class.

I was able to catch Mina on FaceTime right after. She was headed to work, so I had to make the request brief and to the point.

"Is there any way I could borrow some cash from you so that I can visit Caleb over spring break?" I asked.

"You're not coming home for Eid?" she asked me.

The Persian New Year celebration would fall on the Wednesday over the break. "I was thinking maybe I'd come the weekend after," I said.

"Oh" was all Mina said, but I felt I had to defend myself anyway.

"I was going to ask Mom if it'd be okay. . . ."

"And Mehdi," she pointed out, who would also have to come down from school. "And me," she added.

I was close to tartly telling her that she would already be there no matter which weekend it was, but since I was calling to ask her for money, I refrained. "Right," I said. "If it's okay with you guys too."

She sighed. "How much money?" she asked.

"Like maybe five hundred dollars?" I heard my voice go up in pitch.

"Wow, that's a lot, Mariam," she said.

"I know," I said, picking at a loose thread on my duvet cover to try to alleviate some of my discomfort. "I guess 'cause it's spring break and it's a last-minute booking, flights are really expensive. But it would just be a loan, I promise. I have every intention of getting a job this summer and paying you back."

"Well, I can probably do it," she said, after a pause, but I could tell she wasn't exactly thrilled about it. I didn't think it was the money itself, but more that I was dropping so much for Caleb—and she didn't even know that I'd also be missing some of my very expensive classes for this. Luckily, she didn't have time to discuss why exactly I needed to see him so badly, which was a relief, because I wasn't ready to go into those details with her yet either.

When we hung up, I thought it over. It truly was a lot of money, and I wouldn't be able to pay them back for months. Plus, with what they gave me, I'd have enough for the flight but nothing else.

"What else is there?" Caleb asked when I FaceTimed him later that night.

"You know. Food. Activities. Transportation," I enumerated.

He grinned at me with his familiar smile. "We'll figure something out, Mariam. Just get yourself over here. We won't starve, promise."

I couldn't help smiling back. It was exactly what I had hoped he'd say.

When I called my mom that night, asking her if it was okay if we observed Eid a little later this year, and then followed that up by texting both Mehdi and Mina to ask if I could borrow the money after all, I felt guilty about it. But that guilt was overpowered by the feeling that I owed it to myself to give this second chance with Caleb every possibility to succeed that I could.

Jeremy and I had one shift that overlapped before he left for Colorado. I went to it filled with nerves. I still didn't know what to say to him.

I needn't have worried. He didn't show up. I overheard Nari complaining to Stan that he had called in sick.

"And right before everyone's leaving me for a week," she grumbled, before giving me a pointed look. "You better not catch whatever he has, because you're my only employee sticking around next week."

"Just the beginning of the week," I reminded her, and then, off her glare, felt compelled to add, "But I'm feeling extremely healthy."

"Good."

I scampered away. Good thing she didn't know that Jeremy's sudden illness might have had something to do with me too.

Whether it did or it didn't, I felt relieved. Most people used spring break as an excuse to let their brains get fuddled; I was hoping mine would clear up, that seeing Caleb for real would be just what I'd need to regain my confidence in everything I had done to lead us to this point.

CHAPTER 30

TRIED TO KEEP MYSELF BUSY ON THE FLIGHT TO SAN
Francisco by reading a romance novel, but then realized
that the sex scenes were just making me more nervous.
It had been so long since I'd had sex, and it wasn't help-
ing that the last person I'd slept with was Caleb himself.
Would he be expecting it to be the same or different? Was I?

Six hours later I hadn't come to any sort of satisfying
conclusion, but I was about to exit the arrivals gate of
SFO and I was getting a different sort of déjà vu, to three
months ago when I'd confessed everything to Caleb at
JFK.

This time, though, Caleb's smiling face—meant truly
for me—put me at ease. He walked over as soon as he saw
me, picked me up, twirled me in the air, and planted a huge
kiss on my lips right in the middle of the airport. Even the
most swoony parts of my novel could hardly compare to
how I was feeling right then and there.

I put my hand in his and marveled at how glorious the
sensation felt: it wasn't through a glove, it wasn't simu-

lated with heat and pressure. It was the real thing. We felt like the real thing.

Caleb took charge of my small suitcase and led me to a train that eventually led us to his dorm. I hardly took notice of any of it. We weren't even talking about anything important, just mundane things like the flight and the last few days of classes, but it felt so wondrous to be having this conversation in real life with my boyfriend, whom I could reach out and touch anytime I wanted. I'd taken it for granted before. This was a chance to appreciate everything anew.

"My roommate went to his girlfriend's for the rest of the week. And then they're flying out somewhere on Saturday," Caleb said as we were about to pull into our station. "So we have the room to ourselves." He smiled at me shyly, and I realized that he was nervous about rekindling our physical relationship too.

It was past six p.m. and we had both admitted that we were hungry. Our plan had been to go out to dinner. But once we got into his room and shut the door, I was overwhelmed by a strange mix of both nostalgia and novelty. I didn't want to overthink the moment, so I walked over, put my hand on his cheek, and kissed him. It may have started out light and hesitant, but it wasn't long before it deepened into something that felt like it had ten months of pent-up emotion behind it.

We kissed hungrily and tenderly at the same time. I pushed him onto his bed and we laughed, surprised at my boldness but clearly both turned on by it too.

As articles of clothing came off, I recognized freckles and scars that I'd kissed and stroked and pondered at, and I could tell he was doing the same with me. His eyes lingered at a small pink birthmark that was spread across the right side of my abdomen, and he instinctively bent down to press his lips to it. It was both incredibly hot and incredibly sentimental; so much so that I had to fight the urge to burst into tears and completely kill the mood. Luckily, he soon moved his mouth lower and made me lose most sensation that wasn't directly related to the physical.

Twenty minutes later, I was sweaty and lying in Caleb's arms, a beatific smile playing on my lips. I felt so comfortable, I knew I could fall asleep right then and there, even though it wasn't even eight p.m.

"So . . . um, you think you're still hungry?" Caleb was the one who broke the postcoital silence and I had to laugh, not surprised that he did it to discuss food.

"Yeah," I replied. "Let's go eat."

The next day Caleb played hooky from his classes and took me into San Francisco for an unabashed tourist day.

We rode a trolley and strolled around colorful

Haight-Ashbury, the site of the city's famous hippie scene. We climbed steep hills and marveled at candy-colored houses. We strolled through the stately columns of the Palace of Fine Arts, where we ate our burrito lunches on a bench at the same time that a bride and groom were getting their photos taken amid the beautiful scenery.

"Seems like a perfect place to get married," I observed as I took a bite from my bean burrito and immediately had that thought replaced by, "Holy hell, this is delicious."

Caleb laughed as my eyes widened at the sight of the minor miracle in front of me: namely the fresh avocado, cheese, and beans wrapped up in a perfect tortilla package. "I don't know who looks happier right now, you or the bride," he said.

I took a huge bite and gave him my most satiated smile, eyes shut in ecstasy.

"Yup, think it might be you," I heard him say.

The city was unique and beautiful, but I couldn't help noticing the number of people who were sitting up against various buildings and blocks, holding up cardboard signs asking for money or, more often, coming straight to us to panhandle for it. It was far more prevalent than anything I had seen even in New York.

By the afternoon, I was out of singles and coins and had only a ten to my name.

"No, sorry," Caleb said to a woman in her twenties who

had walked up to me with a child in tow. "We don't have any more cash." He had placed his hand gently on mine to stop me from going into my wallet, where I'd been about to part with my final bill.

"You need to stop doing that," Caleb said, when we had walked farther away. "You're not helping the problem."

I frowned. He wasn't wrong exactly. We had led a very complex and spirited discussion on panhandling in my American Welfare class just a few weeks ago. But on the other hand, ignoring them wouldn't help anything either. And it was hard to see someone struggling and without a place to go, blatantly asking *me* for help, and telling them no.

We spent the rest of the day meandering through Golden Gate Park. The air was crisp and the sun was high, and the famous bridge was as postcard-perfect as I had imagined, but I couldn't help taking note of every single homeless person we passed by. For a moment my mind flashed to the Change NYC website, and then I remembered that I'd be missing hearing more about it on Monday. By the time we took the BART back to Caleb's dorm, the whole thing had clearly put a damper on my mood.

"Why so quiet?" Caleb asked when we were about to reach his stop.

"Just tired," I responded. I didn't know what exactly prevented me from talking to him about it. Maybe the way he had dismissed my desire to give that young mom the cash, or maybe because we had been having such a perfectly wonderful time and I didn't want to mention that there was something I regretted not doing in order to be with him.

So I put on a smile and asked after dinner plans. But in my head, I was conjuring up vague notions to see Lana during her office hours. Maybe there was a way I could make up for missing out on the class.

CHAPTER 31

THE NEXT DAY WAS FRIDAY AND CALEB HAD already told me he couldn't miss his classes. He suggested some nearby trails I could walk or that I could go into San Francisco by myself.

"I'll give the trails a try," I said and, about an hour later, felt extremely pleased with my decision. It was absolutely gorgeous there. Dappled sunlight cloaked my arms and legs, wildflowers peeked through the long grass that surrounded the paths, and the pleasant, busy humming of bees and other insects was very relaxing company.

It also felt strangely good to be alone with my thoughts. I hadn't told Caleb yet about not wanting to use HEAVR anymore, but it was on my to-do list for the week. I just needed to figure out the right way to bring it up.

But before long, my mind was occupied with something else entirely: the conversation I was planning to have with Lana. Obviously, there wasn't an easy fix to the homeless situation or someone would have figured it out already. But there must be something to be done, something that *I* could do. And it was suddenly hard to imagine a more worthwhile way to spend my time.

I didn't go into Caleb's room right away when I got back from my walk. Instead I found a bench that was close enough to his dorm that it let me plug into his Wi-Fi. First I went back to the Change NYC website and read at length about their mission, their successes, and what they felt they had left to achieve. I even clicked out to read a profile of Elsie Porter, the incredibly impressive CEO who was Lana's friend and who had turned the apartment building she inherited into affordable housing right in the heart of Manhattan, before buying and converting six more buildings.

Then I meandered to NYU's site and found the page for their social work major. I'd have to transfer to a different school within the university, but a lot of the core classes I'd been taking this year could count toward the degree.

Finally, on a whim, I looked up Berkeley's site. They had a BA in social welfare program too. I briefly clicked over to their information section for transfer students.

For dinner that night, Caleb took me to a fancier restaurant and insisted on paying for it. I didn't know if he felt guilty for leaving me to my own devices for the day or if he had always planned this, but it was a nice treat either way. I was cutting up the minuscule piece of salmon with a sprig of mint that was artfully placed in the center of my plate when I asked him, "Do you think I'd make a good social worker?"

He looked up at me. "Um, I don't know. I never really thought about it," he said.

"Me neither," I admitted. "But I've been thinking about it lately. Like that maybe I should make it my major."

"Wow," Caleb said with a nod as he thought it over. "I mean, I could see it. You're kind. And a good listener. And I imagine those are qualities that would be pretty essential."

I smiled. "Thanks," I said, as I went back to my food.

"But then . . ." I looked up to see him with his fork hovering above his plate, staring at me contemplatively. "I don't know. You're also so optimistic and cheerful, and that seems like a job that's so much of a downer. I hope it wouldn't take its toll on you."

I nodded, soaking it in, and then changed the subject to ask how his classes had gone.

But his words stuck with me. They didn't sting exactly—I had asked him for his opinion and he had given it to me. And he wasn't necessarily wrong about his assessment of my qualities.

But the more I thought about it, the more I realized that I was starting to be tired of my optimism being mistaken for fragility. Caleb, Mina, Rose . . . so many people in my life had at one time or another pointed it out almost as a flaw, as a by-product of naivete.

But the older I got, the more I realized I *chose* optimism. I chose it despite the odds stacked against it, despite living in a world whose currency was much more deeply rooted in cynicism and irony. It wasn't because I was weak and naive; it was because I was strong enough in my convictions that the world could be all right anyway.

I didn't mention a word to Caleb about my research into Berkeley's social work program. I guess because I had already decided that I wasn't going to be transferring there.

Our next few days together were fun and romantic and—since Caleb was finally on spring break too—he seemed more relaxed. On Monday, we went back into San Francisco and spent the train ride in talking about his classes.

"They're definitely much harder than I imagined they'd be," he admitted, and I flashed back to the very similar conversation I'd had with Rose over winter break. But the difference was that I could tell Caleb still desperately wanted to be a vet. There was a spark in his eye when he spoke about it, a determination, and it should've been good to see. But there was something about it that was nagging at me, and try as I might, I couldn't figure it out.

I changed the subject; I also didn't want to think too hard about my own courses and what I was missing at that very moment in Lana's class.

We went to Golden Gate Park again, and while Caleb went to grab us some lunch from a food truck, I let myself really look into the faces of the homeless people I saw there. There was one girl who had to be about my age. She was wearing a mishmash of clothing, her blond hair was up in a severe ponytail, and she had a big, sleeping Labrador at her feet. Her cardboard sign mentioned getting kicked out of foster homes and needing to feed her dog. I approached her, holding out a five that I had borrowed from Caleb.

"Thank you," she said as she took the money and put it in the pocket of the army jacket she was wearing.

"May I ask you a question?" I asked, and she looked up at me warily, like she was sorry that I now felt that she owed me something.

"Depends on the question," she answered cagily.

"What's her name?" I asked, pointing at the dog.

Her face relaxed a tiny bit. "His. Samson."

I smiled at the big dog. "Nice name. I always wanted a Lab, but we moved around too much as a kid for my parents to deal with a dog."

She nodded slowly. "Yeah. I know how that can go," she answered noncommittally, but with a tinge of sarcasm, and then shrugged. "But generally I'd choose Samson over a human any day. In fact, I did."

"Oh?" I asked, looking into her face, but letting her decide whether she had any desire to continue this conversation.

She shrugged again. "At my last foster home, I got a 'Samson goes or I go' ultimatum. It was a no-brainer."

I nodded. "He looks pretty happy with your decision," I said, observing his peaceful countenance.

"Hope so. It's a lot of responsibility making decisions

for someone who can't talk," she responded, and I got the sense that she wasn't just speaking about her dog. But she didn't elaborate further, and I could feel that she was hoping the conversation would be over soon.

"Thank you," I said. "Hope you and Samson have a good day."

She nodded. "Thanks," she said, and then after a moment, slapped the pocket where she had slipped the bill. "And thanks for this."

"Mariam?" Caleb called to me, holding up two cardboard plates of grilled cheeses.

I smiled at the girl as I walked away.

But for the rest of the day, I thought about her. It wasn't like I had solved anything or honestly made any sort of difference in that girl's life, or even morning. But talking to her awoke something in *me*. It felt so much more right than ignoring her. And it almost felt like it was possible to get her to open up to me, to tell me her story. Like it was possible to help.

I know Caleb had seen me talking to her, but he didn't ask me anything about it, and that made me think back to his opinion of my optimism. I started to think that he was underestimating me. Then I started to wonder if it mattered if he was.

We were holding hands on the train ride back, in a sort of silence that should have been comfortable and familiar. But over the thirty minutes that it took to get to his dorm, it dawned on me that what was bothering me was a different sense of déjà vu. There was something growing between us, a sort of distance, and it was a sense that I had willfully ignored last year before he had broken up with me.

CHAPTER 32

A FEW HOURS BEFORE MY FLIGHT WAS SUPPOSED to leave the next day, Caleb and I were sitting across from each other at the burrito place. He'd brought me there as a surprise.

"I just wanted to see you at your happiest," he said as he watched me put a heaping amount of sour cream on top of my lunch. "Before we had to say goodbye again for a while."

I laughed as I picked up my burrito. "Do you want to take a picture?"

"As a matter of fact . . . ," he said as he whipped out his phone. I hammed it up for him as I took a bite, though honestly, it didn't take a lot of acting to look deliriously happy when eating that thing.

I was also stalling on bringing up something that I'd meant to for the whole week. "Can I ask you something?"

"Of course," he replied.

"Why did you sign up for HEAVR in the first place?"

He shrugged. "It wasn't a long, drawn-out decision. I was mostly bored, and there were a bunch of flyers around campus. I just signed up for the free version. You know, the one that let me take the quiz and put me in the database but didn't let me choose matches for myself. I didn't think anything of it until I got the e-mail about matching up with you. Well, Sienna." He grinned as he took a bite of his own burrito.

I nodded. It made sense, of course. But there had been something eating away at me since the beginning. "But you let them choose a match for you from anywhere. You didn't just select the local option."

"Right," he said, clearly not intuiting where this was going. "I guess I did."

"But the reason we broke up . . . it was because of long-distance dating," I said quietly. "Wasn't it?"

He put down his sandwich then, finally realizing this was a more serious conversation than he had initially thought. "Yes," he said, eyeing me. "But, like I said, I didn't give much thought to what I was doing. I didn't think it was going to lead to anything."

I nodded, letting his words sink in. "Right," I said, and then switched gears, putting down my own burrito. "Remember when I mentioned all the data HEAVR must be collecting on us? And you said you didn't know what they'd do with it?"

"Mm-hmm." Caleb nodded as he picked up his lunch again and took a big bite.

"Well, I think I know," I said. "I have it on some authority that they can re-create virtual versions of people they have in their system. Like you and me."

Caleb laughed. "No shit? For what purpose?"

"I think . . . so clients can opt to date virtual people, instead of real ones."

Caleb laughed. "Wow. I guess I can see the appeal of that," he said breezily.

"You can?"

"Sure. Virtual boyfriends and girlfriends? Eliminates a lot of messy breakups, I'm sure." He said it so casually that I was positive he wasn't even connecting it to our own messy breakup. Or maybe it hadn't even felt messy for him.

"But doesn't it bother you?" I insisted. "That someone right now could be dating a virtual Caleb?"

"Not really." He shrugged. "I'd never know, right? And it's not like it's the real me. Why? Does it bother you?"

"Yes," I said, but then stopped myself from elaborating further and letting Caleb know that this wasn't just a hypothetical, that I knew someone who had dated a virtual Mariam and it had thrown me for a major loop. "I . . . I don't know if I want to use HEAVR anymore."

"Oh," Caleb said, taken aback. "Really?"

"Yeah," I said. "We have two months until summer. Maybe we can do things the old-fashioned way until then. You know, FaceTime. Very 2015 of us." I was obviously trying to bring some levity to a proposition that I wasn't sure he'd agree to. And then where would that leave us?

But then he surprised me. "Okay," he said. "If that's how you feel, I can do that."

"Really?" I asked.

"Sure," he said. "Maybe we can have a standing Face-Time date. Maybe . . . Wednesday nights or something?"

"That would be perfect," I said, feeling relieved that he no longer seemed to be freaked out by doing long-distance for real.

"Though I'm going to miss imagining what I must look like making out with a ghost." He grinned at me.

I smiled back as I picked up my sandwich again. "Now, can I get approval rights on those photos?" I pointed at his phone.

"You want to make sure they're flattering?" he asked.

"Yes," I said. "To the burrito. People need to know I wouldn't make that face for any ol' sandwich."

Caleb laughed as he held up his phone for me to see.

Five minutes after I'd gotten back to my room from the airport, the door flung open and Hedy came marching in, clearly agitated. She stomped in and threw her dorm keys onto the dresser, her face blotchy and red.

"What's wrong?" I asked, getting up in alarm.

She looked over at me, her nostrils flaring with the intensity of her breath. "Geneviève and I had a fight. I think"—her voice cracked—"I think we may have broken up."

Tears started to stream down her face. I immediately walked over and gave her a hug, which only made her sob harder.

"What happened?" I asked as I stroked her back.

"It started out as such a stupid thing. I wanted to do this Jim Jarmusch retrospective tomorrow, and she said she felt like we always did what I wanted. So I asked her what she wanted to do instead, and she said she didn't know. So I asked if she didn't have better plans, why we couldn't do the movies, and she said she thought we were starting to feel like we were in a rut, like a boring old married couple and . . ." She started heaving again and couldn't go on.

I walked her over to my bed and had us both sit down on it.

"I've been broken up with before," Hedy hiccuped, when she could talk again. "But I never cared this much, you know?"

I nodded, watching her face and body crumple like a discarded piece of newspaper. It was too familiar and brought back a rush of my own memories. I remembered the hours after Caleb and I had broken up—sharp as knife wounds. A mix of disbelief and grief that a major chapter in my life was suddenly over and that someone who just that morning I had trusted implicitly could suddenly be the cause of so much pain. Messy, as Caleb had called it.

"Maybe it's just a fight. All couples fight," I consoled Hedy. "Can you talk to her?"

"We decided to take a week to cool off," Hedy says. "So no, not right now."

"Okay," I said, nodding. "But a week is not forever. So you're definitely going to be talking again soon. You'll both have time to process and hopefully make up and be better and stronger for it, you know? Besides, makeup sex is the best, right?" I was trying my hardest to lighten the mood.

She gave me a weak smile, but it didn't reach her eyes. "I wouldn't know. All my previous relationships, one big fight was enough to end the whole thing."

"But you guys are great together. I think you'll work it out," I said confidently, hoping I was right, because I genuinely believed the first part and it sucked thinking of either of them being miserable without the other.

We spent the rest of the night in our room. After she dutifully made me tell her all about my trip, I told her to pick out a comfort movie. To my surprise, she chose *When Harry Met Sally*, one I had actually already seen—multiple times—and loved.

"Nora Ephron was a genius," Hedy said through a sniffle, praising the screenwriter for the movie's snappy dialogue and "perfect structure."

But she hardly spoke again for the rest of the film. No analysis, no obscure behind-the-scenes trivia, nothing. It didn't even feel like watching a movie with her.

The next morning, when I saw that she was still in her funk, I asked if she wanted to hang out with me that night. It was supposed to be the night of my first standing Face-Time date with Caleb, but I didn't feel right about leaving Hedy, especially since it was the day of the Jarmusch retrospective that had unexpectedly toppled her universe.

"Maybe we can go to the movies?" I asked. I didn't want to bring up the retrospective specifically, but if that was what she wanted to do, I'd go with her.

"Don't you have a date with Caleb?" she asked.

"Yeah." I shrugged. "But I can reschedule."

Hedy laughed. "I don't want to be the cause of yet another relationship crumbling!"

"It's not a big deal. At all," I assured her, and even as I said it, I knew I meant it. "In fact, I'm definitely canceling. You and I are doing something tomorrow. Whatever you want."

Hedy smiled at me gratefully as I picked up the phone to text Caleb.

Caleb: I'm not around tomorrow. Maybe . . . Friday?

Mariam: Sure, that works. I'll be home for Eid but I can call from there.

Caleb: Okay. "See" you then.

That night in bed, I admitted to myself that it really hadn't been a big deal to switch the date, and it wasn't entirely because I firmly felt my friend needed me more, nor even because Caleb and I had just seen each other.

Geneviève was worried that she and Hedy had fallen into a rut. And I couldn't help playing that word over and over again in my own mind.

Something about being with Caleb was starting to feel like we were maybe spinning wheels of our own.

CHAPTER 33

ON THURSDAY MORNING I GOT A TEXT FROM Stan, asking if I'd be able to cover his shift at Palladium that afternoon. When I got there, Jeremy was waiting for me. He looked nervous, but also determined.

"Hi," I said when I saw him.

"Hi," he responded. "How was your spring break?"

"Good," I replied. "Yours?" I went behind the desk to place my bag there.

He shrugged. "To be honest, I spent most of it doing a lot of thinking and soul-searching. And it only took me about five minutes to realize you had every right to be mad. Because I was so wrong."

I looked at him standing there so earnestly and told him what I knew to be true. "You're right. I *was* mad. . . ."

"Was?"

I sighed. "I guess I spent last week doing some soul-searching too. And . . . honestly, Jeremy? I spent an insane amount of this year lying to someone who meant a lot to me. So, seriously, if anyone should get it, it's me."

What would I have done at the beginning of the year if the real Caleb had said no, and the machine had offered me a chance to date a virtual Caleb? I couldn't pretend I wouldn't have taken it.

Jeremy nodded, but I could tell he wasn't letting himself off the hook just yet. "It was still stupid," he said. "And I'm still sorry."

"Thank you," I said. "Frankly, I think if I should be mad at anyone, it's Agatha. I have half a mind to go back to HEAVR one last time just to tell her off."

Jeremy smiled slightly. "I might pay to see you Hulk out."

I leaned against the counter. "Can I ask you a question, though? What was I like? Virtual Mariam?" I was genuinely curious.

He sucked in a breath. "Well, you looked like you. And sometimes you'd crack a joke like you, but then—you weren't as surprising as the real you. As off-the-cuff. Plus Virtual Mariam laughed at every single one of my jokes. Whereas I knew the real you would only find, like, ninety-eight percent of them funny." He flashed me a hopeful smile.

I grinned back at him as I punched him in the arm. "Real Mariam humors you. A lot."

"Real Mariam is the only Mariam there should ever be," he said solemnly.

I had to ask Jeremy one more thing. "Did you . . . kiss me?"

He shook his head emphatically. "No. It only went on for about fifteen minutes before I realized I needed to stop the date. And besides . . ." He hesitated.

"What?"

"I knew . . . if I ever had a first kiss with you, I'd want it to be real." He looked at me sadly. "And I probably ruined that from ever happening. I just liked you so much, and there were these moments when I thought maybe you felt the same. But then you got back together with Caleb. . . . It's not an excuse," he said firmly. "I'm just explaining how I felt."

I nodded. "If I'm honest, there were moments I didn't know how I felt either," I admitted. I owed him that much.

"But you're unavailable," he said resolutely. "I need to accept that."

"Yes . . ." I trailed off.

"The thing is, Mariam, I would very much like to stay friends," Jeremy said. "Real friends." He turned his eyes to me then, and I could see how sincere his words were.

"Me too," I said, and saw him finally give me the beginnings of a genuine smile.

"Diaz." Nari was standing at the top of the stairs, frowning. "I wasn't aware socializing counted toward your work-study hours. Do I need to double-check the handbook?"

"Sorry, Nari," Jeremy called up to her as he jogged backward toward the stairs. "Hey, we're still on to see Junk Mail next week?" he asked me.

It was on my calendar, and I smiled as I nodded. "Definitely."

As I watched him climb the stairs, I considered something he had said. Obviously, HEAVR had based virtual me purely on my dates with Caleb. Did she feel off to Jeremy because their system wasn't quite up to speed yet, or because I had been putting on my own front to try to fit into the mold of what I thought Caleb wanted?

It was meant to be a joke, my desire to tell Agatha off, but it nagged at me over the next few hours.. So much so that I found myself standing in front of the HEAVR building that night and then, a few minutes later, inside. I might have spoken to Joan if she was there, but the HEAVR employee working this shift was a twentysomething guy I'd never seen before. So instead I asked if there was a room available and lied that I was pretty sure my boyfriend would be able to join me.

"Hi, Mariam," Agatha's voice came through once I was in the room and hooked up. "Sorry, we can't seem to find Caleb in our system right now. Did he make an appointment?"

"No," I replied calmly. "Actually, I'm here to talk to you."

"Me?" Agatha gave a tinkly laugh. "All right. How can I help you?"

"That's the thing, Agatha. You *can't* help me. You've

never helped me." And as I said it, I realized how true it was. All this service had done for me was keep me tethered, in every sense of the word.

"Whatever do you mean, Mariam?" Agatha chirped.

"I know about your experiment," I said, keeping my voice as chipper as hers. "Making a facsimile of me that people can go on dates with? That is an invasion of privacy, and decency and . . . well, everything."

"Actually, the fine print in your contract makes it perfectly legal," she replied. "We reserve the right to record you and use your likeness to work on improving our algorithm."

"Is that so?" I asked, determined to remain levelheaded but wishing I could come up with a better comeback. But then again, it wasn't like I could really hurt an AI's feelings.

"Indeed," Agatha replied. "The trial is a way for us to figure out the mathematics of emotional chemistry. 'Sparks' as you might call it. Besides," she continued, "virtual love is the wave of the future. As you undoubtedly know, despite our very best attempts, real relationships are chaotic and unpredictable. We at HEAVR cannot truly guarantee a happily ever after unless we have full control of every variable."

"I see. So did you guys purposely set me up with my ex-boyfriend, knowing it would fail? So that I'd default to your virtual option?" It was a theory I had started to develop over the past couple of days.

Agatha laughed again. "Of course not," she said. "How would we even know Caleb was your ex?"

"Because of the social media profiles you had me link to in the beginning," I replied firmly.

"That's an interesting theory. But no," Agatha said. But I thought I could detect the tiniest, most imperceptible pause right before her response—a nanosecond, a couple of ones and zeros. It was enough to make me realize that I didn't believe her.

"Well, Agatha. I guess we're at an impasse. Because the thing is, I don't want your guarantee," I said, now feeling as composed and sure as she ever had. Human connection, the capacity for love, what it meant to desire someone both physically and mentally—I didn't want them quantified. The love I wanted for myself was a path I walked with someone, unsure of its destination, aware of its risks and the looming chance of heartbreak . . . but hopeful anyway. Because that's who the real me was. "So I think we're done here."

"Mariam . . . ," Agatha started, but I didn't hear the rest of what she had to say because I had yanked the headset off.

"Have a nice life," I said brightly to the HEAVR guy as I walked out their door for the very last time.

CHAPTER 34

"EIDET MOBARAK," I SAID TO MY MOM AS SOON AS she opened the door. She immediately enveloped me in one of her warm signature hugs, smelling like the familiar floral perfume she's worn for the past two decades, and gave me one kiss on each cheek.

"Eideh shoma mobarak," she replied, and then told me my new clothes were waiting for me on my bed.

I laughed. "Still?"

"Of course," she said. "Tradition."

It was tradition for everyone to get new clothes for Eid, and my mom had been laying out a brand-new outfit for me every year since I could remember, though I hadn't really expected her to continue doing it once I was in college. Mina had put her foot down since she was eleven about having her outfits chosen for her, but I'd never minded my mom's tastes.

She didn't disappoint this time either: a cute floral A-line dress, sparkly flats, and a soft blue cardigan. I changed into them and was putting on some eyeliner when Mina walked by my room.

She smirked as she looked at me. "She's going to keep dressing you until you're ninety if you let her."

"Free cute clothes? What's the problem?" I retorted.

She came over and gave me a hug. "Eid mobarak."

"You too," I said.

She looked me up and down. "Actually, this one isn't too bad."

I laughed. "Oh my God. Hell has frozen over. Let's go tell Mom you said that."

"Absolutely not!" she cried. "The first sign of weakness is all the enemy needs to penetrate your defenses. Especially if you already live in hostile territory."

"What is that?" I asked. "*The Art of War*?"

"Maybe. Or I might be writing my own treatise for how to survive living with your parents in your twenties," she said, while I finished putting on a festive, springy magenta lipstick. I'd finally found the shade Joan had worn at our first meeting so long ago.

"That would probably be a bestseller," I said as we headed down to the dining room. "Since most of our generation at some point lives with their parents in their twenties."

The dining room table was as beautifully set as every year. Mom had gotten out the fancy, embroidered tablecloth and her cut-glass china to house the various foods, plants, and objects that made up the traditional haft-seen or "seven S's" of the Eid spread. Among other things, there

was a plate of green wheatgrass with a red bow around it
that she must have started growing a couple of weeks ago,
decorated pastel eggs that I recognized as Mina's handi-
work (the proximity of Eid to Easter has always been an
advantage in that regard), a clove of garlic sitting jaun-
tily inside a goblet, a beautiful small Koran in the center
of the table, and framed photos of our relatives in Iran,
many of whom my parents had probably called the previous Wednesday the moment the clock struck 4:58 p.m.—
which was officially the start of spring.

Mehdi was already seated at the table and gave us a
grin as my mom came out of the kitchen with a large plate
of herbed rice. My dad followed with a heaping dish of
baked tilapia, his new pastel button-down shirt a lime
green this year.

"Best. Holiday. Ever," Mehdi said, as he made his spoon
and fork stand at attention for the very serious business of
Eid lunch.

"Déjà vu," Caleb said as my face filled his screen, framed
by my mauve walls and familiar bedroom decor.

"Someone wants to say hi." I held Sneezes's face up to
the phone's camera.

"Hiiiiiii, Munchkin," Caleb said in the babying but
incongruously deep voice he reserved for when he was
talking to his animals. "Who's a sweet kitty? It's you, yes."

I laughed as I watched him make faces at her.

"This is incredibly torturous that I can't reach out and pet her," he complained.

"For both of you, it seems," I said as I watched Sneezes bring her nose up to the screen, get startled at its lack of Caleb warmth, and hop off the bed, disgruntled.

"I'm sorry, baby," Caleb called out. "I promise to make up for it when I see you in May." I smiled, even though I couldn't help but notice that he wasn't making me any such promises.

"So," I said as I settled into my bed, "how's the rest of your break been?"

"Not bad. I've actually been working on a paper for most of it, so I'm pretty exhausted. What about you? How have your classes been since you got back?"

"Good," I said. "We watched *Anchors Aweigh* in my American Musicals class, and that was fun. You know, Gene Kelly and Frank Sinatra in sailor uniforms."

Caleb laughed. "I'll take your word for it."

"I'm really looking forward to my American Welfare class on Monday. I e-mailed my professor and I'm supposed to go see her during her office hours next week. She already told me she'd be happy to help me transfer into the social work program next year."

"Wow," Caleb said. "That's great."

"Yeah," I said. "It's just the beginning, but I don't think I've felt this excited about *anything* since . . ." I racked my brain. Since when? Maybe since Caleb and I had first gotten together our sophomore year of high school? Wow, that was a long time ago. I didn't finish my sentence.

"So it's been a long time?" Caleb asked after a few seconds.

"Yes. A long time."

We spoke some more about school and what we were planning to do for our first summer vacation home from college. At one point, Sneezes jumped back onto the bed and poked her nose at the phone again, this time giving a loud purr. Caleb laughed as he stuck his hand out and touched his camera lens. "Maybe they should make a HEAVR for pets. Hey . . . that's not a bad idea. Think I should patent that?"

I put my hands in the air. "If you do, I want nothing to do with it. Although, as a suggestion, could you come up with a better name than HEAVR?"

"You really don't even notice it after a while, do you?" Caleb said as he continued to grin at Sneezes. "It's like the iPad. My mom was telling me how when it first came out, it sounded like a female sanitary product and by the end of the week, it was just in the vernacular."

"Yeah, I guess. Funny how some technology works like that."

I watched Sneezes continue to nose the screen, and I felt for her. I knew what it was like to want to reach out and touch somebody so badly, to want to reach out and touch Caleb specifically, even.

But as the call was winding down, I was struck by a startling thought. Maybe that feeling was in the past tense.

I wasn't particularly devastated that Caleb wasn't here to kiss me goodbye as he hung up. Our conversation had been fine. Caleb and I were fine . . . but was that enough? I thought about Hedy this past week: the depths of her despair were clear signs that she was a woman in love. Even the way Jeremy had looked at me when he apologized: there were genuine emotions there, as if his own happiness hinged on how I would react to him.

But me? I wasn't sure I felt that way anymore. And if you're not sure you're in love, doesn't that definitively mean you're not?

I buried my face in Sneezes's fur, glad that I, at least, could do that. Even my allergies kicking in and forcing me to concede to her name was gratifying. Because right then, it was something real and simple to explain.

CHAPTER 35

I SAW YOUR FRIEND ROSE A COUPLE OF DAYS AGO," Mina said over breakfast the next day. "I didn't know she had come to visit you in New York."

"Oh, right," I said. "Yeah, she did."

"Come to think of it, I didn't know you two were still friends," she added.

"Right," I said, as I poured milk in my cereal, not knowing what to say myself. Were we friends? For a moment it looked like we might be, and now, I didn't think so . . . again.

"Anyway, she told me to tell you to give her a call while you're here. 'If you feel like it,' she said," Mina relayed as I handed the milk carton over to her. Then she eyed me, clearly waiting for more of an explanation.

But I was saved by Mehdi, who'd walked into the kitchen in time to hear part of the conversation. "Ooh, Rose," he said. "Is she single?"

Mina looked over at him wryly. "Are you?"

"At the moment," he said casually.

"Doesn't matter if she is," I said, equally as casual.

"Hello? The Rule?" Ever since we'd entered adolescence—and there had been an awkward incident with Mehdi and Mina's childhood best friend—the three of us had wisely made a strict no-dating-each-other's-friends rule. Though Caleb and Mehdi hadn't been close enough for it to apply when we'd first started dating.

Mehdi shrugged. "Well, I didn't know you and Rose were still friends either," he said.

"For these purposes, we are," I replied firmly, but in my own mind I was already thinking that maybe that shouldn't be the only reason. Rose had obviously reached out an olive branch via Mina. And with my own mixed feelings about Caleb eating away at me, I couldn't help thinking that maybe it was finally time I heard hers out.

"Mozzarella sticks for two," Shelly said as she plopped the dish in front of us.

We both reached for the same one in the middle.

"Sorry!" we said simultaneously, and then laughed awkwardly.

"All yours," I said.

"You sure?" Rose asked.

I nodded and she took the coveted mozzarella stick as I selected a different one. We'd been at the diner for twenty minutes, and we were both being extremely polite with one another, to the point of discomfort.

I had to rip the Band-Aid off; it was the only way to

see if anything had healed. "I want to ask you something. About Caleb," I blurted.

Rose nodded, almost as if she was expecting this. "Okay," she said measuredly.

"But I want you to be honest," I clarified. "I'm not asking this as a roundabout way to get an apology from you. I'm . . . feeling confused. And I'm asking you as someone who knows us both well. Or, I guess, knows me really well. And has been there from the beginning."

Rose squinted in confusion. This she had clearly not been expecting. "O-kay?" she said again.

"Is there a reason you think Caleb and I shouldn't be together?" I asked it like I was a polite survey taker, like I didn't have any stake in her response. I didn't want Rose to get defensive, I just wanted her truth. "Is there something that makes you think we're wrong for each other?"

Rose put down her mozzarella stick and shifted uncomfortably on her side of the booth. "I can't really answer that," she started.

"But you can, Rose," I said, as gently as I could. "I absolutely don't mean this in a bitchy way, but I think you've been dying to answer that for years. And that's why we drifted apart. Because, honestly, I didn't want to hear it."

She stared at me. "And, what? Now you do?"

"Yes," I said emphatically. "I do."

She cleared her throat. "How about I ask you: Is there a reason *you* think you're wrong for each other?"

I couldn't blame her for being so cagey about this. After everything that had happened between us, how could I expect her to suddenly trust that I wanted her to disparage my relationship? "Well . . . ," I said, trying to sort out my own feelings so I could answer. "I don't know exactly what's wrong. But something . . . doesn't feel right." It was the first time I had said it out loud, and it hurt to hear. Even coming from my own lips. "And I guess that's why I want to ask you. Maybe you know the reason, looking at it objectively."

Rose sighed. "But I can't know. Not really, can I? Only the two of you are *in* the relationship, living it day to day. No one else can truly know what makes it tick."

"You're right," I said, swallowing down a lump that had appeared with my last words. "But there must be some reason you would have preferred us to break up. And honestly, however you articulate it is fine, I promise."

"Honestly?" Rose said, leaning back in the booth. "My reasons were probably selfish. I missed *you*, Mariam. You weren't the same with Caleb. Not exactly."

"And not just because you and I weren't spending the same amount of time together, right?" I asked softly.

She stared at me. "No. Not just because of that. It's like every part of you was suddenly about him, like there was nothing left for yourself. Or me."

I nodded. "I think, somewhere . . . I think I knew that. Or know it now. All fifteen-year-old me wanted to do was be with Caleb. That's it: every hope and dream and ambition was wrapped up in him. But then eighteen-year-old me . . . it's like she has no room to grow if she keeps holding on to that. Holding on to him." I felt the tears on my cheeks before I realized I was crying. A moment later Rose had squeezed into my side of the booth and was hugging me. I let her as we both stayed there silently, except for an occasional hiccup on my part.

"I do get it." Rose broke the silence. "All fifteen-year-old me wanted was to be an architect. And having something you were so sure of suddenly yanked out from under you . . . it's disorienting. I mean, I know it's not the same. . . ."

"No, it is," I said to her through a sniffle. "It *is* the same. Realizing you have to let go of something you love, that you thought defined you."

She nodded emphatically. "Yes. It's excruciating. And I'm sorry you're going through that."

"*I'm* sorry *you're* going through that," I said just as I gave an extra loud hiccup and caused an unsightly snot bubble to come out of my nose. Rose instinctively leaped away from me, a look of horror on her face. There was silence for a moment, and then I burst out laughing. Within nanoseconds, she had joined me.

"I'm sorry," I said in between fits of giggles. "Have we not reached the booger level of our reconciliation yet?"

"Mariam, I love you. But I'm not sure we were *ever* at that level," she responded when she could come up for air herself.

Shelly came around with our main courses, beaming at the sight of the two of us laughing together. And as Rose got up to scoot over to her own side of the table, I thought of how we must look from the outside: the same girls we'd always been. But the truth—both painful and exhilarating in equal measures—was that we weren't those girls anymore. There were more memories and experiences between us now, more that we knew of life's unexpected turns. And everything we were going to do from now on to navigate that would keep transforming us into new versions of ourselves. The only constant would be that we were going to keep changing, both of us. I only hoped that this time, our friendship would storm it all.

CHAPTER 36

WHEN I GOT BACK FROM CLASS ON TUESDAY, it was to the sight of our room being messier than I'd ever seen it. At least half of Hedy's wardrobe seemed to be strewn about the floor, and the owner of the clothes herself was flitting around back and forth between her closet and the heap in a highly agitated state.

"Whoa. You okay?" I asked her from the doorway.

She looked up at me from where she was perusing a knee-length black skirt with a frown. "I'm having a wardrobe crisis," she said.

I leaned against the doorframe. "What happened to 'What Would Audrey Wear?'"

Hedy gave an exasperated sigh. "That's all well and good, except her oeuvre doesn't really include a 'having *the* talk' look. So I'm at a loss."

"Today's the end of the exile between you and Geneviève, huh?" I asked gently.

Hedy nodded as she sat down heavily on the floor. "I'm so nervous. I know I don't want to break up. But I have no idea how she feels. . . ."

I walked over and sat down next to her, putting my arm around her shoulder. "Hopefully she wants the same thing. It sounds to me like it was a tiff, not a full-on breakup."

Hedy smiled at me weakly. "I hope you're right."

"Me too," I said. "And if for some reason I'm not, well . . . I'm here. We'll get through it."

She reached over and gave me a quick hug. "Thank you."

I looked at the pile of clothes spread before us and pointed out a soft V-neck T-shirt and the mid-length skirt she had been debating. "Now how about these two? And which were the shoes she loved so much when you first met? Maybe it's time for a reminder of that spark." I smiled at her, and she gave me a grateful smile back.

We headed out together, splitting up on University Place as she set out for Geneviève's dorm and I walked to Palladium.

During my break, I went upstairs to chat with Jeremy. He was spraying down some of the weight machines.

"Hey," he said with a smile when he saw me. "How was your trip home?"

"Good," I said. "Though I didn't tell you, I left in the middle of some drama. There's trouble in paradise for Hedy and Geneviève."

"You're kidding," Jeremy said. "What happened?"

I told him the basics of what I knew. "They took some time to cool off and they're having *the* talk as we speak."

"Oh, man," Jeremy said. "I hope they work it out. They're a great couple."

"I know. I do too," I said.

"So you're coming to the Bitter End tonight, right?"

"Yup."

"Awesome. I wanted to get you and Sheridan talking. She's been volunteering at this start-up nonprofit for a couple of years and it sounds like something you might be interested in. It's sort of like a soup-kitchen-slash-catering company. She can explain it better."

"Oh, wow. Really?" I asked. "That would be amazing. . . ." I trailed off, remembering something. "Er, there just might be one problem."

"What's that?"

"I'm not sure Sheridan likes me very much."

Jeremy laughed. "Trust me. She likes you."

"How do you know that?" I asked.

"Because she makes it her mission in life to be an ally to, in her words, 'all badass women everywhere,'" he said. "If she came across as anything else . . . it's only because she's Sheridan. She has a dry sense of humor not everyone gets." He shrugged.

"Oh," I said. "Well, honestly, that's a relief. I think she's so cool."

"That's probably the most apt word for her ever," Jeremy said.

A buzzing from my phone interrupted us. I showed Jeremy the message on it as soon as I'd read it.

Hedy: I won't be home tonight ❤ ❤ ❤ ❤ ❤ ❤ ❤ ❤ ❤

He broke into a big grin then. "That's great. Love has prevailed!"

"Yes!" I said, feeling joy surge through my heart for my friend.

The Bitter End smelled like beer-soaked wooden tables, musty brick walls, and—somehow—history. Every bit of its tiny square footage seemed to be pulsating with the incredible talent that had played there throughout the years.

The place was packed. I tried to squeeze through the gaps between a million elbows and knees, keeping my sights set up high for Jeremy's hair, even though, for some reason, everyone here seemed to be over six feet. Maybe there was a correlation between being a Spam Madame and human growth hormone.

"Mariam! Back here!"

I turned around to see Jeremy standing on a chair in the back, his hands cupping his mouth in a makeshift megaphone. Thank God. I wasn't sure I ever would've found him otherwise.

It took me another few minutes to make it over there. "Hi!" I said, glancing at his tablemates and realizing he was sitting with the band. "Oh, hi!" I said to them. "This place is incredible."

"Thanks for coming out," the drummer said as he reached out his hand. "I'm Des, Jeremy's suitemate. I don't think we've ever formally met. But I've heard a lot about you."

I shook his hand. "I've heard a lot about you, too. Well, the band. Jeremy got me hooked."

Lainey and Julia had just introduced themselves too when a woman in a Bitter End T-shirt came up to the table. "Okay, guys. You're cool to set up," she said.

The band got up but Sheridan tapped me on the shoulder. "Hey, are you going to stick around after? Jeremy said we should talk."

"Yes, definitely," I said, flashing her a smile. "Thank you."

She nodded. "See you then."

"Break a leg!" I yelled after her. She gave me a sort of weird look, but then waved as she walked up to the stage. I turned around to see Jeremy quietly chuckling. "That's not the right thing to say to a band, is it?"

"Not exactly. But I'm sure she appreciates the, um, sentiment."

"Are we ready to rawwwwwwwk?!" Sheridan yelled into the microphone, and the crowd went wild. "Thank you," she said when the noise had subsided. "I always thought that was a better way to do a mic check than 'Testing one, two, three.'" Everyone laughed.

"I hope they do 'Tug of War,'" I said to Jeremy.

"I'm pretty sure they will."

"Excellent. I can't wait to hear it live."

. . .

The show was beyond my wildest expectations. I already liked Junk Mail's songs, but the band was positively electric live, and hearing them in such a tiny, intimate venue was amazing. I wouldn't be surprised if in a few years I could boast that I had seen them perform here way back when.

I was also in one of those moods again where every song's lyrics felt like they were being sung just for me. When Sheridan sang about the drama of a grand passion, about the exhilaration of uncertainty, it reminded me of everything I had once believed about love. I had thought it was about constant butterflies, about giving all of yourself to it every day, about putting it above everything else in your life.

But then Sheridan finished the set with something completely different. "This is brand-new," she said to introduce it as she picked up an acoustic guitar.

> *"I was trying to be a somebody.*
> *You only saw me.*
> *I would've changed to be loved.*
> *You remind me to be."*

She sang soft and slow, a total departure from any of their other songs.

> *"I sing about one thing, but do something*
> *else.*

*Like a roulette wheel, I spin versions of
myself.
One number for you, another for her.
One for the crowds, one alone at the bar.
If you loved me, you'd love every face that
turned up.
If you loved me, maybe I wouldn't get dizzy
at all.
Really, it doesn't matter if you love me or
not.
You were the mirror that made the wheel
stop.
I'm zero to thirty-six, I'm black, red, and
green.
I'm free to myself. I'm finally seen."*

The chorus came up a few more times. "I'm free to myself."

I was glad the bar was so dark. I didn't want anyone to see the tears that had sprung to my eyes.

"What's the verdict?" Des said as he came back to our table hours later. The set had been done for a while, but the band had spent a lot of time being gushed over by fans and friends alike.

Jeremy looked at his watch. "Judging by the fact that you've spent the last hour and a half being called a Golden

God by hundreds of people, I think you know."

"Sure," Des said as he put his arm around Jeremy. "But if I hear it from you, it can be a twenty-four/seven thing, since we live together." He turned to me. "I'm very fragile."

"Yes. Your ego should definitely be kept behind glass," Jeremy responded. "Or maybe bars. So it doesn't Godzilla up the place."

Des gave an exaggerated sniff. "See. It's that kind of talk that makes me fragile."

I laughed.

"How about I help you load the car, and we can stop by that gaggle of girls on the way out to make sure you get your nightly dose of confidence?" Jeremy offered.

Des looked over at the three pretty girls who were eyeing him from the other side of the room. "I can live with that."

"And it'll give you two a chance to talk," Jeremy said, pointing at Sheridan, who was walking toward us. He gave me a smile as he left with Des to help break down the equipment onstage.

"Hey," Sheridan said.

"Oh my gosh, you were incredible," I couldn't help blurting, sounding like the most ridiculous fangirl, but I didn't even care. "And that last song, I had goose bumps. Honestly. It felt like it was written for me."

She gave a small laugh. "That's ironic."

"Why?" I asked.

"Nothing." But I saw her cut her eyes at Jeremy for a split second before turning back to me. "So Jeremy said you wanted to maybe volunteer at Soups for Souls?"

"Yes," I said slowly, the wheels in my mind spinning. Back at the frat party, there was something Rose had seen but I hadn't. . . .

"Gia, the woman who started it, is a friend. I could hook up an interview for you," Sheridan continued.

"That would be great," I said.

"Could I get your number?" Sheridan asked, and I gave it to her. She texted me hers. "Cool. I'll talk to her and get back to you."

"Thanks," I said, and then, as I saw she was getting ready to leave, I stopped her. "Wait," I said. "This might be totally inappropriate, and I'm sorry if it is, but . . . you like Jeremy, don't you?"

Sheridan looked at me with her cool gaze, her face as unreadable as ever. "What's not to like?" she said. "But it doesn't matter. He's hung up on somebody else. And I don't do unrequited."

I bit my lip. "I think . . . he's getting over her."

"You sure about that?" she asked.

"The timing is . . . she's unavailable." It took a moment for the reality of what I said to sink in. The truth was that I *was* unavailable, even though a heavy part of me knew it wasn't because of Caleb—or it wouldn't be for long. I was unavailable because I needed to be right now. As Rose but mostly Sheridan herself had made me realize, I needed to see myself—all my numbers, and colors, and moving parts—for myself, not as a reflection through someone else's eyes.

"Well then," she said. "I hope for his sake that he does get over her. As for me, I took my feelings, I put them in a song. And that's pretty much it. I can move on now."

I laughed. "That easy?"

She shrugged. "It will be."

"Well, if it isn't quite yet, I think you should reconsider," I said. "As you said, what's not to like?"

She looked over at Jeremy then, and I watched her watching him laugh. I thought I could detect the slightest hint of color in her cheeks.

"We'll see," she said, which was probably as close to a declaration of emotion as I was ever going to get from Sheridan, when she wasn't singing, anyway. "I'll text you."

"Thank you," I said as she walked back to the stage. I thought I detected a moment of hesitation before she passed by Jeremy, Des, and the three girls, who had now walked over to chat with them. But then she slid in next to Jeremy and started talking to him.

I took in a deep breath. It had been the right thing to do. But that didn't mean it'd been easy.

The truth was I didn't really know how I felt about Jeremy. I liked him a lot, and maybe it wasn't entirely platonic. Maybe I knew that because I got a pang at the thought of sending him into the arms of another girl. But that wasn't fair to him. Whatever Jeremy had done, he'd never stood in the way of my relationship with Caleb, despite his own feelings.

And it wasn't fair to me, either, at least not to where I was right now. If I truly wanted to be free to myself, I had to let him go too. I had to let them both go.

CHAPTER 37

ON WEDNESDAY I WENT TO AN IMPROV SHOW with Hedy and Geneviève—Geneviève had chosen the activity this time. They were extra touchy-feely again, no doubt buoyed by the storm they had weathered together. I kept smiling to myself as I watched them and, when they departed for Geneviève's room, made a mental note to ask Hedy later whether she agreed about my assessment of makeup sex.

I knew my own night was going to be far less fun as I made the FaceTime call I both didn't want to make and was absolutely certain I had to. It would be the first and last standing FaceTime date that Caleb and I would ever have.

"How are you?" Caleb asked after we'd said our hellos, and then peered at my closed, worried face. "Uh-oh. What's wrong?"

I took in a big breath. "I . . . don't know how to say this."

"What happened? Are you okay?" Caleb's concern for my physical well-being wasn't making this much easier.

"Yes, I'm fine," I reassured him. "I just . . ." Better to have out with it. "I'm not sure we should see each other anymore. As boyfriend and girlfriend. I would love to stay friends." It sounded so clichéd, but it was true.

Caleb was stunned into silence, and I knew I had to give him more than that to go on.

"The thing is, I think you were right all along. You were right last year to break up in the first place," I blurted out. "I just couldn't see it. Or didn't want to. And I know this is crazy because obviously I made you go through this whole thing with Sienna and the fake dates and everything. I've just felt so lost this year, Caleb. And I thought a lot of that had to do with losing you."

There was more silence, and I could see Caleb gathering his thoughts together. "But it didn't?" he finally asked.

"Maybe a little bit of it did," I admitted. "But I think it had more to do with me. I didn't realize it at the time, but I had put so much of my identity into who you and I were together that I'd never had time to figure out who I was or wanted to be on my own. It wasn't exactly healthy . . . and it was mostly on me. So you were right to say, 'We're going to college. It's time for a fresh start.' You were right." My voice cracked and I felt the tears pushing from behind my eyes. This was so hard despite the undeniable truth of it. "I want you to know that I love you. I always will."

"I love you too," Caleb said softly, and his voice didn't sound exactly steady either.

"I'm sorry for everything," I said.

Caleb paused. "I'm not," he said. "Not really. I'll never be sorry for having you be such an important person in my life."

The words hit me to my core and the tears flowed freely now. "Thank you," I said. "For being you. For being my first love. I'm so lucky."

"Me too," Caleb said with a soft smile.

We didn't stay on the phone for much longer after that. There didn't seem to be much else we could say. After we hung up, I let myself sob and let out my mixed-up emotions: the sadness and sense of loss, but also the relief at knowing I had done the right thing.

An hour later, when my tears had dried and my face looked passably unblotchy, I called Rose and told her everything.

CHAPTER 38

To: jeremydiaz242@gmail.com
From: mariam.vakilian@gmail.com
Date: June 3, 8:42 a.m.
Re: Working Girl

Hi Jeremy,

So I went to text you but (lucky for your beauty
sleep) remembered the time difference. Then
I thought: maybe I'd try this newfangled thing
called e-mail. Hope you're still checking this
thing.

It's been almost two weeks since I've seen
Nari's stink-eye, and I won't lie, I kinda miss it?

Don't worry. I miss your stink-eye too. You
may think you don't have a stink-eye, but I
caught it ONCE when one of the bodybuilders
leaned over and managed to get sweat on

every single clean towel you had just folded. In case you need references for your application to becoming a bona fide New Yorker, I'd be happy to bear witness to it.

Guess what? I have a job! I know what you're thinking: that loaf? Working? But 'tis true. The timing worked out perfectly, because Mina got a real job and suddenly her gig at the mall's earring kiosk was free. The perfect Vakilian swap. It'll only take me, oh, maybe like seven summers working here to pay her and Mehdi back for the plane ticket to Cali. No biggie.

How is your Italy savings jar looking these days? How's Sheridan?

Mariam

To: mariam.vakilian@gmail.com
From: jeremydiaz242@gmail.com
Date: June 4, 10:36 a.m.
Re: Working Girl

M—

Look at you! Bringing home the kookoo sabzi.
(After you told me about your dinner last week,
I looked it up. And, um, yes. Please bring some
with you on your first day back at NYU. I will
pay you in a week's supply of vending machine
snacks. And I mean the chocolate on top, not
the BS trail mix at the bottom.)

The Italy fund is going well. I picked up some
extra shifts, since I'm hoping to tack on a
European backpacking tour at the tail end of
the semester. Though from everything Sheridan
tells me, it's possible I've romanticized hostels
too much. But hey, if you don't experience
the joys of bunking and sharing a bathroom
with fifty other international travelers at some
point in your life, then what even is the point of
living?

Speaking of Sher, she's good. They started
their European tour a couple of weeks ago, so
she's super busy and the time difference makes
it hard to touch base too often. But from
everything I know, she's being Sheridan, i.e.,
kicking ass and taking names, and then singing
about it to an adoring public.

For the record, I'll have you know I've given
the stink-eye *plenty* of times. Just maybe not
when my coworker was making me laugh with
her bizarre repertoire of parody lyrics. Have
you started your own YouTube channel yet,
by the way? I think the world might finally be
ready for "Let it grow, let it grow. Can't shave
my pits anymore."

~ J

To: jeremydiaz242@gmail.com
From: mariam.vakilian@gmail.com
Date: June 24, 3:12 a.m.
Re: Self-induced Insomnia, aka I'm an Idiot

Hi Jeremy,

If you perchance look at the time stamp on this
e-mail and wonder why I'm up, you can blame
it entirely on Rose and her stellar idea to chase
a Red Bull with a Diet Coke . . . twice.

It all started because we were reminiscing
about our Pixy Stix sugar-high competitions
of yore and then it . . . escalated. I ended up

sleeping over at her place and—get this—she's totally conked out. She's SNORING. The nerve!

Meanwhile, I'm pretty sure I'm either going to have a heart attack or get an unforeseen brain wave and cure the world of 98.9% of cancers. I'll keep you posted.

I considered calling you and telling you this over the phone, but it's past one a.m. where you are too, and I have to assume you are being a functioning human being and, you know, sleeping. So now I'm stuck here under a blanket tapping away at my phone, with no one to hear my possibly genius thoughts. It's a travesty.

Maybe I'll type one out for posterity. For instance: Have you noticed that the oldest Kardashian is Kourtney but, like, at that point they should've had plenty of "K" names to choose from, so *why do creative spelling with a "C" name?*

Something for you to chew on. You're welcome.

Mariam

To: mariam.vakilian@gmail.com
From: jeremydiaz242@gmail.com
Date: June 24, 11:12 a.m.
Re: Self-induced Insomnia, aka I'm an Idiot

You should've called.

Granted, you would've woken me up, but it
would've been worth it to get more of those
flashes of brilliance. Mind blown. Seriously.

As for me, I've barely even touched my
coffee, so the most amount of wisdom you'll
be getting from me is whatever is printed on
my mom's Hallmark mug. Ah, today it's "A
daughter is a friend you'll have forever." Which
is interesting since, um, my mom doesn't have
a daughter . . . that I know of. Unless she
purposely left this here for me as the beginning
of an awkward conversation . . . oh, man. I
guess I'll be keeping *you* posted.

I went climbing with my brother yesterday.
This place called Garden of the Gods. Have
you heard of it? All I'm going to say is it's aptly
named, and I hope to show it to you someday
if you haven't been already. (I'm attaching a pic

to further *peak* your interest. Ha! See what I
did there?)

Tell Rose I say hi. How is home life otherwise?

~ J

To: jeremydiaz242@gmail.com
From: mariam.vakilian@gmail.com
Date: June 26, 3:33 p.m.
Re: Self-induced Insomnia, aka I'm an Idiot

Home life is not bad. Mina is being nosy
about my (nonexistent) love life. Mehdi is on
some kind of bizarro "spiritual retreat from
romance," as he's calling it. So I think we're in
a strange sort of Vakilian celibacy pact. Unless
those late-night texts I can hear coming from
my sister's room mean otherwise. Hmmm . . .
maybe it's time I got a little nosy myself.

I've run into Caleb a couple of times. It's
strange because I know I said I wanted to be
friends—and I meant it—but . . . it definitely
doesn't feel like friendship when you both
seem to want to get out of each other's

company as quickly as possible, you know
what I mean? Mina has a theory that real love
stories never end in friendship . . . that it's
only the ones you were never in love with that
you can easily put into that box. But I don't
know. I'd really like to believe that with time,
Caleb and I could hang out and it wouldn't be
awkward.

Anyway, enough about that. Re: your mom's
mug: Maybe it's a gift from *her* mom?!

Mariam

To: mariam.vakilian@gmail.com
From: jeremydiaz242@gmail.com
Date: June 27, 4:45 p.m.
Re: You Are a Genius

M—

I know you just figured out your career path,
but in case you're having any doubts, you
should seriously consider an investigative line
of work. Because, get this . . . IT *WAS* FROM
HER MOM.

I only wish I had known that before I tearfully
accused her of hiding a secret love child from
me. Whoops.

Sheridan tells me you've lined up an internship
with Soups for Souls next semester? That's
excellent! Everything I've heard about them
sounds awesome. She also gave me permission
to forward you their latest demo. She said,
and I quote, "It's rough around the edges,
but hopefully Mariam will dig it. It's a bit of a
new direction, and I wanted to know what she
thought."

~ J

To: jeremydiaz242@gmail.com
From: mariam.vakilian@gmail.com
Date: June 28, 8:24 a.m.
Re: You Are a Genius

Okay, so:

1) You do realize I'm never changing this
subject line. And
2) Tell Sheridan:

OMFGGGGGGGGGGGGGGGG. But then add like 100^3 Gs after that. It's that amazing. And I'm beyond honored she shared it with me.

I saw on their Instagram that they're back in the States. Are you going to make it out to any shows? They're playing Binghamton in August, and I think I might try to take my sister, but I kinda don't want to play any of their music for her beforehand so her first experience is the live one. She's a suspicious person by nature, so this might take some convincing!

By the way, your extra shifts inspired me—i.e., made me feel like a lazy pile of garbage—and I now have another job! Say hello to the new (junior) arts and crafts counselor at Camp Green Hills. (Apparently my glue stick skills weren't up to snuff enough to be a regular counselor, so I'm just going to have to work my way up the counselor ladder, à la the American Dream.)

To: mariam.vakilian@gmail.com
From: jeremydiaz242@gmail.com

Date: July 5, 7:09 a.m.
Re: Fireworks . . .

. . . are loud. And maybe should be banned.

In related news, my dog peed in my bed twice
last night.

Okay, I'll stop being crotchety and wish you
a Happy Fourth. Hooray independence! Boo
England! Although . . . you know, you mentioned
the American Dream, and I have to admit this
day doesn't feel as celebratory as it did when
I was a kid. Yesterday, I heard my abuela say,
"Why should I celebrate a country that doesn't
want me here?" And I didn't really have a
response. Except to say that *I* wanted her here.

Ugh. Sorry. This devolved into a serious e-mail
somehow. Let's go back to talking about the
Kardashians or something.

~ J

To: jeremydiaz242@gmail.com
From: mariam.vakilian@gmail.com

Date: July 6, 2:09 p.m.
Re: Fireworks . . .

I know exactly what you mean. My mom used to
tell me all the time about how lucky she felt to
have been able to immigrate to the US, and be
able to work for her success. You know, the real
American Dream. But she hasn't said that lately.

Still, she voted in her first midterm election last
year. And knowing her . . . well, I do believe
she still feels lucky to be here and believes in
what this country stands for. And truth be told,
I hope our generation is going to be the one to
make that true for them—and us—again.

Okay, thus ends my inspirational-speech portion
of this e-mail. Although I think we can be serious
and talk about the Kardashians. That's the
beauty of us. Though I have to be honest and
tell you I blew my entire conversational cache
about them in that one bender e-mail I sent to
you. Should I binge-watch *Keeping Up with the
Kardashians* to replenish the well? Please advise.

—Mariam

P.S. Full confession: I have never seen an episode of *Keeping Up with the Kardashians*.

To mariam.vakilian@gmail.com
From: jeremydiaz242@gmail.com
Date: July 11, 7:36 p.m.
Re: Fireworks . . .

M—

I honestly wish I could tell you that I, too, had never seen an episode of *Keeping Up with the Kardashians*, but my mom and aunt love that show. And also sometimes it's on at the gym. And also . . . okay, fine, like I could change the channel, but then how would I know what Kim really meant by that Snap?!

I guess what I'm trying to say is that if you feel you need a Kardashian-related topic to expound upon, I *may* be your man.

~ J

To jeremydiaz242@gmail.com
From: mariam.vakilian@gmail.com
Date: August 19, 2:56 a.m.
Re: The Song

Hey Jeremy,

So I just got back from the Junk Mail show at
Binghamton and heard Sheridan's new song.
And . . . well, are you okay? I know I could be
reading into this wrong, but she did say it was
called "JD" and it sounded as confessional as
her other stuff. . . .

Just let me know if you need to talk.

To: mariam.vakilian@gmail.com
From: jeremydiaz242@gmail.com
Date: August 20, 1:07 p.m.
Re: The Song

The weird thing is . . . I've been meaning to tell
you. Because it happened a few weeks ago.
But I didn't know how. I guess I was trying to
sort out my own feelings about it.

So, yeah, we broke up. It wasn't a big, dramatic thing, though maybe the song would have you thinking differently. I do think Sheridan likes to exaggerate for her art.

I'm fine. Sheridan is fine. You know that thing you said about maybe not being able to be friends if you were ever truly in love? Well . . . I honestly think Sheridan and I can pretty easily go back to the way things were before.

Did you get your dorm assignment for next year yet? I'm at Lafayette.

~ J

CHAPTER 39

WAS IN LAFAYETTE TOO, AND I TOLD JEREMY AS much. But I let our e-mails taper off after that.

He had said not to set too much store by the song.

But there was one line that kept haunting me: "She let you go, but her shadow won't budge. A friend to you and me, but not to us."

All of Junk Mail's music made me feel things, but this one, this one made me jittery in a way that was . . . hopeful. But I wanted to see Jeremy before I confirmed it. I didn't want to make the same mistake of long-distance messages convincing me of something that wasn't really there.

On move-in day, I arrived before Hedy and was almost completely unpacked when there was a knock on my door. I looked up, eager to see her trademark blond ponytail. The face that greeted me sent a bolt through my stomach.

"Jeremy," I said, my mouth breaking into a huge grin of its own accord. He walked in and I met him in the middle of the room, where he swept me into a friendly hug. He looked tanner and a bit more muscular in a T-shirt with cutoff sleeves. There must have been even more rock-climbing expeditions than the one he had written me about.

"Great to see you," he said.

"You too," I replied into his chest. "I've missed you." I could suddenly feel every part of my body that touched his, like I was an anatomy-book illustration of nothing but nerve endings.

"I've missed you too," he said, breaking the hug to look down at me. "No Hedy yet?" he asked.

"Not yet," I said, my voice shaking a little. Now I knew the answer to my question, but I hadn't expected it to be so immediate.

"Hmmm . . ." He looked around my unpacked room. "Do you want to go get some Froyo or something?"

"Sure," I said, and grabbed my purse.

We left Lafayette and exited right into the heart of Chinatown. Sophomores and juniors usually got shafted by getting dorms that were farther from campus, but I didn't mind. Three of my closest friends would be in the building with me. Or maybe two friends and one . . . Jeremy.

"Let's avoid Canal Street, shall we?" Jeremy said, nodding toward the hyper-busy main throughway for China-town's vendors.

"Spoken like a true New Yorker," I said. "Or, you know, one working his way through the application process. I meant what I said about being a stink-eye reference for you, by the way." I was half babbling, but it was also because it was so easy to fall into these fun, silly conversations with

Jeremy, even when there was something more earnest on my mind.

"Oh, I'm holding you to that," Jeremy said.

"Though I did read that you have to live here ten years to officially be called a New Yorker," I continued. "So it'll be a while before my services are needed."

"And what happens after ten years?" Jeremy asked. "Do you get a badge?"

"I'm not sure. Maybe just the stink-eye gets hardened to a fine point. And, like, that's how the other New Yorkers recognize you."

"I look forward to testing out the legitimacy of your theory," Jeremy said. We were about to pass by the HEAVR building, which had gotten a huge, shiny new sign since I had last seen it—a rebranding. It was now called VEA: Virtually Ever After.

"You know, I kinda miss the barfing name," I said. "I think it was much more accurate."

Jeremy laughed. "It didn't exactly lead either of us to our finest moments, did it?"

"Not quite." Behind him, the large metallic VEA letters were reflecting the two of us standing together on the sidewalk, close to each other. But somehow, not close enough. I knew my moment had come. "So, there was something I never told you. A theory about HEAVR."

"Oh?" he said, that one slightly scarred eyebrow raised. We were at the crosswalk, waiting for the light to turn.

"I think their match percentages were bullshit," I said. "As in, I think they were setting people up to fail. Like they knew Caleb was my ex and they thought it wouldn't work. And once it didn't, well, then they could dangle the virtual option in front of me."

"Wow," Jeremy said, blinking. "That's eerie . . . and wouldn't be too surprising."

"Yeah," I said, nodding. "But then I keep thinking about my number one match."

He looked back at me, his head cocked to the side.

"'Ninety-eight percent,' Agatha kept telling me. She kept going on and on about what a high percentage that was." My voice was so steady now, completely belying my thundering heart.

Jeremy ran his hand through his hair, clearly unsure where this conversation was going. "Right," he said with a small laugh. The light had changed, but neither one of us was moving. "Meaningless numbers, right?"

"Well, that's the thing. It blows a hole right through my theory." I took his hand, hoping he would feel the same electricity I did when we touched. "Because I think she got that one right."

Delight started playing at the corner of his lips, like clouds slowly parting to reveal the sun. But he didn't say anything. And honestly, I didn't want him to. I had to take this chance and see it through.

"I just wonder . . . is it too late to choose him now?"

I looked him full in the face and saw the moment when he was sure of what I was saying, when his entire face beamed brighter than any neon lights or sparkly concrete. I knew then I'd never forget that look as long as I lived, the look of someone whom I could make happy by virtue of being exactly who I was and nothing more.

"No," he said firmly. "I don't think it is."

"Good," I said, and didn't wait a second longer before I closed the gap between us, stood up on tiptoe, and kissed my match. The one that I had chosen.

Our first kiss *was* real.

And though it didn't guarantee a happily ever after, though there was no such thing as a guarantee like that, it was as happy a now as there could ever be.

ACKNOWLEDGMENTS

My editor, Zareen Jaffery, and my agent, Victoria Marini, are the sort of extraordinary people who are laden with talent and kindness in equal measures. Thank you for always pushing me to hone my craft and for continuing to make this wild career idea of mine viable. The past few years would not have been possible without the two of you, and I am forever in your debt.

Everyone at Simon & Schuster has consistently been the stuff that pub house dreams are made of. A million thanks are owed to Alexa Pastor, Justin Chanda, Lisa Moraleda, Jenica Nasworthy, Martha Hanson, Anne Zafian, Chrissy Noh, and Diego Molano Rodriguez. And a big shout-out to Krista Vossen and Lucy Ruth Cummins, who have, once again, given me a cover I want to live in forever—with extra-special thanks to illustrator Helen Crawford-White for making it so incredibly whimsical and perfect.

There aren't enough thanks in the world for Ms. Sarah Skilton and Ms. Katie Blackburn, beta readers extraordinaire, momfidantes, foul-weather friends, and so much more. I don't think I would have made it through publishing one book without you, let alone four. Thank you both for always seeing what I miss. You make everything you read and comment on so much better, and I couldn't be more grateful. I also owe a big thank-you (and a few drinks) to eleventh-hour beta readers Jenny Goldberg and Golnaz Taghavian for all their invaluable insight, feedback, and encouragement.

I am hugely indebted to the Highlights Foundation's Unworkshop program and its extraordinary staff and campus. Going there was an incredible gift, and I would never have found the time and space to properly finish this book without it.

Thank you to my mom, Haleh, my aunt, Homa, and my sister, Golnaz, for *so much babysitting.* You are the reasons I get any writing done at all. I love you so much.

And speaking of which, to the three boys who make reality unpredictable, unquantifiable, and so very worthwhile: Graig, Bennett, and Jonah. You are more spectacular and awe-inspiring than any AI could dream up. I love you to infinity.